ammer

ALL SUMMER

Claire Kilroy

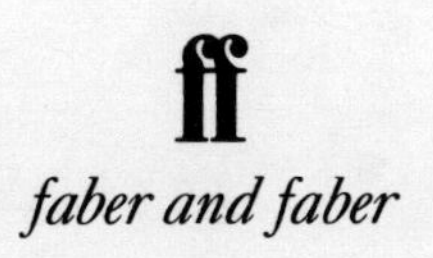

faber and faber

First published in 2003
by Faber and Faber Limited
3 Queen Square London WC1N 3AU

Typeset by Faber and Faber Ltd
Printed in England by Clays Ltd, St Ives plc

The text contains quotations from:
The Deeper Picture: Conservation at the National Gallery of Ireland, Andrew O'Connor and Niamh McGuinne. © 1998, The National Gallery of Ireland.
Container Gardening for All Seasons, ed. Brenda Houghton. © 2001, The Reader's Digest Association Ltd, London.
Fever, Peggy Lee

A CIP record for this book
is available from the British Library

ISBN 0–571–21562–9

2 4 6 8 10 9 7 5 3 1

For Helen, Jim & Mia

fugue: *Psychol.* loss of awareness of one's identity, often coupled with flight from one's usual environment. [French or Italian from Latin *fuga* 'flight']

The Oxford English Reference Dictionary

I

The Island, Winter

ONE

I didn't arrive on the island with much. The clothes I wore. The keys to a cottage I had never seen. Some money, not a whole lot, and a matchbox containing a small piece of canvas.

The piece of canvas is about the size of the heart of a daisy. It is rough to the touch and as brown as mud. It is woven out of a flax that grew on the banks of the Rhine nearly four hundred years ago. Without the rest of the canvas from which it is cut, my piece is no better than dirt. And in a house as full of rubbish as the one I have just rented, if I am not very careful, it will get lost for ever. I will keep it on the top shelf of the dresser, where it should be safe.

I took off into the storm this morning. Had to stumble along the coast road like a drunk. I was soaked within seconds. The Atlantic waves crashed thirty feet into the air as they collided with the sea wall. Each collision boomed in the sky like cannon-fire. At first it was a thrill to hear wind blow so hard.

The shop is painted blue and cream. MACKEY'S PETROL COAL GAS VIDEOS NEWSAGENT FRESH MEATS it says on the wall. The newspapers flapped in the blast of wind that burst in when I entered. I heaved the door shut and blinked rain out of my eyes. Two women were smiling at me. One was behind the counter, the other in front. I'd seen the one in front before. She had made breakfast for me in the pub the morning I had arrived on the island.

'Awful day,' the woman behind the counter said.

'It is,' I agreed, and shook the rain out of my hair. My hands were numb. So was my face.

'Shocking,' the one from the pub said. 'And what's more, it'll get worse.'

'Will it?' I rubbed my hands together and blew on them. They had turned purple.

'You haven't seen the half of it. All the chickens blew away one year. Every last one of them. We woke up and they were gone.' The barmaid again, still shaking her head. I made an appropriately appalled face, and then grabbed a wire basket from the pile that sat on the newspapers as paperweights. I disappeared down the first aisle. The women began to chat behind me. I wasn't sure what to buy. Bread, I reckoned, and threw in a loaf of sliced white. Butter to go with it. Jam and tea. Old-fashioned food. I hadn't eaten jam in years. I moved through the aisles quickly, throwing items in. Milk and a can of beans. Two cans of beans. Four altogether. Toilet roll. Soap. Cat food. And the makings of a big fry: rashers, sausages, eggs and tomatoes. The whole process took only a few minutes. Soon the basket was full. I was comforted by how heavy it was. It knocked against the side of my knee as I walked.

I hesitated in front of the fruit and veg stand and stared at the potatoes. I knew I was forgetting something important. The two women were still chatting away in the background. One of them laughed. Beyond them, the wind howled like a wounded animal. *Firelighters,* I remembered, whispering the word aloud. I needed firelighters and a box of matches.

I worked my way back through the aisles. I couldn't find the firelighters, though the shop was quite small. I had been doing so well. I doubled back a third time. The drone of the women's conversation stopped. Only the hum of the refrigerators was audible. And, of course, the relentless wind. I looked up at the convex mirror that was mounted in the corner. I was set, taut as a spider, right in the centre of it.

'Are you all right, love?' the shopkeeper called out. She could probably see me hovering in the deviant mirror; was likely addressing herself to that stringy reflection. 'Do you need a hand with anything?'

I emerged from the canned goods. 'Firelighters?'

'Just behind you, pet. Bottom shelf.'

I turned around and there they were, at least twenty boxes of them, stacked up in neat piles. I smiled stupidly at the shopkeeper. 'Thanks,' I said, adding a box to my basket. I approached the counter and stood behind the second woman.

'Don't mind me, chicken,' she said, stepping out of my way. 'I'm not queuing.'

'Thanks,' I said again, and hauled the basket onto the counter. The shopkeeper – I shall call her Mrs Mackey – reached across and grasped the other side of the basket. She helped me manoeuvre it into the slot beside the register, grimacing under the weight of it.

'Jesus Christ, love,' she said, 'are you stocking up for a war?' Another stupid smile from me. She fished out the fire-lighters and turned the box about, looking for the price sticker. I tore down a plastic bag from the pile hooked onto the counter, and packed the box when she had rung it in.

'And matches, please,' I said, 'before I forget.' This produced a smile and a nod from the customer, or the barmaid, or whatever she was. The landlady, the publican. Mrs Mackey turned to the cigarette shelf and took down a box of matches. She shook it before placing it on the counter. I dropped it into my plastic bag and selected a bar of chocolate from the tray by the register. I looked down at the stacks of newspapers. I didn't recognise any of them. They were all local ones.

'Have you any of the national papers?'

'No, pet,' Mrs Mackey told me. 'The boat can't sail in weather like this.'

'Ah. I'll try tomorrow.'

'You'd be lucky. This one won't die down for a couple of days.' Mrs Mackey hummed a tune as she rang up the goods. The other woman picked up one of the local papers and flicked through it. I filled up my plastic bag and tore down a second one.

'So,' Mrs Mackey began, her voice that bit less casual than it had been before. 'How are you getting on?'

I looked up and turned around, hoping that a fourth person had emerged from somewhere. But there were just the three of us, forming a tight little circle around the cash register as if it were a hearth. Mrs Mackey keyed in the price of the loaf of bread, her eyebrow arched towards me, then she met my eye. I turned to the other woman, and she smiled encouragingly. I shrugged.

'I'm getting on fine, thanks.'

Mrs Mackey nodded and handed me the bread. I put it in the bag. 'And what brings you to our remote corner at this time of year?' She rang in the eggs, then the milk.

A few months earlier, I'd have thought something up. 'I'm doing some research.' 'I'm on a retreat.' 'I'm . . . I don't know, painting, or writing, or bird-watching, or something.' But right then, I couldn't so much as answer. I opened my mouth, but nothing came out. So I shut it again and packed up my goods. I threw them in any which way. The eggs would get broken. The carton of milk would burst. There was a steady straightening up of the two women as they watched.

'I'm –' I said after thirty seconds or so, searching desperately for a suitable word. 'I'm waiting,' I eventually managed. The two women nodded sagely, as if my explanation had made perfect sense. Mrs Mackey put the bar of chocolate into the bag for me. She hadn't rung it up on the register. She told me how much I owed her, and her voice was quiet. I handed over the money.

'Thanks,' she said, handing back my change. 'Will you be able to carry all that back on your own?'

'I will, yeah.'

'Are you sure, honey? It must weigh a ton. And in this weather. Why don't I get Michael to run it up to you later? He's to go up that road anyway.' She knew where I was staying. I shook my head as I divided the bags between my hands.

'I'm grand,' I told her, holding the bags up for her inspection. My arms seemed a yard long. 'See?' The two of them looked on, unconvinced.

'Take care now, love,' the other woman said as I turned to leave. I paused for a second, my bag-entangled hand already on the door handle.

'Sorry,' I whispered hoarsely, and smiled crookedly at the floor. My mouth felt awesomely big, quivering and throbbing on my face like an exposed vital organ. I hurried out.

Painkillers, I remembered when I was halfway down the road. I stopped walking and tucked my chin in against the driving rain. The stretched handles of the bags cut into my palms. I had forgotten to buy painkillers. I turned back towards the shop and stood there for a moment, my headache already returning, but I couldn't face going back.

The priest was sent up to me after that. An hour or two later. He was quick off the mark. Perhaps he had been waiting for the signal, and Lord knows but I had triggered it that day. The storm had not abated when I heard his knock. I opened my door and there he was, his back hunched against the October rain. Fantastic, I commented under my breath. My headache was full-blown by this stage. I thought about asking him if he carried painkillers. Ministering to the sick, and all that. But he didn't have a bag, and his pockets were small. I knew immediately that he would be of little use.

He gazed at me in an absentminded manner, as if I was not the person he had expected to see. Then, deciding to make the best of a bad situation, he smiled. His teeth were tiny and white. His wind-stung face was the colour of his gums.

'Forgot my cap,' he said cheerfully.

'Oh right,' I replied, as if this explained his appearance on my doorstep. He, too, even had he remembered his cap, was poorly dressed for the weather. This made me feel less of an idiot myself. Strength in numbers.

The priest shifted from foot to foot on the doorstep, making a show of being cold.

'Come in out of the rain,' I said. And he did, without hesitation. Did he even introduce himself? If he did, I missed it.

He behaved as if his visit was self-explanatory, which it no doubt was to him. Not to me, though. I kept waiting for him to state his business. I certainly didn't introduce myself to him. He didn't ask to be introduced. He already seemed to have the measure of me.

He slipped off his jacket with a deft swagger and hung it on the hook above the telephone seat. I looked at the hook in surprise. I hadn't noticed it before. It was camouflaged by the swirling pattern of the wallpaper. My own jacket was thrown in a wet heap on the back of the chair. The priest made a note that the hook was new to me, and proceeded with authority.

'Right, then,' he said, adjusting his cuffs. He headed for the kitchen. I followed along behind.

'How are you settling in?' He had seated himself at the table. I stood in the doorway and leaned against the doorframe. The priest stretched out his legs and clasped his hands behind his head. 'Come in, for God's sake!' he said, and I did. I placed myself before him in the middle of the room. 'Now tell me this: are they treating you well?'

'They are,' I replied.

'Oh, poss-poss,' said the priest. 'Oh, pretty poss-poss.' I looked at him aghast, and retreated towards the sink.

The priest retracted his legs and bent down. The previous occupant's cat had trotted up to him, and was weaving himself in and out of the priest's legs. The priest tickled him under the chin. The cat threw himself onto his back and twisted kittenishly. 'Good,' said the priest, sitting up again. 'They're a nice lot.'

'Who, the islanders? Yeah. The islanders are great.'

'The islanders!' bellowed the priest happily, and he snorted. He slapped his knee. 'The islanders!' he bellowed again, and snorted again. The cat sprang up onto his lap before he could slap his knee again.

'Get down!' I snapped, jumping forward.

'Ah, leave him. Sure, isn't he fine where he is? Aren't you, little poss-poss? Aren't you just grand?' The cat settled, and turned its yellow eyes on me. I retreated back to the sink.

'Would you like a cup of tea or something?'

'I would. And a few biscuits to wash it down.'

'I'm sorry. I have no biscuits.'

'Ah, not to worry,' he said. 'You'll remember the next time.' I turned around and flicked the switch on the kettle. It hissed at me angrily. There was no water in it. I called it a bastard and filled it at the tap.

'I see you like art?'

I glanced over my shoulder. The priest was flicking through the pages of the Renaissance book that I'd left on the table.

'Yes,' I said, and then: 'No. I found it in the cottage.'

The pages shuttled by in the priest's hands. Grey stone nudes. Enraptured cupids and sylphs with no body hair. The priest frowned at them thoughtfully. I had to look away.

'It was great, though, wasn't it?' he said, slamming the book shut so loudly that I jumped. 'The Renaissance?'

'I suppose, yeah.'

'They recovered that painting that was stolen last January. You know that painting. The one with the face. They found it the other day.'

My mouth started making funny shapes again, so I turned back to the kettle. 'They got it back, then, did they?'

'They did. It turned up in a bank somewhere. They never caught the second thief. They caught the first one, but he was already dead. Wouldn't have been very hard to catch him in that state, heh heh.'

'Did they say who found it?'

'Ah sure, how would I remember such details?'

The priest belched softly and pushed the Renaissance book away. Then he shifted on his seat with a grimace of discomfort and extracted something from his back pocket. A cigarette lighter. He lit it. The flame was tall. He watched it burn for a second, and placed it on the table. I didn't take my eyes off him, which didn't unsettle him in the least. 'Anyway,' he said, with another gummy smile. 'No friends or family in the area?'

'Why would I bring my friends?'

'I didn't ask if you brought them. I asked if you had any here.'

'Well, I don't.'

'All right then.'

I shook my head in bewilderment. 'I don't understand you,' I told the priest. 'Why are you here?'

The priest dismissed my question with the air of one clearly used to dismissing questions. The kettle was taking an awfully long time to boil. Everything looked damp in the rain-mottled light.

'It's a grand little house, though, isn't it, Anna?'

'Yeah,' I conceded. It was nice hearing my name pronounced with the country accent. I wanted to repeat it back to myself with his exact intonation. I knew I'd forget how to as soon as he was gone. It irritated me that he knew my name, though. Of course he knew it, but I wanted him to ask me, just as a formality. I hadn't told anyone my name, except for the man from whom I'd rented the house, and he lived on the mainland.

'Have you an ashtray for me?' The priest fished a packet of tobacco out of his other back pocket. He had to heave himself up onto one buttock to do so. I gazed at him for a second (how bizarre to have a priest sitting at my table) and then I turned to the dresser. The drawers were full of old things, things that I would never have bought, nor would ever find a use for. And there was an ashtray amongst them somewhere. I had seen it one night. I started with the top drawer. Folded tablecloths and faded aprons. A dusky pink tea cosy. Pieces of heavy silver cutlery that left a metallic tang on the food. Recipes for mutton. And hundreds and hundreds of square cardboard tokens cut out from the back of tea-bag boxes.

'Bottom left,' the priest instructed me, whilst rolling his cigarette, and there it was. A big amber glass thing that had been nicked from the pub. I placed it in front of him with a clatter. He whispered his thanks and lit up.

I took up my position in front of the sink again. The priest looked more comfortable sitting at my kitchen table than I ever had. The cat on his lap, one hand scratching its back, the other arm propped up on the elbow, the smoke weaving around him. I was the odd one out in the house, not him. The kettle finally boiled behind me and I unplugged it from the wall.

'I'll have your tea for you now.'

'Milk,' he said, 'no sugar.'

Something hit the window with a moist thud. The cat leapt off the priest's lap to investigate. A small brown bird, a sparrow perhaps, had crashed into the windowpane and was sliding down to the sill. It fluttered once, weak and stunned, its wing twisted around its head. I lurched towards the glass, but as I did so, the little thing was swept up by the wind and carried out towards the sea.

'Jesus wept,' said the priest.

How long was he there? The guts of an hour. What did we even talk about? The usual things. The weather. The rough seas. Whether the boat would sail or not. At least half an hour of such chat. I cannot remember the specifics. We each got through three cups of tea. Possibly four. I was determined to keep up with the priest. I held my cup with both hands in front of my face like a little shield against the world. He played with the cigarette lighter, turning it over and over in his hands. The gold of the print on the side kept flashing at me. MACKEY'S STORES, it said, and the phone number. That was when the priest asked about the scar. The rain was pelting hard against the window. I was staring out when he said it.

'That's an interesting scar you've got under your eye,' he said. 'I don't believe I've ever seen one quite like it.'

I slammed the cup of tea down on the table. It splashed onto my hand. I cried out in pain, though it hadn't much hurt. The cat sprang from the priest's lap again and stalked out of the kitchen with a poker-straight tail. I shoved my hand under my arm.

'Put it under cold water,' the priest said.

'No.'

I pushed the cup away. The priest finished his own tea and we sat in silence. Eventually he nodded up at something over my shoulder.

'I see you have the Sacred Heart still burning.'

I glanced back and saw what he was talking about. A painting of Jesus Christ, like a girl with a beard. A small red lightbulb burned inside the glass capsule that was attached to the wooden frame. It lit the room up cavernously at night, gave it a satanic appearance. I had tried to unplug it when I'd first moved in, but couldn't find a switch. I'd eventually discovered that the thing was hard-wired into the wall.

The priest whispered something sibilant up at the image, and waved his hand about himself in a blessing. Then, as if reading my thoughts, he shook his head sadly.

'It'd be a shame to extinguish it now,' he commented. 'It hasn't stopped burning for so much as one second since the island first got electricity in 1966.'

'Really?' I muttered. 'Not even when there's a power cut?' I wanted to sneeze, but couldn't quite manage it. I reckoned I was coming down with something. Some virus to which the locals were immune. I got up from the table and stood over the sink. Filled it up with hot water for some reason. There were no dishes to wash yet. I plunged my hands into the sink and stood there staring at them, suddenly very unhappy. My skin looked green under the water. I'd had about enough of the priest, and he was showing no signs of leaving. My head started to pound again.

Suddenly I was blurting out that I was not a religious woman. I was surprised when I heard my words. It was not a thing that I had chosen to say. I turned around and looked at the priest and found myself saying it again.

'I am not a religious woman.'

'Ah, don't mind that,' he said with a flick of his wrist. I turned back to the sink and put my hands into the hot water again. The rest of my body seemed to get colder as I did so.

'It's not a priest I need, Father. Do you understand that?' I addressed myself quietly to the kitchen taps. I doubted that the priest had heard me. But he had. Used to confessions whispered in the dark. Ears attuned to that sort of thing.

'What is it you need?'

I stared at my submerged hands. The priest's voice had come from somewhere else. He had moved away from the kitchen table, though I hadn't detected the sound of him standing up, nor heard his footfall. I couldn't turn to face him. My chin dropped onto my chest. I sucked in air through my teeth. Here we go again, I told myself. Tears welling up once more. None for ages and then twice in one morning. I bit them back and looked up at the ceiling. Waited for the salty water to ebb back down into my eye sockets. The usual intense pain in the crook of the jaw. A toothache where there is no tooth.

'What is it you need, Anna?'

His voice was softer this time. Softer and closer. It filled up the room. He is not one foot away from me now, I told myself. He must be standing right behind me, about to lay a hand on my shoulder. What was I to do? If he'd put his hand on my shoulder, I'd have wailed out loud.

My head sort of listed to one side, as if all the blood in it had swung to the left. My headache was getting vicious. I waited for the hand on the shoulder, and it did not come. Was the priest just standing there, looking mournfully at the back of my head? I waited a further few seconds and then took a deep breath. I turned around, carefully, so as not to bump into him.

The priest was not behind me. He was still sitting at the table. It was his turn to stare out the window. He was entirely lost in whatever he saw. His hands were wrapped around the empty teacup. The cigarette was gone. So was the lighter. He had forgotten his question. What is it you need? I decided to answer him anyway. My voice had a peculiar resonance, as though I spoke in a church.

'To apologise,' I said evenly. 'I need to apologise.'

The priest didn't move. He was a million miles away. I knew that he had not heard me this time. He had not heard a word that I had said, but I didn't mind. I didn't want to make myself heard.

Well. Not to him.

TWO

So how had the priest known that they'd found the painting? The news must have broken. I tuned in the old radio and listened to every bulletin. Not a word. I turned the cottage inside out looking for the television. There was no television. Was it the kind of story that would make it onto the television? I didn't think so, but what would I know? The priest had probably read about it in the papers. I dragged myself back down to the shops every morning on the pretext of buying biscuits. I asked which ones the priest liked. 'He likes them all,' Mrs Mackey told me, smirking. The papers took two more days to come in. If the shop didn't have them, how had the priest read them? It didn't add up. I took one of each of the national broadsheets for the four days that had elapsed since the boat's last voyage. Sixteen in all. Twelve of them were out of date, but that hadn't stopped the boat from bringing them over.

'Don't you want the local one, pet?' Mrs Mackey asked when I heaped my papers on the register. She was all proud of the colourful tabloid that she held up for my inspection. 'It's only 50p.' I shook my head as I counted out my change. She carefully put the paper back on top of its pile, giving me plenty of time to relent and buy the bloody thing. I did not relent.

I rushed back through the wet wind, the pile of papers tucked under my jacket. I sat down at the kitchen table and tore through them. Couldn't find anything, so went through them again, more carefully this time. Word by word. No sign of my name. No sign of yours. Not even of Kel's. So how did the priest know? I wondered, for one ludicrous moment, if *you* could have told him. But that is impossible. How would you know where to find me?

I read the papers a fourth time, a fifth, the wind raging around the cottage like a trapped animal. The doors rattled and the windows shook. The sun had come and gone by the time I had finished, and I had neither breakfasted, nor tidied the house, nor even brushed my hair. The fireplace remained empty and the evening's chill set in. I pulled the blankets off the couch. Have I mentioned that I sleep in the living room? I couldn't face the bedroom with its crucifix and sagging double bed. Mother of God, the lives that get led behind closed doors! Sometimes I think I catch the tang of urine in the air. It could be just the smell of the rotting window frames. The lace curtains are mildewed. Something yellow is growing up the wall. It has stained the ceiling above it. The wardrobe is all shadows and corners that daylight cannot reach. The hinges creak and open only so far. I peeped into it on the day I moved in. There was a collection of squat grey handbags mouldering away on the bottom shelf. The handbags had not always been grey. Something grey had grown onto them, a thick clammy skin of it. That was all I could see in the narrow shaft of light that the door allowed. Like opening up a crypt to examine in what ways the contents had rotted. Garments were hanging to the left and right, but I did not disturb them. I am not as brave as I used to be.

I returned to my newspapers, the bedclothes wrapped around my shoulders like a cloak. I didn't turn on the light, so had to strain my eyes to see the print. I squinted at the small ads for an age. The papers all spread out on the table, and me with my finger tracing out the words. All kinds of religious stuff. 'O most beautiful flower of Mount Carmel, fruitful vine, Splendour of Heaven, Blessed Mother of the Son of God, Queen of Heaven & Earth, I humbly beseech you from the bottom of my heart to succour me in my necessity.' 'St Clare, grateful thanks for favours received and about to receive.' I had never read through the small ads before. Never knew that people wrote such things, or that such things were allowed to be printed. The foot of each announcement was marked by an initial. Not even the initials matched up to yours. I went through the 'SITUATIONS VACANT' and 'MOTORS FOR SALE'. Made it to the PERSONALS. Heart rate got faster. Hoped I might find a message somewhere. A message from you. Thought I saw my own name in the 'LOST AND FOUND'. First just patterns on the page, then the four letters of my name screaming out at me. Got that fright, that thrilling bolt of fright that I haven't had in a while. The heart did its usual trick. Stopped altogether for a split second, and then hurled itself right at my ribs. A downward plunge in my insides, as if gravity had collapsed. That was when the first knock on the door came. I recoiled so violently that the chair nearly tipped over. The bedclothes fell onto the floor. Practically dark in the kitchen by then, except for the demonic glow of the Sacred Heart lamp. I jumped up from the table and sat back down again. I wondered whether I was visible from outside. A black silhouette against the faint red light. I listened hard. The seagulls were screaming at each other on the roof. Their cries echoed down the chimney flue. The foghorn moaned in the distance. I got up and skulked out to the hall. There was no one to be seen through the window. My visitor was either already gone, or standing directly behind the door.

A second knock then, almost as alarming as the first. This knock was more insistent – six or seven sharp raps on the door, as if they could see me standing there and were fit to spit at me. How could I have answered the door then? My visitor would realise that I had been lurking alone in the dark. I flattened myself against the swirly wallpaper and counted to ten. My visitor did not knock again. After a time, I heard the scrape of shoe on cement, as he or she turned away and disappeared back into the drizzle. I crouched in the hall a little longer, then crept back to the kitchen. I wrapped myself once more in the bedclothes, and started to sneeze. The sky was the colour of charcoal. A few blurred lights flashed out on the sea. A milky patch of cloud concealed the moon. I turned my attention back to the paper. I could barely see it, but I didn't switch on the lights in case my visitor cast a backward glance. I took the page up to the Sacred Heart and squinted at it in the red light. Found the message again after an awesomely tense search. 'Anon' it said, not Anna. As I had known it would.

I had first seen it in near darkness, the island, and I will never quite shake the impression it made. I saw it from a distance across the water, more like a sea monster than an outpost of land. The island was black against the sea. The sea was as smooth as oil. It reflected the dawn light of the sky, and the dawn light was ultraviolet. The island was matt and inscrutable. It could have had fields and valleys and farms. It could have had barren plateaux. It gave away nothing of itself as I approached it. I was unprepared for the stillness. A day later, the first storm arrived.

The painting, at the exact moment of my arrival on dry land, was also still. It stood in the emptiness of a locked room, awaiting the forecasted storm. The studio would be its new home for the next three months or so. Almost twenty-four hours had passed since I had last laid eyes on it. I had parted from it without ceremony. I had merely left it behind on the table, and walked away.

Shortly after my departure from it, the painting is collected. The conservator from the National Gallery supervises the transportation. He remains close to the painting at all times. He travels in an armoured van with two policemen. The three of them sit up front. Two unmarked Toyotas escort the van, one ahead, one behind. In the back of the van is the painting, wrapped in a non-stick plastic film. It is sandwiched between two foam-padded boards. The boards are secured together with masking tape, and the whole thing is placed in a wooden crate that had been collected a few hours earlier from the gallery. The painting is in an especially delicate state, but there is not enough time to organise proper packing handlers.

The priority is to remove the painting to a high-security location. It is decided to bring it directly to the National Gallery. The media are informed, however, that it is being kept overnight in police headquarters.

The conservator is silent for the duration of the journey. The two policemen look bulky and round-shouldered beside him. They are the same height and build as him, but they seem to have distributed their weight differently. Perhaps it is because the conservator wears a well-cut suit. The policemen are wearing navy ribbed wool jumpers that cling to their bellies. And perhaps it is because the conservator is sitting ramrod-straight. The muscles are standing out on his jaw. One hand grips his knee, all knuckles. The other is in his pocket. He judders around between the two men like a propped-up corpse. He has never had to travel in a police vehicle before. He looks tired. He looks gaunt. He is aware that the guard to his left – Tony – he is aware that Tony is surreptitiously trying to eye him. He is aware that he is making both men tense. He is aware that if he weren't there, the two men would be chatting away.

'Watch this,' the driver says, nudging the conservator as they near the city. He points up at a hill. There are two stationary cars parked at the top. When the convoy reaches the bridge, the two cars descend from the hill and join them, sirens blaring. These police cars are marked. The rest of the journey proceeds with full sirens in all five vehicles. The convoy makes its way to the centre of the city in less than fifteen minutes.

The four cars leave the armoured van once it has entered the back gates of the gallery. Security personnel are in place. The van is driven through blue metal doors and onto a lift. The doors are locked behind it, and the van is shunted up to the unpacking area. The policemen wait until the crate has been opened and the presence of the painting confirmed before turning to shake hands with the conservator. The conservator steps back. He pulls his right hand out of his pocket and holds it up apologetically. It is bound in what looks like a tea towel. Sorry, he says to the policemen, and thank you. The same masking tape that had been used to secure the painting is wrapped around the conservator's hand to hold the tea towel in place. He has not wrapped his hand with anything like the care with which he packed the painting. You should get that hand seen to, Tony says. Next thing on the list, the conservator assures him.

The painting is ushered through the back corridors and lifts of the gallery to the studio. It is placed on a trestle table that is covered in green felt. I, meanwhile, am somewhere in the midlands, driving down the motorway as fast as I can. The quality of the daylight has changed. It is no longer hazy, but lucid and sharp. I lean forward over the steering wheel and peer up at the sky. Black heavy clouds are gathering overhead.

The upstairs of the gallery is usually a quiet place. It is usually even quieter than the display rooms below. The noise generated by the arrival of the painting pinballs around the walls hours after the security men and handlers have gone. The studio is on the top floor. There are no windows. The ceiling is a complicated Victorian iron structure, infilled with hundreds of panes of glass. It forms a pyramid above the room. The conservator needs natural light. Vertical natural light. Daylight is required for colour matching and retouching. It is the first week of October and the days have already perceptibly shortened. The conservator is keen to get started on the painting as soon as possible.

The camera has already been set up. It has been rigged above the table on which the conservator will restore the painting. It is at this point that the conservator will notice that a tiny piece of the canvas is missing. A piece about the size of the heart of a daisy. The conservator will note that the edges are freshly cut. He will also note that no damage has been done to the painting by this small theft. The piece has been taken from the tacking edge.

The painting can't be mounted on an easel – the stretcher frame was stripped from it when it was stolen. Photographs are to be taken at every stage of the restoration. This information is valuable to the police as well as to the conservator. The present condition of the painting will help identify the perpetrators of the theft. The conservator's opinions will be vital in this regard.

The telephone rings. The conservator's Nordic assistant answers it. It's Detective Inspector something or other, she tells him, her hand covering the mouthpiece of the phone. The surname is unintelligible to the conservator. All he has gathered is that it begins with an 'm'. Every name sounds foreign when the Nordic assistant pronounces it. She finds additional syllables floating in the air, and drops them into her sentences. The conservator has never felt so tired in his life. He waves the phone off, and his assistant turns to the wall clutching the receiver. It is an old-fashioned handset. It looks huge in her possession. He isn't here, she whispers into the mouthpiece, and nods, then nods again, as if the caller can see her. She transcribes a phone number onto a yellow post-it, and promises the Detective Inspector that she'll pass on the message. Thank you, the conservator says when she hangs up. She looks at the makeshift bandage on his hand, and wonders if some of his fingers are broken. He leaves the room before giving her a chance to relay the detective's message. She sets it down in her geometric handwriting, and leaves the message and the phone number on the conservator's desk. She sees the message later, balled up in the conservator's wastebasket. Did her message puzzle him? It would not be the first message of hers to puzzle the conservator. Her English is excellent, but the foreign names cause her difficulty. She tackles them phonetically, using too many consonants. There is no sign that the phone number has been written down elsewhere. The Nordic assistant hovers over the wastebasket, wondering what she should do. She decides to do nothing. I am no secretary, she tells herself, and turns on her heel. The policeman will just have to ring again. She relents minutes later, and goes back and picks the message out of the wastepaper basket. She looks around the room. Where should she hide it? She drops it into her purse, feeling foolish.

The conservator's meeting with the director of the gallery is brief. He comes out from behind his desk when the conservator enters the room. Welcome back, he says, placing a hand on the conservator's shoulder. He pushes him gently towards a chair. The top of the director's head is bald. The black hair on the rest of his head is glossy and thick. He wears it so that it is long enough to touch his shirt collar. The director is one of the many men in the gallery who never married.

The two men sit. The director puts on his reading glasses and clears his throat. Is the conservator in a position yet to authenticate the painting? Almost, says the conservator. He explains that the canvas is still covered in overpaint, but he doesn't envisage difficulties. He'll be able to confirm tomorrow. Excellent, says the director. He sits back and folds his hands serenely in front of himself. He smiles. He is the *Mona Lisa*. Excellent, he says again.

Then he notices the bandage on the conservator's hand. He sits up and his chair creaks mightily. The reading glasses are whipped off. He peers at the hand with narrowed eyes, notes that it is the right one. Have you had that hand seen to yet? he asks. It's nothing, the conservator tells him. It's only a bit of a bruise. It does not look like a bit of a bruise to the director. He can't see much under the bandage, but he suspects from the way that the conservator has wrapped it that the hand has been crushed. Perhaps even broken. There appears to be some sort of splint under the tea towel. How can the director allow the conservator to restore such a significant painting with a broken hand? He looks worried. Don't worry, the conservator says. The director nods, but he still looks worried. He leans forward and puts his elbows on his desk. He clasps his hands together. Now he is one of the apostles in *The Last Supper*.

The director clears his throat again. Would you like more time off? he begins. Perhaps you should complete your sabbatical? The conservator has come back two weeks early from a three-month sabbatical. The discovery of the painting is a circumstance that was unforeseen. The director would prefer to ease the conservator back into his job. He cannot take chances with this painting. Nor with the conservator.

We could arrange for someone else to . . . The director doesn't finish his sentence.

The conservator smiles politely. He spreads his good hand out flat on the desk, as if preparing to swear on a Bible. I don't need any more time off, he states. The Conservation Department does not require additional staff. I'll take care of this. I'll take care of it properly. You have my word.

The director makes steeples with his fingers. Okay then, he says, after a long pause. If you think that's best. I do, the conservator quickly affirms, removing his hand from the desk and glancing at his watch. It is already after two. Okay then, the director says again, sounding even more unsure. But you should get that hand seen to as soon as possible. The two men stand up. The meeting is over.

It is mid-afternoon before the initial photographs have been taken and the conservator is at last left alone with the painting. He moistens a cotton swab in chemical solvent and applies it to the canvas. No one sees how he does this with his bandaged hand. The conservator has been anticipating this moment for some time.

He starts on the top left of the canvas. The blue overpaint lifts easily enough. A relatively weak solution is all that will be required to remove the modern paint. The seventeenth-century paint beneath has oxidised and hardened. It won't be affected by the solvent. The conservator can proceed immediately with the cleaning process. I, by now, am in a port town on the south-east coast, thinking of the painting. There is a wasp dying on the windowsill beside me. The sun has disappeared for the first time in months. I have been put in a chair that swivels about on a central pedestal. The chair must be at least twenty years old. The towel that is stuffed down the back of my neck is older than I am. My hair is being chopped off. I look at it on the linoleum floor. There is so much of it. What have I done?

The conservator is reluctant to leave the painting alone that evening. He stays working in the studio as I begin my journey west. The mountains tower up as if they're going to topple over and crush me. It is dark by the time I arrive at the coast. I arrange to take a room above the pub. I choose a seat in the corner nearest the fire, and order a bowl of soup. A man at the end of the bar sidles up, and tells me that he has a cottage to rent. I don't know why he offers this information. Perhaps he was eavesdropping as I booked the room. His teeth are too big for his head, and they are not one bit clean. The front two incline towards each other, like the pages of an open book. The information he brings me is unsolicited, but welcome. I listen, pretending not to. The cottage belonged to his aunt, he tells me. His great-aunt. Her old cat is still living there, looked in on by a neighbour. Do I like cats? he asks. I do. I must feed the cat if I take on the cottage. It doesn't require much care. It is a nice old moggy. Its name is Bert.

I give the man a month's rent and another month's deposit up front. It makes me nervous to hand over so much money when I have so little, and no guarantee of more. The man is oblivious to my anxiety. He counts out the cash and tells me that the key is under a stone by the back door of the cottage. He writes the address on a beer mat. The address is just the name of a house. There's no street name on this, I point out. Turn left with your back to O'Leary's pub, he instructs me, and keep walking. Is this O'Leary's pub? I ask. The man laughs. You can't miss O'Leary's, he says. Ask anyone. He holds out his hand and I shake it. It is covered in black bristly hair. His other hand is fastening the button on the shirt pocket in which he has placed my money. He mentions, as he's rising to go, that I can catch the fishing boat over for free if I get up early enough. He says that the fisherman is a friend of his. Fishing boat? I ask, looking at him in horror. What do you mean, *fishing boat*? The cottage is across on the island, the man explains, jerking his thumb at the darkness outside. The *island*? I repeat in disbelief. What *island*? My eyes are blinking involuntarily. I am finding it difficult to remain seated. I am finding it difficult not to shout.

The man raises his hand as if calming an angry animal. The island, yes, he says, backing away as he speaks. Did he forget to mention that the cottage was on an island? Presumed I knew. A beautiful place. Away from it all. He'll look in on me in a month or so. Good luck.

The door clatters shut in his wake. There is no point in going after him. He will have vanished into thin air by the time I get outside. I am left with my beer mat and my soup. A flaccid skin has grown on the soup. I break a hole in it, then push the bowl away. I have made my bed, and will lie in it.

I retire to my room at ten that night, about the same time as the conservator leaves the studio. It is normal for the conservator to remain at the gallery long after the others are gone, especially under such exceptional circumstances. He hasn't actually been working on the painting. He doesn't want to touch it in artificial light. He has simply been staring at it for three or four hours. He has also been postponing having his hand seen to. He finally decides that it is time to go to Accident and Emergency. The queues shouldn't be that bad on a Monday night. He switches the lights out. The night sky leaves the studio in blue shadow. I sit down on the bed. There are white sheets and wool blankets on it. I realise that I have forgotten to ask my new landlord what became of his great-aunt. He has left me with no way of contacting him. I don't want to live in a house in which somebody has recently died. Perhaps, I tell myself, she has retired to a nursing home. Perhaps the rent is needed to pay her keep. If she were dead, the grand-nephew would surely just sell the place. Wouldn't he? Of course he would. The great-aunt must be alive.

I get into the bed and fall asleep quickly. I dream that I am part of a crowd on the steps of the National Gallery. We are waiting for the painting to arrive. Presumably, I have this dream because of the sound of revelry that is coming from the pub. It rises through the wooden floorboards, and is muffled and dull. The other people on the steps are having great fun waiting. They all seem to know each other. They tell jokes, and one of them sings a song. Someone falls off the step. Apparently, this is the funniest thing that ever happened. I try to tell the crowd what I know about the painting, but they don't listen to me, so I give up.

Five-fifteen and the morning is cold. The morning, to my mind, is still night. Daybreak is at least another hour off. I climb onto the boat, thinking how awful it must be to have to do this several times a week. The fisherman seems cheerful enough. He says that he doesn't feel the cold. Never did. I should eat more fish, he tells me. We both laugh at this. I hate fish.

There it is, says the fisherman after half an hour or so. He points at the darkness. I look, but can see nothing. It's the island, he says. I still can see nothing, and tell him so. You'd be able to see it clearly, he tells me, if you ate more fish. Something black begins to loom out of the navy sea and sky. It takes shape, and is resolute. It looks like it is approaching us with more speed than we are approaching it. What have I done, I ask myself again.

Three hours later, and I'm walking down the road to my new cottage. The gulls are doing battle above my head. They clash in the sky like rocks. I have had breakfast in the pub nearest the harbour. O'Leary's, ask anyone. Perhaps it is the only pub, I speculate. I have little idea yet of how big the island is. I don't know if the pub was officially open when I wandered in. The door was unlocked. It was 7 a.m. The sunlight was streaming in through the stained-glass windows. The woman who was washing up behind the counter greeted me warmly and pulled off her rubber gloves. Breakfast? I asked, and she nodded and disappeared into the kitchen. I was the only customer during the two hours I spent there. It was the best breakfast I'd ever had. It was the best meal I'd ever had. I only realised how hungry I was when the plate of food arrived. Rashers, sausages, eggs and tomato. Two pots of tea. No fish.

I leave the pub at nine o'clock in the morning and turn left, as instructed by the grand-nephew. My stomach is swollen and happy. I feel calm for the first time in days. I yawn. The conservator yawns too. He is parking his car. He has a parking space assigned to him with his title on a placard: Keeper of Conservation. He parks between the Director and the Keeper of the Collection. The conservator's space is to the front of the gallery. He has one of the best parking spaces in the city.

He enters the foyer and mock-salutes the man in the security office. The conservator's hand is now in plaster. The security man mock-salutes back, and buzzes him in through a steel door marked 'Private'. The conservator takes a left and makes his way down the corridor. This is the part of the gallery that the public never sees. It's the part that runs behind the façade with the blind windows. There are five floors in the private part of the gallery, but from the outside it looks like three. The conservator runs a card key through the slot on the wall, and the doors of the lift slide apart. Like all the lifts in the gallery, it is huge. It could carry a small car. The lift goes up to the fifth floor and the conservator steps out. His Nordic assistant is already at her desk, bent over a large gold-leafed picture frame. She is remoulding the baroque swirls and flourishes that have splintered off over the years. She smiles; says good morning. She has perfect skin, and I am jealous of her. I don't know if the conservator has a Nordic assistant. If he does, I know that I am jealous. I know that I would never take to her. I'm still wandering down the road, clutching last night's beer mat. I am searching for the great-aunt's cottage. I should have asked the woman in the pub if she knew where it was. Or if she had even heard of it. If such a place actually existed. I cannot believe that it is only occurring to me now that there may not be any such cottage. I cannot believe that I have been so stupid. A light drizzle has started. It is not heavy enough to make me turn back. I have to go through all the cottages, peering at the names on the walls. A flat white face stares out at me from the window of one of them, like a stingray in an aquarium, and I look away, flustered. The cottages are set half a mile apart. Not all of them have names, but the grand-nephew assured me that my cottage does. Gull Cottage. How much money have I given him? A fairly large portion of what I had. Have I been ripped off? Is that why there was so much laughter in the pub that night? I am exhausted. I want to lie down on the side of the road. I must be getting older. I feel like I am older.

I eventually find the cottage and unlock the back door. The cat comes trotting out to have a look at me. He has tears running down his face. Judging by how congealed his eyes are, he has had the infection for some time. The cat turns away when he sees that I am the wrong person. The conservator unlocks the studio door. The rain is falling heavily on the glass ceiling now. He walks up to the trestle table. There it is, *Girl in the Mirror*. He has only cleaned the top left corner of the painting, but it is enough. Already he can confirm that it is the real thing.

I want to write a letter to the conservator. I have no conception of how the conservator would take it. His relationship with the painting is so wholly different to mine. Dear Sir, I would write, for I would not know how to address him. I cannot write his Christian name. I cannot write Mister, because then I'd have to use his surname. I don't want to use his surname. Any intimation of familiarity would be inappropriate. The conservator is not interested. The man does not want to know. It'd be easier to just say Sir. I don't think that the conservator and I will see eye to eye. He will open the letter in the studio with his broken hand. His Nordic assistant will not notice that something is amiss. I will write my new address in the top right corner so that the conservator will know where to find me. And then he can tell the police where to find me. Everyone will find me. Dear Sir, the letter will say. My name is Anna Hunt. I am the woman who stole *Girl in the Mirror*.

II

The Stables, the Preceding Spring

THREE

They say a fugue state is like a safety valve. When it gets too much, you become someone else. The detachment, I can now say with a reasonable amount of certainty, began last spring, six or seven months before I ended up on the island. I am estimating the time of the year by the weather. I will never be sure of the exact date. It was a clear bright morning when I first found myself in the stables. Found myself, yes, because I had no idea how I got there, though the state of my clothes would suggest I'd been dragged backwards through bushes. I just looked around and there I was. I remembered nothing from before that moment. That is the truth. I had managed to detach myself from my own past. I had forgotten every part of it. My memory was gone. Though I didn't understand that as such. Not at the time. You cannot miss something you've forgotten you ever had. At least, you cannot miss it properly, though you know that it's lost. You pat your pockets over and over without knowing what it is that you're hoping to find.

The painting itself had been stolen approximately two months before I arrived at the stables. The twelfth of January, I later found out, and shook my head – the date sounded like someone's birthday, not the day on which my life had gone wrong. The twelfth of January. Nine months ago now. Paintings, I should say – there were three of them, of which I kept one. Everyone seems to know this already. I know it too. I just didn't know it last spring. I knew nothing last spring. I didn't know my own name. I had become someone else by the time I'd reached the stables. I did not know what was in the briefcase that I carried in my hand, but I decided it was mine. Which, of course, it certainly wasn't. I absolutely did not know that I had stolen a painting. Three paintings, even. Kel and I: together we had stolen three paintings.

The entire operation was masterminded by Kel. He conceived the plan to steal the paintings, and with my help he executed it. He was the one who organised selling on two of them for the briefcase full of money. I think he believed he was selling them to private collectors. I was not involved in the sale. The paintings didn't go back to the collection from which they'd been stolen. They ended up in the National Gallery. They spent some time, no doubt, in the custody of the conservator, who gave them the once-over to see what damage we'd done. There was damage all right, but not to the paintings. I had nearly lost an eye. Kel had sliced me with his knife. The details of the incident are still unclear in my mind. There had been the inevitable fight between us once the sale of the first two paintings had been completed. Kel couldn't control himself when money was close. It was the first time he had turned on me, physically at least. Unfortunately, it was not the last time. I believe now that part of him had always hated me. Perhaps he hated me because I reminded him so much of himself. Perhaps I was just part of his hatred for the world in general. I never hated him. And I never will. It is easy to say that now, after all that has happened. It is easy to have mercy for someone who has already been punished. I escaped from Kel with my bleeding eye, taking *Girl in the Mirror* and the money with me, but the shock of the physical attack, the shock of blade on skin, of blade sinking into skin and moving fast, the shock must have wiped my memory clean.

It goes without saying that the next time I saw Kel, maybe four months after he had knifed me, I had no idea who he was. I did not know Kel from Adam. Unfortunately, he knew exactly who I was. Though it took me a while to figure that out.

So there I was. It was that simple. I didn't question it at the time. *There I was*. In these stables. Strangely unperturbed. No past tense, no future, and I didn't care. I had woken up in the hay barn. I immediately stood up and looked around. I was alone, and that was good. Everything drowsed in warm shadow. I brushed myself down, all business. No idea where I was. No idea who I was. That didn't trouble me, not one bit. I picked up the briefcase and went marching towards the door, but there I stopped to appraise the situation. The barn door glowed orange, as if a fire burned behind it. I held my hand out to see if I could detect heat. No heat. It was too early in the morning for heat.

I heaved the door open. I had to put the briefcase down to do so. It took all my strength to get the door to budge – the barn was a great wooden construction that had, over the years, sagged to one side. The door had to be lifted off its hinges to get it to move.

The light on the other side of it was unbelievable. It was blindingly white and flooded into the hay shed. I stepped outside and blinked. I saw nothing for several seconds. Then the scene assembled itself before me with a downward movement. The buildings slotted into place like falling snow. I was in the courtyard. The horses all stood to attention behind their stable doors. They were astounded, as astounded as I was. We regarded each other in astonishment. I already had the scar, though it wasn't yet a scar. Still a wound. I could see the mound of the scab in my peripheral vision. I squinted up at the sun. It was low in the sky. The day was very young.

'Are you here about the job?'

I turned and saw an old man shuffling towards me. The figure he cut – a bedraggled ogre. The horses shifted about in excitement, and turned their attention to him. One of them whickered hopefully. He ignored them and continued to approach. His white hair stood on end. His fly was undone. The trousers were made of some coarse fabric. Hemp, maybe. One of his shoes had burst at the toe. What was it he carried in his hand? I can't say with certainty. A hatchet, or something. Some sturdy deft implement that had a thick wooden handle. A hatchet or a small lump hammer. He swung it about in a businesslike fashion. There was a dog at his heel. A great matted dog with a twig caught in its underbelly hair. The twig dragged along the cobbles like a withered leg, and the dog high-stepped around it. It looked up at me, all worried eyebrows, and hesitantly wagged its tail.

The old man laboured towards me, as oblivious to my state as he was to his own. He did not appear to notice my torn clothes. He did not look twice at my wounded eye. I took a step back as the little procession drew near. The man stopped walking and the dog collapsed by his feet, its pink tongue aloll. One of the horses kicked shyly at its door. The dog abruptly jack-knifed, and bit at the twig on its belly.

'Oh, for God's sake, are you simple?!' the old man bellowed. 'Or are you foreign? Did you not hear what I'm after saying? Are you here about the job?' He waved his hammer in the direction of the horses by way of explanation. My briefcase was still in the hay barn. I would have to come back for it later. There was a five-bar gate to my left. I could get to it in ten paces, and clear it in one swing. The dog, for no apparent reason, jumped to its feet, barking so shrilly that my teeth hurt. One of the horses whinnied. The door-kicker kicked the door again, less diffidently this time.

'Shut up!' roared the old man, and a mutinous silence descended upon the place. Two of the horse heads disappeared behind the half doors. The dog flattened itself onto the ground. The old man turned back to me.

'The owners only come up on the weekends. You have to mind them the rest of the time. Feed them, exercise them, keep them alive. Money's not great, but lodgings are provided.' He sniffed resentfully, as if I had contrived to insult him somehow.

At this point, as I remember, I turned around. I forgot about my escape route, and turned right around so that my back was to the old man. What made me do so? Perhaps I heard something, though if I did, I cannot recall it. Perhaps the old man threw a nervous eye over my shoulder, though I don't recall that either. Just one of those things, then. The intervention of fate. There was a paddock beside the courtyard, flanked on one side by trees. Wooden fence about the other three sides. Grass-less and pockmarked by thousands of hoof prints. The chestnut mare wasn't there yet, but she was almost there. I watched the shadows between the trees. It seems we all did – me, the horses and the dog, even the old man. We all concentrated fiercely. Not a sound in the air, which was swarming about the branches like petrol fumes. Then she came plunging out from them, the mare rampant, all mane and flashing hooves. It was as if we had conjured her up by force of will. I took a step towards her. She didn't notice me. She came dancing through the morning light, literally dancing beneath the shimmering leaves. We all watched this lightsome performance, until it became too much for the dog. It leapt up again and ran in a tight circle before us, yelping hysterically at its own tail. The old man roared and swung his foot at it. He missed. The dog wailed. The mare stopped short and came to earth again, thrusting her hooves into the soil. She took us in and flattened her ears. She kicked at the air and squealed, just out of badness, and then disappeared back into the woods. An angry twist of tail, and she was gone.

The dog shrank away. The old man sauntered up behind me. It was what he said next that sold me on the idea.

'That animal,' he grunted, and spat on the ground. A gob of yellow saliva landed to my left and I looked at it expectantly, as if it, and not the old man, was the one that had spoken. The saliva bubbled on the stones.

'You can have her if you want,' said the voice. 'That animal's mad.'

'I'll take it,' I said. 'I'll take the job.'

The old man grunted once more and walked away in the direction from which he'd come. His shoulders were shuddering. The bastard was laughing at me. Whatever the job was, apparently it was mine. I turned back to the paddock. The chestnut mare watched me through the trees, and moved off.

*

Lady, I think her name was. I think that is the name that the old man gave me for the chestnut mare. Something instantly forgettable, which I instantly forgot. I waited for her to come out of the woods, but she never did while I was around, no matter how well I hid myself. She was on to me, and knew to stay away. But I was persistent. I tried tempting her out with food, and with the promise of the company of the other horses. (Think of it! I wheeled them all out and lined them up on the other side of her paddock fence. The lot of them watched the gap in the trees, briefly enraptured, then restless. They began picking fights with each other, so I marched them back in. They sighed and snuffled and pulled at the straw in their stables.)

In the end, I chased her out with the lunging whip. She bucked and she reared and she shrieked at me in indignation. I dropped the whip, and wrapped barbed wire around the gap in the trees. The mare was quiet behind me. Ominously so. She hung back at the far end of the paddock. I hurried on with my reel of wire, wrapping it around the two trees a third time, a fourth, cutting my hands as I tightened it into place. I shot a glance over my shoulder. The mare was running full tilt at me, gauging how high she'd have to jump to clear the wire. I threw myself out of the way, arms clamped to my head. She lost her nerve at the last second, and skidded to a halt just before crashing into my blockade. When I looked up she was standing over me, the whites of her eyes levelled at mine. I reached for the whip. She struck out her foreleg and missed. Then she galloped back to her corner. That was it. I had her.

But I couldn't get near her. So I starved her for a while, all the time talking to her and holding out a bucket of food. I shook the contents, and she flattened her ears at the sound. It became too much for her eventually. She held out for about three days. The shadows of her ribs were creeping up her belly. She picked her way up one evening, head high and alarmed. Stood just shy of me while I tormented her with the bucket. She swallowed hungrily and ground her teeth, but she did not step forward. Her head ducked up and down as she stretched out her neck and pulled back again. Out and back, out and back, never actually reaching the food. An age of this. My arm was nearly dead from the weight of the bucket by the time she put her nose into it. She snatched a mouthful of food in such haste that most of it spilled, and then she galloped back to her corner. That was enough for one day. I emptied the bucket into her trough, and left her for the night.

The day after that, she was up to me within minutes. Head into the bucket, and then she was gone. But she came back, almost immediately. I started talking to her. I told her that she was beautiful, that she was the most beautiful creature in the world. She listened attentively and picked at the food. She disappeared when the bucket was empty.

We did that for three days, each time spending over an hour standing in the middle of the field only a few feet away from each other. The old man came down from his house on the hill. He stood in the courtyard watching us, all the time shaking his head. He informed me later that I must indeed be simple, for I was wasting my time. He ambled off, muttering under his breath. Bad words, and lots of them. No sign of the dog.

And then on the fourth evening, I showed up without the bucket. My pockets were full of food. I stood in the middle of the paddock with my back to the mare, holding out a handful of oats. I was all the time talking to her while gazing at the woods, pretending not to notice her, pretending not to care. She came up behind me, wondering where the bucket was. I didn't turn to look at her. I couldn't see her shadow on the ground. I just told myself that she was there, and that she was listening to my every word, ears tilted towards me while I talked and waited.

A nervous snort investigated my hands. Her breath was warm. Some of the oats spilled onto the ground. I heard her step back and snort again. Beautiful creature, I said. Stunning creature. Why do you make it so hard on yourself?

She considered my question intently, and stepped forward once more. A sort of lunge at my hand that knocked off more oats. I braced myself, terrified that she'd bite my fingers. She could take them right off if she set her mind to it.

Deadlock for some moments. I waited for her to gallop away like an animal insane, but she didn't move. She stood with her neck arched like a seahorse. I had no idea how she stood – I couldn't see her because she remained behind me – but in my mind, she stood as tautly as a seahorse. At any second, she might have snapped like an overstretched wire and gone whirring through the air. The tension was unbelievable. The tension was exhilarating. That was when she chose to eat from my hand, my poor mad Lady. She ate from my hand and I wanted to run around and whoop. But I didn't. Her muzzle was smooth as velvet. I could see it too in my mind's eye, her soft warm muzzle with its twin curlicues of nostrils slanting upwards towards her face. She gathered up the food and withdrew her head. But she did not step back from me. I waited to see what she'd do next. She did nothing. Nor did I. We both stood there doing nothing until I was ready to collapse.

That was when she let me place my hand on her neck. She lowered her head, and I smoothed down her poor mane. Her poor torn mane. It hadn't been attended to in months. Next thing, as if shot by a pellet gun, she was galloping and bucking down the field, sending mud-clumps hurtling like meteorites through the air.

I believe in fatal flaws. There is a Greek term for it. The conservator would know precisely the word I need. The conservator is full of information of this nature. An 'unsound constitution' is what the old man called it in the chestnut mare. 'That mare is of an unsound constitution,' he said. 'The animal is mad. There is nothing that can be done with her. Not worth feeding.' She had been given to him by one of the women who kept horses in livery with him. 'The hoor toppled over backwards,' he remarked one evening, 'and broke a paying customer's hip.' He shook his head bitterly and spat on the ground. He was going to put her down, just as soon as he managed to catch her. 'That animal can see the devil in the wind.'

All that rage and constant fury! My God, the animal was filled top to tail with unfocused wrath. She provoked something in me though. Something I didn't think I had. Compassion. If I could rescue her, I told myself. If I could just manage to do that much, then, I don't know. Then I'd have earned myself a little grace. Or so I told myself. So I chose to believe.

FOUR

'Detek-a-tive Inspek-a-tor Macadona,' the Nordic assistant announces. Perhaps she is Oriental. Perhaps she is a tiny Japanese girl, with a doll's round face and shiny bobbed hair. No: it is important that she looks like she could have fallen out of a Raphael painting. She is definitely pale and blond.

Today she wears open-toed clogs that would look bizarre on any other woman. Certainly something bought in her own country – the conservator has never seen anything like them before. Her feet are white and pretty. She has varnished her toenails an iridescent blue. On one of her toes is a silver ring. She smiles sweetly at the conservator, then steps out of the doorway to reveal a well-dressed man in his forties.

'Sebastian McDonagh!' the conservator declares. He puts down his tools and rolls his chair back from the desk. 'I was wondering when you'd show up.' The Detective Inspector comes forward, offering his hand.

'Oops,' he says, when he sees the conservator's bandage. 'Been sticking them where you shouldn't have?'

The noise that the conservator makes in answer to this is a cross between a cough and a grunt. There is a degree of embarrassment in it. Possibly even of disapproval. The conservator is too conscious of the Nordic assistant's presence in the background to run with the Detective Inspector's innuendo. Sebastian is not overly impressed with his old friend's response. He withdraws the offer of his hand, placing it instead on his hip.

'And here she is at last,' he says, peering over the conservator's shoulder at the painting on the desk. The conservator stands out of his way. Much of the overpaint has been removed from *Girl in the Mirror*, but she is still a hybrid of two paintings. There is sky and field on her face. The detective bends over the canvas, his face only inches above it. He scrutinises it for several moments, then turns to the conservator. 'As lovely as she ever was,' he comments, nodding gravely.

The conservator cannot help but smile. There are times when he feels an almost paternal pride in the accomplishments of the paintings he restores. Something about removing the overpaint from *Girl in the Mirror* has moved him. At first it was like chipping away at a face frozen under ice. Gradually it thawed, and the young girl's features emerged.

'You have yourself your first talisman painting,' Sebastian says. He rattles the coins in his pockets and leans back slightly, closing his eyes and letting the light from the glass ceiling diffuse onto his face. He can sense that the conservator is watching him. He enjoys this bit. The display of insider knowledge. Lecturing of the uninitiated. The demonstration of the capacity to never be surprised.

'How lucky we are,' remarks the conservator. 'What in the name of God is a talisman painting?'

'*Girl in the Mirror* is now regarded as a prestige theft. Because she has been stolen so many times, it would now be an honour to steal her again.'

'Well now, that's just what the collection needs.' The conservator is already aware that *Girl* has become something of a celebrity since her recovery. He has helped Detective Inspector McDonagh with previous enquiries. They go back about ten years. Last time the painting was stolen, it was Sebastian who found her, stashed in the boot of a car in an airport in Rotterdam. He had to pose as a black-market dealer to get her back, a task he appeared to relish, and in which he excelled.

'So, what can you tell me about the perpetrators of the theft?' Sebastian asks questions as if he already knows the answers, and is just checking that the examinee is on the ball. He crosses over to the conservator's desk and sifts through the photographs that are scattered upon it. The photographs document the painting during the various stages of its restoration.

The conservator regards Sebastian for a few seconds. Detective Inspector McDonagh is half French. Always seemed more of a London banker-type than a policeman to the conservator, what with his stylish clothes and knowledge of fine art. The conservator goes to the filing cabinet in the corner. He unlocks it, removes something, locks it again. He returns with a page of white paper, which he hands to Sebastian.

'I have received a written confession from a woman called Anna Hunt. After stealing the painting, she appears to have spent some time working in livery stables situated fifteen miles to the north of the city. It's not clear what she was doing there. Hiding, probably.' The detective runs an eye over my handwriting.

'And the painting? Did she have the painting in her possession during this time?'

'The condition of the canvas would suggest that *Girl in the Mirror* was subjected to minimal exposure to the elements. I would say that there was very little, if indeed any, movement of the canvas for the duration of its disappearance. It is more likely that it was stored in a safe-house somewhere.'

Naturally, the conservator says nothing of the kind. Nor does he give the detective my letter. There is no letter. I have not written one. When asked what he knows, the conservator turns away from the detective and picks up a knife. He cuts off a piece of wax and applies it to the canvas. He eases it onto the craquelure with an electric metal spatula. His absorption in the task irritates the detective.

'It's hard to tell anything at all,' is the only comment he eventually makes. The conservator does not look at Sebastian as he speaks.

FIVE

It was all there unravelling around us, the wide open space of the yellow meadows that rolled and curved as they strained for the sea, the cliff path that tightly belted those meadows in, the raucous scream of the kittiwakes that reeled above us, but I was concentrating on the chestnut mare's hoof beats. She had a great white blaze staked like a javelin onto her face, and a golden tail that shredded the air behind her; made that air whistle and sing. A tall animal, maybe seventeen hands high, and very strong. She whirled around in circles beneath me, practising the steps of her restless dance.

'Stand.'

Her ears flicked back and forth at the sound of my voice. She fell still and chewed on the bit. We had reached the bottom of the meadow. She was reluctant to stay there, and inclined her head warily towards the crashing waves below. Thirty feet beneath us, the inlet sea water was as black as ink. I leaned forward and peered down. The temperature of the air fell by a few degrees. The land seemed suddenly hollow then, as if we stood upon a vast cave that delved into the underworld. The meadow was stretched tightly over that cave like the sprung dry skin of a drum, and it was upon that resonant surface that the mare's hoofs played rhythms.

She stamped down hard with her back leg. I turned her away from the cliffs. We stopped at the foot of the hill, yet she never really stopped beneath me, that exquisite animal, but sidestepped, and fixed her eyes upon something in momentary fascination, and realigned her feet carefully beneath her. I tried to see what she saw, but there was nothing there. Her eyes darted and froze upon that nothing, and then seized upon other nothings. I never tried to discipline her on such occasions, just watched her start and stare. Her nothings were as real to her as mine were to me. They whispered threats to her on the breeze, and then examined her reaction with narrowed eyes. The whole world was alive with them. The whole world itched.

A basking fox regarded us calmly, half blind in the sun. He raised his wet snout to the air. I held my breath, and watched his black nose pucker and contract, but the fox smelled just horse smells, and lazily dismissed us. The mare took up her impatient jig again. I drew up the reins.

'Stand!'

She wanted to be good. That poor horse, God love her, she tried so hard to be good. Her muscles trembled like plucked guitar strings. It took the tiniest signal from me – I was amazed that she could even feel it – and we were launched at last into air and light. Her hoofs rumbled upon the face of the hollow yellow earth, and the air gushed up at us as though we were falling through the sky. I glanced over my shoulder at the land that we were covering. It was difficult to get a proper look, because of the speed with which we travelled. It was her hoof prints that my eyes sought. I needed to see her prints, just her prints, cut into the grass, and to know that there were none of mine amongst them. I needed to know that I had not yet set foot in the outside world, so to speak. I rode upon air, and was there and yet not there. I was practically invisible, and I knew that I had done it. I had fooled someone somewhere into believing I was gone.

A derelict cottage stood at the top of the hill where the meadow levelled off for a few hundred yards before beginning its downward slope towards the river and the quicks. The roof of the cottage was long gone. Two gabled-ended chimneys pronged the sky. The cottage was surrounded by a small birch wood, and at that time of the year, the leaves were almost translucent. The sun shone through them, casting green light on what had once been the floor. It was within this still pool of light that something roused itself as we galloped past. There was a man crouching behind the broken wall.

The mare twisted in fright. I swung out of the saddle at speed. Saw my legs above me swinging through the sky, then I landed hard on my shoulders and tumbled. I was face down in the grass before I realised that I'd come to a stop.

I lay there without moving and wondered if I was okay. No pain, so I got to my feet. Very dizzy – I tottered forward to keep my balance. Ahead of me, the mare was disappearing down into the quicks. The empty stirrups jabbed her in the sides, goading her on like a phantom rider. I looked back at the cottage. The man was no longer visible. He was probably standing on the other side of the wall, not ten foot away. I ran off through the long grass.

The chestnut mare was waiting outside the gate to her paddock when I got back, the reins caught under one of her forelegs. Her coat was wet through and dark brown with sweat. Her mane was plastered to her skin. She snorted loudly and back-stepped at my approach. It's all right, I called out to her as soothingly as I could. She didn't look like she believed me.

'There was someone here asking about you while you were out.' The old man, Jerry, had appeared by the well. He used to do that sometimes. Just appear.

'Who?' I asked, trying to lay a steadying hand on the mare's neck. 'Who was asking about me?'

'Tie that damned animal up before she kills us all!' The mare gazed at Jerry uncertainly, her nostrils quivering.

'Who was asking about me?'

'I don't bloody know, do I? I told him to get off my property. I don't want any of your young men hanging around here, do you understand that?' Jerry stalked off in the direction of his house. His dog was back with him, one of its ears turned inside out. It looked at me apologetically, then trotted after its master.

SIX

He was back that night, the man who had been asking about me. I woke up and he was standing at the foot of the bed. I couldn't make out his features in the dark.

'Who are you?' I demanded, sitting up. The man moved towards me with lizard speed. He seized my throat and I gasped.

'Shush,' he whispered. His hands were large and tipped with long nails. The nails cut into the back of my neck. He angled my face to the right and leaned over me. My scar. He was looking at my scar.

'Who are you?' I choked out again. I grabbed his wrists and tried to push him away. He reacted with such force that he practically lifted me off the bed. It was probably the fright more than anything else that made me black out. The man's fists released my throat, and recoiled like snakes. There were footsteps around me. Cautious and stiff. The man was checking if I still breathed. He poked me in the ribs. He slapped me once or twice. I heard myself groan and I rolled onto my side.

When I came round, I saw that all the stuff in my room had been rifled through. The drawers were overturned. My few belongings were strewn about. Even the boxes under the bed had been pulled out and emptied, though they weren't mine, and were only full of old rosettes. I was amazed that I had stayed unconscious throughout the whole thing.

'You'll have to manage without me.'

It was the first time in the two months or so that I'd been working for Jerry that I'd called to his house. I pressed the doorbell. It didn't make a sound. I banged on the brass knocker, and stood waiting in the noon sunlight. There was no sign of life inside. An old horseshoe was nailed to the door. The horseshoe had rusted, and a mouldering brown rivulet ran down the paintwork. I pushed open the letterbox and saw the foot of a threadbare stair.

Some creaking and scraping noises came from the open upstairs window. 'Jerry?' I called up, standing back on the doorstep. There was a jangle, like that of a brass bed, one of those huge antique affairs that you are born and die in. The old man must have been heaving himself out of it and scratching around on the floor for his shoes. I turned my back to the door and waited.

The garden hadn't been attended to in years. A network of fox runs wormed through the undergrowth. Midges swam in the moist shadows. A blackish-green bush to my left shook with sudden fury. A haggard bird tumbled out, complaining loudly. A rook perhaps, or a jackdaw. Whichever is the more wretched of the two. It flew a short distance and settled upon the gutter, eyeing the place malevolently, beak agape. I saw its tongue in silhouette. It was thin and leathery. Still only May, and the garden was already out of control. Within a month, it would spring up without warning, and swallow the entire house like a poisonous fog.

Jerry's dog came round from the back, and sat before me. 'Hello,' I said. It thumped up a dust-cloud from the doormat with its tail. I placed my hand on the bony dome of its skull, and it gulped and moaned sadly a number of times. The skin on its head was loose and soft. A frail shuffle was lumbering towards the door. I straightened up and smoothed down my hair. The door opened and the dog scuttled away. Jerry emerged with slow deliberation, like something floating up from the muddy depths of a lake. Before he had even registered who I was, I had blurted out my bad news.

'You'll have to manage without me.'

Still as stone as he inspected me. I knew immediately that there was something wrong with him. Something had happened to him since the day before. He realigned his feet and tilted back his head.

'Miss?' he responded, after some hesitation. He had never addressed me as 'Miss' before. His eyes were red. His face sagged on one side. He seemed to be at a loss as to who I was. It is likely, I realised, that the man has had a stroke. I stared at the frame of the door. The paint was chipping and blistering in the heat. I began to pick at it.

'You'll have to manage without me.' Delivered with a shrug this time. I wasn't sure why I'd said it again. It hadn't made sense to him the first time. Jerry squinted at me. 'I can't look after them anymore.' I squirmed on the doorstep. 'The horses. I can't mind them. I'm just telling you so you know.'

Jerry's huge cat came out to see what the commotion was. It stood at the old man's feet and blinked at me with fierce eyes. It was a good mouser, that cat, the old man had once told me fondly. As was its mother. A good family of mousers. The smell of neglect wafted out of the house. I turned my attention back to the flaking paint.

'I have to go away soon.'

I waited for him to ask how soon, but he didn't open his mouth. I wondered if he could hear me. Had he gone deaf? He had heard the brass doorknocker from upstairs, though. He couldn't have been that deaf. I finally stopped picking at the paintwork, and looked the man straight in the eye.

'It's just not working out anymore,' I said decisively.

With anomalous energy, Jerry swatted at my face. I flinched backwards and came off the step. A guttural snigger from him. He opened his hand and held it before me. I got back up on the step to have a look. There was a fat bluebottle in the centre of his palm. It was stunned, but not dead. He dropped it on the ground. The cat sprang forward and swallowed it whole. We looked at the cat. Then Jerry jutted his chin out in a scoffing way, as if he had been proved right all along in his suspicions about me.

'I'll be around for a few more days,' I offered.

'Don't mumble!' he roared and I came off the step again. He stepped back into the gloom and slammed the door.

The horses began to disappear, one by one. Every evening, there was one less head watching me. I felt sick at their loss. I really did. I'd help their owners box them up, and hand over their tack and their grooming kits and rugs. Don't forget his lead-rope, I'd say. And here's his head collar. I hope he likes his new home! Then I'd stand in the yard and watch the horse-box trundle down the dusty road. I didn't have to make any calls. Jerry took care of it all. Then one morning I came down, and there was just the chestnut mare, and she was quiet.

'Someone will come for you too. Don't worry,' I promised her.

The noise woke me the morning after that. Jerry was gouging out a hole in the far corner of the paddock. He had hired a digger from somewhere, a big unwieldy yellow thing that moved like a dinosaur. Metal screeched against stone as he tore at the bedrock. The mare was galloping up and down along the perimeter. She had torn up the ground and wouldn't come near me. The hole was huge. About ten feet deep. *For Jesus' sake*! I screamed at Jerry across the paddock. The claw of the yellow digger reared up in my direction. It jolted and lurched as if it was going to strike me down. Behind the glass of the little cabin, Jerry was screaming back at me as he pulled madly at the gears and levers, but I couldn't hear him over all that noise.

The courtyard was empty the night I left the stables. The lights in Jerry's house were off. Only the chestnut mare watched me from her stable. Not a sound out of her. Her head lifted hopefully as I approached. I kept walking.

The briefcase was exactly where I had hidden it, buried under several bales of straw in the corner of the hay shed.

The leather handle creaked as I approached the five-bar gate. I saw the big hole that Jerry had dug in the paddock. He had heaped up the soil in a neat mound behind it.

I turned back to the mare, the last living thing in the courtyard. She was no longer to be seen. I went up to her stable and peered in. She stirred darkly in the shadows. Only the liquid reflections of her eyes were visible. I slipped in the door and put the briefcase down. She backed off when I approached.

'Someone will come for you,' I whispered, and held out my hand. Her nose came out of the shadows to investigate. I rested my palm on it and pressed my forehead into her mane. She took hold of my hand with her teeth. She held the flesh between thumb and index finger. I wanted her to bite me then, but she did not bite me. She did not bite me, though she should have. I pulled my hand away and turned to the door. I picked up the case and left the stable. Absolute silence behind me. The mare didn't move. She didn't come to her door to watch me go. I headed once more for the gate. I left it wide open behind me. There was no need to close it anymore, though I wanted to close it. I looked at it, agape and off its hinges, and it seemed the worst thing yet. Then I started to walk. It was several days later before it occurred to me that I should have released the mare back into the woods, where it would have been impossible for Jerry to get near her. She knew better than to be caught by him.

SEVEN

It would be difficult to tell the conservator's age from the small black and white photograph that is printed on the back cover of his book. His stern expression makes him appear older than the thirty-eight years I know him to be. Or perhaps he is still only thirty-seven. The short biography beneath the photograph gives only the year of his birth. Perhaps the conservator was a winter baby, in which case, his thirty-eighth birthday is still to come. In fact, the conservator has all the signs of having been a child whose birthday presents were lumped in with those of Christmas. There is something hawk-like about him, despite the absence of an aquiline nose. And despite the fine eyebrows. It is the forehead that gives him away. It is the wall of a forehead that dominates a full third of his face that indicates that the conservator is a razor-sharp man.

The meetings with the detective have trailed off. The investigation has already begun to slow down. 'If you don't catch them immediately, you sometimes never do,' Sebastian said to him one morning on the other end of the phone. The conservator murmured what a shame that was, and replaced the receiver in its cradle. The detective looked with resignation at the phone in his hand. The dial tone wafted out of it. This was precisely the kind of abstruse bullshit that he had lately come to expect from his old friend. It was irritatingly easy for the conservator. What did it matter to him? *Girl in the Mirror* was back.

If I did write to the conservator, what, I wonder, would he do with my letters? I want to believe that he would not turn them straight over to the police. I want to believe that he would mull over them for a time. I would send them to his studio, care of the gallery. I would not tell him my name, nor where to find me. That way, my letters would be of little interest to the police. That way, the conservator might just keep them to himself. I would talk to him about *Girl in the Mirror*. I would tell him all that happened. The conservator is a man who'd understand the allure of a painting. The conservator would comprehend the predicament I am in. He would keep my letters in the locked filing cabinet in the corner of the studio, but then one Friday evening, he might just take them out. He might just slip them into his case and bring them home for the weekend.

Then what? He probably lights fires at this time of year. He strikes me as the kind of person who would rather light a fire than flick the switch of an electrical heater. He is a methodical man. He would derive satisfaction from the process of setting the hearth. Every task is performed with care. He has long thin fingers, some of which are now broken. But they will heal soon. And they will be as good as new. I presume. I don't know much about broken bones. And I don't know much about the conservator, but I doubt he would throw my letters in the fire. He is too sentimental for that. No, not sentimental. Too keenly aware of the value of artefacts. And of evidence. That is what comes of spending your time amongst silent things that demand interpretation. To the conservator, my letters, if I wrote to him (which I won't) would be evidence. He would keep all of them. The conservator would study my letters in silence. They would yield knowledge to the conservator.

I awoke the next morning in a field. I was curled up like an animal in a nest of flattened ferns. The grasshoppers stopped chattering as soon as I moved. I was embracing something in my arms. The briefcase. I had used it during the night as a pillow. I had thought in my sleep that it was something else, and I had wrapped myself around it, lovingly.

I propped the case up onto its spine. A spider with a green balloon for a body clambered across the lock. I blew it away and tried to open the case. It was locked. There was a rock on the ground beside me. I picked it up and took aim at the lock. It cracked open on the first go.

That was when I found out about the money. There were piles of it, in stacks of fifties. There was so much of it that I had to think of it in terms of physical mass. It would have taken too long to count it. In fact, now that I think of it, I never did count it. I estimated its quantity by simple equations: 50 by 2½ inches equals 100,000, and so on.

I slid my fingers along the inside of the storage folder. There were two things inside: a passport and a key. I opened the passport and looked at the photograph – the face was like mine, only with different hair and no scar under the eye. It was like my face, but it was not my face. I read the name. Isolde Chevron. I had never heard of her. I swear to God, I did not know that name.

An hour or so later, I began my journey towards the city. The ferns gave way to meadows of a long flaxen crop. Maize, perhaps. It lit up in the sun. Gold everywhere. The gold of the sun, of the yellow crop, and of course of the money. Yes, the golden glow of a truckload of cash. It is not a glow that is easily outshone. The maize yielded to my step. It parted before me like the Red Sea. I strode through, leaving it flattened and broken in my wake. I was oblivious to the trail I was leaving behind me. I was oblivious to the target circles drawn on my back.

It was dark by the time I got to the city outskirts. I hailed a passing taxi and told the driver to take me to the best hotel the city had. The driver told me that there was no money in taxis, and he recommended the Grand Plaza Hotel. The Grand Plaza Hotel. Even at the time, those words sounded promising. Yes, there, I said to the back of his head. Take me there. He picked up his radio and informed it where he was going, and the words sounded even better the second time around.

The hotel porter surveyed my disarrayed state as I made my way up the steps. He tried to prevent me from entering. I told him that I had just been mugged, and while he stood there faltering, I pushed on past him. The clerk behind the desk was another story. He told me politely that he needed to know my name. I laughed heartily, and told him that that made two of us. He didn't see the humour, and then *the* name popped out. Isolde Chevron. I was surprised I'd even remembered it. The clerk wanted identification too, and I handed him the passport. I watched him squint at the photograph, and then at me. I smiled my best smile. He closed the passport, placed it on the counter, and pushed it back across the polished surface. He pushed it with his index finger, as though making a strategic chess move.

'Thank you so much,' he said. I replaced the passport in my back pocket. He told me the price of the room. That's fine, I nodded. Where do I sign? The clerk paused, and then enquired, with lowered eyes, whether Madam would care to pay in advance.

I heaved the briefcase up onto the marble counter. The clerk raised an eyebrow at the broken lock. I took out one of the wads. He watched me count out the specified figure in fifties. Then I multiplied the figure by seven.

'I'll stay for a week.'

I put the money on the counter and slid it over to him as he had slid my passport over to me. The clerk made a show of holding several randomly chosen notes up to the light. I had not thought of that. I had not entertained the possibility that the money could have been fake. But the money was not fake. It was the only thing that was not fake.

'Thank you so much,' the clerk said again. He gave me the key to my room.

'Thank you,' I said.

The clerk gave a pretty bow. 'Thank you so much.'

*

I threw the passport on the hotel room bed, and the page with Isolde's face fell open. I couldn't stop repeating the name to myself, as if hearing it enough times would make it fall into place. Isolde Chevron. I thought of antique lace and black silk. Wrought iron and roses. Long-stemmed roses with their thorns still intact. A tight fist had taken hold of my heart – like the one that had seized my throat that night at the stables, only smaller and more insidious. I knew that there would be a price to pay. Her name on my lips, the shape it forced my mouth into, that carnal pout: Isolde.

III

The Hotel, Early Summer

EIGHT

I must have walked by him on the street. Kel. A week or so after arriving in the city. I must have seen him or, at least, he must have stolen across my field of vision. My eye did not alight on his face, as such, but my brain registered his presence. Perhaps he lurked for an instant in my blind spot. He was maybe standing in a doorway, following me with his gaze, displaying nothing more than a mild interest in the shambling figure that I cut. Barely surprised that I should turn up there, bad penny that I was.

He must have followed me back to the hotel. How else would he have materialised the next morning? The thought of him behind me, observing me off-guard, keeping track of my aimless trajectory – I am amazed by the patience he displayed. It was not a quality I would have noted him for. I remember nothing suspicious. It was just a street. That's always the way though, isn't it? Everything looks so innocent and idyllic in the moments before the bomb detonates. But then the past, and the ordinary perfection of the past, recedes from your grasp with great velocity. He would have been like a fox. He would have fallen still the way foxes fall still, with bristling hackles and one foot held ready in the air. But I am flattering myself now. I did not have that much of an effect on him. It was me who froze. I found, inexplicably, that I could not take another step. I stopped dead in the middle of a street. I don't know which street. I could never locate that exact spot again. Any street, every street. That is the impact that Kel had on me. I looked around and saw nothing familiar, nothing that should have made me stop, but while I was standing there, in the achingly bright sunshine that accompanies so many of my memories of then, I sensed, or was assaulted by, a smell. It wasn't even a smell, as such – it was more like a chemical borne on the air. It triggered something in me, and I had to bite back tears.

The city was loud around me, awesomely loud. I stood in the midst of footsteps and phones, and summer heat and car horns. There were road works behind me somewhere. They belted away at the tar and cement. The workmen hurled abuse at each other over the clatter. I stood still in the midst of it all, life, or whatever you'd call it, as it swarmed hotly around me, and I was acutely aware of something quite separate. I scanned the crowd for traces of I did not know what. I saw something too. Perhaps it was only in my mind that it was present, and perhaps it was just the glint of a car driving by. Perhaps it was the pane of a window fleetingly reflecting the sun as it was thrown open, but I saw it clearly, and saw just it, not Kel around it. I saw it as though it roamed the streets independently of him, full of threat and of promise and of infinite intrigue. Yes, infinite. I can find no way around it. It will neither dry up, nor be finished, nor ever be gone from me, and I saw it for the first time that day, though it was not the first time, not at all. I saw it once more, and it hurt my eyes: the flash of his daggered smile.

Kel was back. I had found the spoor.

How can I produce him in the middle of my chaos? Where could I possibly place him that he would make the same impact on my words as the impact he made on my head when I saw him in the flesh? (When was it? I was never good on context – these things don't matter.) Maybe he should arise out of the sea, like all things good, but that was not his element, and he was not good. I first saw him in sunlight. I could see right through his body. The morning sun penetrated him and came out the other side. I shall place him by a window. That should do it. I shall place him by a window in the morning light, and that is how I will remember the first time, though it was not the first time, no. He was always a sort of an apparition to me. I never fully believed in him. I didn't want him to be real. I wanted him to be like Isolde, mere ink and paper like Isolde, but he was not like her. He was flesh and blood and bodily heat, in the best and the worst kind of way.

He was there in the breakfast room of the hotel the next morning. Head down, reading a paper. A young man in crumpled clothes. He did not look up when I entered the room. My gut reaction was to run, but I did not run. I found a table nearby. I sat behind him, and I held onto that table with my nails.

He was long and thin and his head was shaved. His skull was intricately boned. So elegant, so at ease within himself. He sat in that room like he owned it, though he didn't own the paper he was reading, and he wasn't going to pay for the coffee he was drinking. The world was his, but only because he'd stolen it. Here was my rival. That was what I thought while I scrutinised him: *here is my rival. Here he comes, with the speed of a meteorite.* I should have known to take cover.

The morning light shone into him. I've said all that. Came out more beautiful for its passage through him. A wraith, a ghost, as though a movie camera projected him down. He sat there alone, listlessly smoking, a mass of different densities of air, a maze of refracted light. He hadn't ordered anything other than coffee. He finished up what he was reading, folded the paper, and then turned in his seat and focused directly on me. He didn't have to look around to locate me. He knew already where I sat. The trap had been laid with care. We locked eyes, Kel and I, and his face broke into a feline smile. He pushed his coffee away and stood up. I panicked and jumped to my feet. The cutlery on my table clattered in loud reproof. The other guests looked up to examine our little drama. I tried to scramble away, but he was already standing over me. He was that quick! He reached out and touched my bare arm. His hand wasn't like the hand that had held my throat back at the stables. I knew from the outset that this was not the same person. Kel's touch wasn't like any other touch. Maybe his fingerprints had been burned off with acid. Maybe he had no lines on his hand at all. Maybe I am trying to absolve myself by demonising him. The things I say to justify how I felt about him. There are no ways of justifying how I felt about him. His touch did not feel like it should have felt, but then, I am feeling it again and again not as it was, but with the benefit of hindsight, if you could call hindsight a benefit. I call it a curse.

I took a breath and looked at his mouth. I looked at his lips, and then he said it.

'I know you from somewhere.'

How did he know that I would not recognise him? How did he know that I had lost my memory? Someone must have explained it to him. The man who had been asking about me in the stables must have explained it to him. *When you find her, she will not know you. She has forgotten everything. Poor fool doesn't know her own name.* I stared at Kel in fright. I could have said no. No, I don't know you. I've never seen you in my life. I opened my mouth to say no, but my mouth said yes.

'Yes,' I said to Kel's mouth, and Kel's mouth smiled. Those teeth! Sharp and white. I blinked at them several times. Another blinding smile, and then he turned and left the breakfast room, just like that, without another word. I sat down heavily and watched him depart, trying to assemble my scattered parts back into a human being. I should have run. I should have fled. But it was summer, and I had no sense.

As soon as I could, I stood up again and followed him. He wasn't in the lobby or the bar. He must have taken himself straight to the telephone, my exquisite Judas.

NINE

'I've found her.'

'Has she the painting?'

'Of course she has the painting.'

'Where is she?'

'I need money.'

'How much money?'

'I don't know. Enough.'

I have difficulty visualising the first betrayal. I imagine it went something like that. I fight with myself over Kel's line. He felt like my accomplice, not my consignor. There is a pain in my ribs. It is a red-hot needle. Perhaps someone holds a wax effigy of me right at this moment. Bits of my hair stuck this way and that onto its shiny white pate. Flea-bitten and mad-looking. No dignity at all. The pain is too low to be anything important. I will not worry about it today. I cannot properly conceive of Kel saying the words that sold me. Yet sold I was.

There was a swimming pool under the hotel. It was set into the ground under the plaza so that the ceiling was at street level. I used to go there in the evening, when it was empty. I would swim on my back with most of my head underwater. I'd return to my room towards midnight, my limbs hanging like dead weights out of me, and I'd collapse on the bed and be instantly unconscious.

Kel must have been watching me from some discreet corner. Nothing moving but his eyes. I never once suspected that he was behind me somewhere.

It is a curious thing about indoor pools – they never fall still. They quiver all night, hours after the last swimmer has gone. That pool quivered the first time it saw me. It seemed to be more than just water. It was too gelatinous and kinetic to be just water. It was alive in its own right. It was a great weeping jellyfish. That funny-bone shimmy that pools do, all exposed nerve-endings and neuralgia – it means something, I'm sure of it. But then, I'm sure of many things. I'm sure that nothing is fully insensate. Every discarded sweet wrapper, every broken-down car, every object that has contact with the human race must feel our vague pain. There are traces of it in the skin we shed, in the breath we exhale. It bleeds out of us into the air and coats all the surfaces around us. It is like dust, like plutonium. Nothing can escape it, we don't know how to destroy it, and yet we are constantly creating more.

And then, and then.

And then one night as I swam, someone dived in. I hadn't seen anyone entering the pool-room. The lights were off at that hour. The pool was officially closed. The only lights that shone were the internal ones on the walls of the pool. The rest of the room shimmered dimly. Two shadows wavered on the ceiling. Just one of them was mine – the one that wasn't moving. I looked down and watched the second shadow circling shark-like beneath me. I trod the water nervously.

He surfaced behind me. He exploded through the water and scooped me up in his arms. I shrieked in relief and delight when I saw that it was Kel. He threw his head back and laughed. I was confronted with his throat. His laughter echoed around the damp tiled walls. He jigged me up and down a little, as if guessing my weight.

'You're as light as a ball!' he said, cradling me. I had my arm around his neck. We smiled at each other, our faces only inches apart. The water had beaded all over his skin. I reached out to a droplet on his cheekbone. The bead gave up its spherical shape as I held my finger over it. It leapt onto my skin and straddled the space between us. I couldn't take my eyes off this tiny transparent conduit. The fathomless distance between Kel's flesh and mine.

I became aware that he was staring at me.

'Don't do that,' he said, and I withdrew my hand. He dropped me into the water, and I tumbled over backwards. By the time I surfaced, with water pulsing up the back of my nose and rumbling in my ears, the pool-room was empty again.

'So, did you manage to place me?' Yes, that is what I said the next time I saw him. He was back in his seat by the window in the breakfast room. I sat down beside him this time, acting all casual.

'Nah,' he replied, without glancing up from his newspaper. 'That was just a chat-up line.' Kel and his miasma of lies. The two could never be separated. Like peering at another human being through fogged-up glass.

'Are you chatting me up?'

He laughed loudly at that and threw down the paper. He swallowed what was left of his coffee and stood up. 'Come on,' he said, and I followed him up to his room, which was exactly the same as my room, but on a different floor. The cherry-wood blinds were shut against the late morning sun. The air was the colour of tea. He lay down on the bed and began rolling a joint. I lay down beside him and watched.

'Here.'

He gave me the joint, and began to roll another one for himself. I smoked it carefully. It was carefully put together. What light fingers the lovely Kel had. Time unfurled gently and the room grew hushed. The hotel around us grew hushed. The whole city grew hushed. Had I ever been so happy? I smiled at the ceiling, and the ceiling smiled back. No, I had never been so happy.

It couldn't have been that late when he asked me to leave. It was not yet dark outside. We had been smoking in silence for hours.

'You finish that,' he said, passing over what was left of his joint. He rolled off the bed and unlocked the door, and stood there holding it open for me. I understood that he wanted me to leave, but I understood more clearly that I had no intention of leaving.

'Up you get,' he said. His voice was too loud for the room. I closed my eyes to shut it out. He came over to the bed and clicked his fingers in my face. 'Come on,' he insisted. 'Get moving.'

'Keep your hair on,' I said, and then laughed. It was a messy laugh, poorly executed and shrill. I was ashamed of myself. I knew I could do better.

'Jesus,' said Kel, surveying the scene. He reached forward and heaved me off the bed, sending me stumbling towards the door. The carpet was treacherous, and as steep as stairs. Some of the stairs went up, and some of them down. There was no clear order to it. It was a matter of taking them as they came. I had difficulty negotiating the door frame. It kept confounding my exit.

The lights in the corridor were excruciating. There was an unpleasant taste in my mouth. I tried to hold onto the walls. The butt of the joint, which was stuck to my lip, started to burn. I spat it out and stamped on it, hurt and offended that it should come to this. Kel closed the door behind me before I could object. I turned and looked at the door for a while, thinking that I was in some way still looking at him, and then I wandered off. The first expulsion was complete.

And then he was by my side again the very next day. I didn't see him until he was right up close. He must have been sitting in one of the armchairs in the lounge, biding his time. He seemed to have a lot of time. He seemed to have even more time than I had. He touched my elbow to say hello, and he accompanied me through the lobby, like it was the most natural thing in the world. And me, like an idiot, delighted to see him back! No mention made of the day before. I wasn't overly keen to refer to it myself. We shared the triangular segment of the revolving door. We had to shuffle along inside it and we got too close to each other. He was behind me and he put his hands on my hips. 'Skinny,' he said appreciatively. I didn't know how to respond. I didn't know where to look. He told me that he had this great idea. We'd get dressed up.

'Like pimps,' he grinned, when we were out on the plaza. 'You can be a pimp too. But only if you're good.' He threw back his head and laughed at the sky. I wanted to jump up and nip him on the throat. His arm was around me, holding me by the shoulder. He steered me down the street and we darted through the traffic. I said, yeah, okay. All right. You know, what the fuck? He said, yeah, what the fuck? Come on.

We went into a large department store and made for the designer rooms. I tried on chokers and tight tops, and Kel tried them on after me.

'Check these out,' he said, wearing a pair of white shoes and doing lounge-lizard moves in them. Lounge-lizard moves and all kinds of shimmies.

'Very nice,' I murmured, with clammy hands. Very, very nice. He clapped his hands once and pointed at me with both index fingers.

'I forgot to ask you your name,' he said, still smiling. Another landmine.

'Isolde,' I replied. The smile collapsed. Isolde was the wrong answer. Too late to change it. We eyed each other carefully. Then Kel stretched his lips back into the smile. He did so slowly enough to indicate that it was not spontaneous.

'That isn't how you pronounce that name,' he said sweetly.

The name sounded even more ungainly on my lips after that, even when he had made me ape his pronunciation and repeat it back to him, syllable by syllable. *Isolde,* he said, and I looked at his mouth shaping the word. I watched it stretch and pout. *Eee zole day,* I said back to that mouth, realising that I was nervous. *Eee zole day eee zole day,* I repeated, until the syllables seemed random.

'Good,' Kel said, after a brief hesitation. *Good,* and then the perfunctory smile.

*

We wore the new clothes out of the shop. Large rectangular shopping bags hung out of us like Christmas decorations. We didn't even bring our old clothes back to the hotel. We dumped them in the litterbin on the street, like it was the most hilarious thing ever. Then we strutted down the high street like peacocks on coke, eyeing up our images in every reflective surface.

I liked the new clothes. Kel liked them too. We tried them all on again that night in his room, and then we got stoned.

'Damn,' he said to me in a Deep South accent as I modelled for him, 'you can be my bitch anytime.' Mah bith, he had said in his street argot. You can be mah bith.

'Are you gay?' I asked.

'No.' He smirked. 'It didn't work out.'

This indeed was welcome news. I took a run and a jump and landed on the bed beside him. He reached over to his bedside table and grabbed a pink bottle. Baby lotion. He squirted some onto his palm and rubbed both hands together. Then he smoothed them over his pale scalp. I felt privileged that he should have done that in front of me. Intimacy, yes. Intimacy with Kel was my quarry. Anything would have done me, any crumb that fell from his table. I propped myself up on one elbow and gazed at him. His scalp still had the paleness of unexposure to the sun.

'What about your head?' I asked.

He gave me an evil look. 'What about my head?'

'When did you shave it?'

'I was in New York,' he began, and a smile came instantly to his very fine lips, a smile for New York, not for me. 'I had been living there for a while, but decided to come back. So, the night before I left, I got as drunk as a rat. I was having a great time, but then I sort of passed out. Anyway, I woke up and dusted myself off and I saw that I was in the East Village, so I went around to one of the Polish diners for a big slap-up breakfast, but when I got in, they all looked at me funny. Like all of them, the waitresses, the customers, looking at me like I was a freak. So I went into the bathroom because I thought maybe someone had written something on my forehead like the time before, but this time they'd got me with the animal clippers.' He paused for a while, nodding in agreement with himself. 'And that's how I ended up with half a head.'

'Half a head?' I asked, showing interest. That would have made two of us.

'Of hair, you idiot. Half a head of hair. Some asshole shaved off half my head of hair, and I had to shave off the other half to stop from looking like a freak-show.'

He was furious. He was really angry. I nodded in sympathy. He shook his head bitterly, ready to thump somebody. He looked at me to see whether I too thought that this was the most appalling thing that had ever befallen a fellow human. I tried to look appalled. And then I couldn't help myself. I started to snigger.

My first thought was that he was going to hit me. The skin on his face tightened and his mouth went thin. I stopped sniggering and tensed up on the bed. A small ember tumbled out of his joint onto the quilt, burning a hole through it. Kel put his finger on the hole. Then he looked up at me, and burst into laughter. I joined in cautiously after a few moments, getting louder and more hysterical as relief set in. Soon the two of us were laughing like the insane. It was the most unbelievable feeling of comradeship I had ever felt. I was so happy to be part of that room. I could not get enough of him. I wanted to embrace him. I wanted to throw myself upon him and hold him tight. Oh, tell me more, I wanted to plead. Tell me about the streets. Tell me about the drugs. Tell me about the women. Tell me about the trouble you were in. Alone at night in my own bed, I dreamt up ways of making him spill.

We looked at each other while we laughed. Right at each other. We didn't break eye contact. I briefly thought I was him. I watched him out of the corner of my eye just as he watched me. It felt good. Really: it felt so good to think I was Kel.

There was silence for a while when the laughter subsided. A ladybird was making its way up the balcony door. I wondered if I was hallucinating it. It was very odd to see it there, so far away from ground level and from any vegetation. Even the tops of the street trees were a good three storeys down. I was flattered that it should have chosen our room out of the hundreds of rooms that riddled the hotel. I should have hated it the way I hated all insects, but I didn't because of its pretty colours. My mind was never democratic where beauty was concerned. I asked Kel how he had worn his hair before it had been shaved off.

'It was sort of like yours,' he said, tightening up again.

'It was dead straight and very dark, wasn't it?' I asked.

'Yeah.' The ladybird spread its wings and leapt onto the wall.

'And to about here?' I persisted, indicating my collarbone.

He shifted his weight on the bed. 'For a while, yeah. Why?'

'No reason,' I said lightly. 'No reason at all.' I was watching an image half forming in my head. It could have been him, I told myself, and then quickly dismissed the idea. How could I have done anything other than dismiss it? I did not know Kel from Adam then. I repeat this knowledge to myself over and over. It is long and thin and very fragile. It wavers back and forth in the wind, and threatens so often to break. It is the straw at which I clutch.

TEN

'I need more money.'

'Already?'

'What do you mean, "already"? It's been a whole week.'

'Where's the painting? Has she got it?'

'I said, I need more money. What don't you understand? God all fucking mighty, grant me strength!'

(Silence.) 'This is the last time.'

There was a pharmacy around the corner from the hotel. A bell rang overhead when I opened the door. The interior was dark. I presumed there'd been a power cut and turned to leave.

'Can I help you?'

The voice came out of nowhere. I had to look around the place a few times before I could locate its source. An elderly woman was standing in the gloom at the end of the counter. Her grey and brown clothing camouflaged her perfectly.

'I'd like to get passport photographs taken.'

Her face fell slightly. The old lady was disappointed. She wanted to sell me prescription drugs. She wanted to know from what illness I was suffering.

It took for ever to process the photographs. The woman eyed me lifelessly while the machine rumbled and heaved. Eventually it spat out its quota of four black and white heads, stacked up on top of each other like a totem pole.

I began by placing an A4 photocopy of Isolde's photograph in the dead centre of the wall. I just wanted to look at her, think about her, rehabilitate her back into my memory. Yes indeed, noble motives. But then I kept going back to the photocopier in the hotel office to do more and yet more, and then larger and yet larger photocopies of her face. I stuck them all together on the wall (unflatteringly out of kilter) so that the pupil of the eye alone took an A4 page for itself. And that page was entirely black. And that was the page that I stared at the most. And that was the page that stared at me the most.

'Why are you taking out the little roundy bits?'

'What, these fuckers? These are the seeds, that's why.'

'Why don't you smoke the seeds?'

'I don't know. Because you don't. That's why.'

'What do they do to you?'

'I don't know. They fuck your shit up. Jesus Christ, Isolde, don't you know anything?'

'Let's smoke the seeds.'

'Okay.'

I watched Kel's fingertips dropping the seeds into the joint. He lit it up and passed it to me, and I couldn't stop smiling. It was the way that he gave me the joint. It was the way that he contrived to pass it without ever making contact with me. We always lay down side by side on the bed with just the ashtray between us, and I never once touched his almond-nailed fingers, just laughed up at them and at the way they flinched from my touch. They fluttered and recoiled above me. They were the cleverest things I had ever seen. I could never outwit them, and I did try. God knows, but I tried. It enraged Kel that I was always reaching for him, but he was always quicker than me. He always got away. Desire is a strange animal. I should know. When he recoiled from me, I would turn my face aside, and instantly comprehend that I wanted him more than ever.

'Tell me about the streets,' I said. His face cracked into a smile.

'The streets were like this undercover industry,' he began. 'Everywhere around you, deals were being struck, and you couldn't even see it happening. It was in a nod, it was in an expression. Territories were outlined, partnerships were forged, mad acts of perversion were consented to, and all of it without words.' I gradually tuned Kel out so that I was just looking at his very beautiful mouth moving, but not hearing the words. The smoke went in and the smoke went out, and I was hearing him say anything that I wanted him to say, until he'd say, you're not listening, are you? And I'd say, of course I'm listening. Look at me listening to you. I'm all ears. *It is impossible to have complete knowledge of the human being beside you,* I thought to myself, and then, after I had smoked some more, *It is impossible to have complete knowledge.* Sentences like that used to drift through my mind while I listened to Kel ramble on. Random abstract sentences that pleased me at the time. *It is not the sky anymore. It is an infinite number of droplets suspended in air.* I nodded with satisfaction, and accepted another joint.

Kel kept talking, not too bothered anymore whether I was paying attention or not. If you left one runner on one stoop, it would be gone the next day, but the day after that, someone would try and sell it back to you, teamed up with another runner of a different brand, but of equal size. That's fascinating, I would murmur, nodding wisely. That's so totally *fascinating.* And the stories went on, and Kel would lie back into the pillow after each anecdote, and I would stare and stare at his profile, wondering who the hell he was. My eyes were always narrowed then, always squinting in suspicion, until he'd turn to look at me, and I'd look away. He knew that I was trying to piece things back together. He'd consider me for a few seconds. He'd roll another joint in silence, and smoke most of it. Then he'd hand it over to me with those awesome fingers of his, and the talking would start up once more, in another direction. Once he started talking, I was free to watch him again. *It is in our falling apart that we are ingenious. It is in our falling apart that we reveal our true complexity.*

Kel often repeated the same stories to me, with all the details changed, so I knew he was lying. Perhaps his point was to show me that he was a liar. Look at me lying to you. Lying to your face. *A liar is just another word for . . .* Nope.

Couldn't finish that one. I never confronted Kel about his lying, lest he stop talking altogether, at which point I was always banished from the room. 'There was a store two blocks down from me in the East Village called H&C,' he would say. 'I lived over this store. There was a plastic sign above the window saying H&C.' 'There's a shop behind the hotel called H&K, you know, just past the cinema. The window is bricked up by a display of breakfast cereals, so you can't see inside. I needed to buy some food. The shop always seemed closed but I knocked on the door one time. It took them ages to open up. I heard them sliding across a load of locks. Hey, you're not listening.' He elbowed me in the ribs and I coughed.

'I am listening,' I protested. 'Shop with plastic sign, you couldn't see inside. They eventually let you in.' *It is his absence that has conquered me. It is more invidious than that. It is what my head has done with him in his absence that has conquered me.*

'Yeah, they eventually let me in and then, like, locked the fucking door behind me. All ten locks again. It took for ever. There was just a long wooden counter inside the shop, and these three fat geezers were standing behind it, waiting for me to say something. So I said: "I'd like a pint of milk." And they said: "Ha ha ha. No milk." So I looked around the room for something else to buy, and it was then that I noticed that the whole place was bare. There was nothing in the shop except for the wall of cereal boxes that blocked up the window. So I stared at this wall and deciphered the name of one of the boxes and said to them: "I'd like a box of Coco Pops." So the three guys all look at me blankly, like they're trying to figure out exactly what breed of asshole they have here, and then one gets up and looks at the cereal wall. And the stupid fuck can't find a box with Coco Pops written on it, so I have to go and get the box myself, and everyone's got their heads in their hands wanting to kill each other.'

My heart is a life form in its own right, a sentient mass that adjudicates within me, independently of me. It will not stop pumping until it is satisfied that I have honoured it, whatever that means, for I do not understand its requirements, only that it has requirements.

'So I get the box down and I put it on the counter, and it's the most fucked-up piece of shit you ever saw. It was, like, antique. The front of it had gone green in the sun. You'd no more eat it, you know what I'm saying? But I thought I'd better buy it all the same, what with them being so hardcore. I waited for them to give me a price, but none of them moved. I'm, like, tapping my fingers, being polite. You know, me, being polite! It nearly broke my face. So I asked them how much for the box, and they all kept looking at me. For, like, thirty seconds. No expressions. Shutters down.' He swept his hand over his face. 'I was looking from one to the other, and all three of them were staring at me. It was like, fuck!'

If I am unable to understand my fellow human beings, how can I even hope to be understood by them? Stop smoking this horrible shit.

'Then one of the geezers shrugged and grimaced and the other two joined in until the fattest guy hit upon the figure of five dollars, and the other two agreed by making seems-fair faces. Isolde, are you listening?'

'That's fascinating,' I said obediently. He elbowed me again.

'I asked if you were listening to me.'

'Of course I'm listening.'

'No you're not.'

'Yes I am.' No you're not, yes I am, no you're not, yes I am, and I was. I *was* listening to Kel, but I was beginning to hear him talk about something else. I was beginning to hear him talk about women. Oh, the women! And one of them in particular! The things that I could make him say! He must have spoken about them at least once when he was particularly under the influence of whatever it was that we smoked from day to night. I had seized on the story and heard it coming out of him over and over, even when I knew he was talking about other things. I used to hear it filtering through the drone of his other words: there was this girl. 'Her blood was thin and I could see right through her flesh. I'd hold her hand up to the light, and her fingers and nails would glow hot red. I'd kiss those fingertips. I'd run them all over my face. I'll never forget how they felt against my skin. Like nothing on this earth . . .' His voice trailed off.

'Don't stop,' I urged him. I was hanging on his words.

'So,' he said, frowning at the fading tip of his joint. He blew on it and it glowed. 'After that I became H&K's best customer. I'd be in every second day. "Hey, Mr Coco Pop," they'd say to me, "how you doin'? You want a hit of H today or you want a little bag of K?" And so on and so on, but then she stopped wanting me. And after that she betrayed me. And I bend over double sometimes with how sick it makes me feel. I know that I will never forgive her. I think that I will some day kill her.' This was the point at which Kel always came to a halt. *I think that I will some day kill her.*

'Do you need any help?' I wanted to offer. I was jealous of her, whoever she was. I was glad that she had hurt him. I was glad that he wanted revenge on her. I wanted revenge on her too. But did I ever wonder if he was talking about me? Not at the time, no. Never crossed my mind. At least, not for some time. His mouth grew ugly when he spoke of her. He covered it up with his hand, and threw a glance at me to see if I had noticed. And I noticed everything. How alike, when it came down to it, the two of us were.

'Are you listening to me?' he asked through his hand.

'Yes.' *Cancer. It always gets itself first in the queue for nourishment. The body does not differentiate between right and wrong. It responds only to demand. If it operates thus, then how should the brain know any differently?*

'Do you understand what is happening in this room?'

I hesitated. 'Yes.'

He wasn't at all pleased with the uncertainty in my voice. 'I mean it, Isolde. Do you understand?'

I considered the question, and then nodded my head. 'Yes,' I lied. 'I understand.'

'Good,' he said, flicking ash onto the carpet. 'Now get out.'

He kept kicking it under the table, but I always managed to retrieve it and roll it back to him before the door slammed shut: my heart.

ELEVEN

Hard to believe it's the same city as the one in which the conservator works. Hard to believe it's the same century. The conservator shuts the door of his studio, and he is in a different world to the one that Kel and I inhabited. The thick granite walls exclude almost entirely the sounds of the city below. The Government Buildings are nearby, and the conservator hears the odd police escort speeding past. That, and the occasional protest march, are the only noises that interrupt the silence in which the conservator restores *Girl in the Mirror*.

The pyramid of the studio's glass roof is visible from the street. The casual observer would not, however, notice it. What draws the eye when first confronted with the gallery is the central portico. The portico occupies a width of exactly one-third of the frontage of the building. Above its three arches are three rose windows. The visitor must climb three steps to enter the building. On either side of the portico are three floors, of three blind windows each. The gallery is a monument to proportion and order. Every detail is symmetrical. Except, of course, for the presence of the glass pyramid on the roof of the west wing of the building. There is no corresponding feature on the east wing. The glass pyramid, which takes up approximately one-fifth of the roof space of the west wing, was added nearly a century after the rest of the gallery was built. It was never intended as a permanent fixture, and was only retained until a more suitable location could be found for the Conservation Department.

The Grand Plaza Hotel, on the other hand, is a completely new building. Kel and I, it transpires, were amongst its first occupants. Unlike the gallery, which two hundred years earlier had been a much welcomed addition, the citizens of the city fought hard against the construction of the hotel, arguing that a building of civic interest should be placed on the site. The hotel would offer nothing to the people of the city. It would be used by those with too much money who were merely passing through. The hotel would become a haven for the likes of Kel and me.

The site on which the hotel is built was previously occupied by the National Maternity Hospital. The hospital was founded in 1825 for the poor women of the city. In the mid-1990s, the board of the hospital calculated that the sale of the site would raise enough funding to construct a modern building in the suburbs which would have a capacity of almost twice that of the original. The sale went ahead and the old hospital, to huge public outcry, was demolished.

The problems for the developers began there. Part of the medieval city wall was discovered beneath the foundations. Outraged people marched on Government Buildings in an effort to permanently halt the construction of the hotel. Perhaps the conservator marched with them. In fact, it is highly probable that he was there. Some day I will look up the press photographs in the archives. I might find his indignant face glaring out of the crowd.

A preservation order was placed on the wall. The developers were ordered to excavate, and construct a glass room around the wall that would be open to the public. The order was implemented at huge expense. Normal foundations could no longer be used. The hotel had to be built on stilts that were bored into the bedrock. The part of the site originally intended for the car park was gone. The swimming pool had to be redesigned on a smaller scale. The projected health spa had to be done away with altogether. The hotel had lost an eighth of its floor space.

All the best materials were used in the construction. The Portland stone came from the same quarry as that from which the Government Buildings were built. The upper floors incorporate both Georgian and Victorian architectural styles. The ground level of the building is wholly modern, however. A large cubic projecting entrance leads into the lobby. The circular base of the revolving door is fitted into the entrance's square floor. A spinning glass cylinder in a white box from which all kinds of creatures used to emerge. The rectangular plaza, from which the hotel takes its name, extends from this entrance. Four six-foot-high glass pyramids built into each corner provide daylight for the swimming pool below. The similarity between these pyramids and the one above the gallery's conservation studio is, I suspect, entirely coincidental. Perhaps I am the only one to have noticed it. All these geometric shapes. The Grand Plaza is like a big stone playground. It must have been designed by an adult child. A flight of wide white steps extends from three sides of the plaza down to the street. Every morning, the steps must be blasted with pressurised water to keep them white. This is done at 5.30 a.m. I managed somehow, during the month or so that I stayed in the hotel, to see it being done twice.

I, of course, when I used to sit on the brilliantly white steps that led up to the plaza, a cigarette between my teeth, the sun beating down on my face, was entirely unaware that I was seated on a huge source of public resentment. I never gave my whereabouts a second thought. Never really saw more than ten feet beyond my nose. I knew that something vaguely official was taking place in the building across the road. A series of black Mercedes drove back and forth through the clanging electrical gates, watched over by guards in navy uniforms. I gazed at them now and then through streams of smoke, and occasionally they gazed back, sizing up my potential as a threat. As for the building beside it, I was, I must admit, entirely oblivious to it. Probably wouldn't have noticed had I come down one day and it was gone. But this morning after breakfast, now that I'm in an empty cottage with little else to do with my time, I took down a map of the city and spread it out on the floor. It took me for ever to locate the street on which the Grand Plaza stands. I really have no sense of the geography of the city. Opposite the hotel are the Government Buildings. And there, diagonally across from the hotel, in all its ordered beauty, stands the National Gallery. Imagine my surprise. All summer, the conservator and I were a mere hundred yards apart.

TWELVE

'Where is she?'

'I need that money.'

'Do you have her?'

'Yes. Do you have the money?'

'Yes.'

The money became the only constant in the equation. In the panic to have something to hold on to, I turned to the briefcase full of money. I did not even use it in the way that money can be used to protect. I needed to hold it, as if it would keep me afloat, as if I could wield it like a club, and beat my enemies off with it. I needed to feel its bulk. I slept in the bed with it. I kept it in my pockets. I hid it in my socks like a fool. I would not leave the hotel room without great fistfuls of it secreted about my person. The hotel staff marvelled at my peculiar shape, yet still I clung to it. As though it could save me! As though it would not also grow water-laden and drag me down when push came to shove. And push was coming to shove. I could hear its steady approach, like a distant stampede. They were all paper, the things with which I set out my stall: Isolde's magnified face on the wall, the cash, the passport photographs from the pharmacy. Mere paper. I had built myself a fortress that would blow away in the first storm. I was shocked at how vulnerable I was in that city. I was full of bullet holes. The wind whistled through those holes, and made my flesh contract. I knew that I would sink like a sieve.

I eventually took Isolde's face down from the wall. I thought that I would have ripped her to shreds and set her on fire, but I took her down page by diligent page and put her in a little pile on the bed. I kept her in the bedside drawer for a few days. She made no sense when she was disjointed like that, an eye here, the corner of her mouth there, a few pages that were entirely unrecognisable, no matter which way you turned them. She stayed in the drawer for a while, and then I took her out and wrapped the money in her. There were twelve packets of it. I transferred them to the hotel safe.

'I want to tell you something.'

'Oh yeah?'

I had never told Kel anything before. 'Yeah. It's important.'

'Yeah?'

'Yeah, it's really important, so you're to listen.'

Kel nodded. I sat up on the bed so that I was facing him. 'Do I have to put this out?' he asked. He had only just lit the joint.

'No.'

'Good.' He put the joint back in his mouth. He screwed up his eyes and inhaled. I spoke evenly, and with conviction.

'I think that there's someone out there trying to kill me.'

No reaction. No indication that he had even heard me. I continued.

'Some guy with long nails. He tried to choke me.' At this, Kel nodded softly. Encouraged, I went on with my description.

'He was tall. Kinda stealthy. He showed up one night in my bedroom while I was asleep and –'

'Yeah,' Kel interrupted, his voice hoarse with the smoke, his eyes streaming as he reached for the ashtray. 'Yeah, that happened to me once.' He started telling me all these stories about people going mental on him and attempting to kill him. I tried to tell him about the man from the stables, but his voice just got louder until I shut up. I sat there in disbelief as he rattled out these stories of drunken debauchery, so I never brought it up again. And he never mentioned the man from the stables again. Nor did he ever say: how did you get that scar under your eye, Isolde? It looks like someone knifed you.

Now who would have done such a thing as that? Surely no one you know? He never even looked at the scar. He avoided it studiously. It was so cloak and dagger, the whole thing. There were masks over masks when we were alone. And if I imagine that I ever got him to shed his mask, then I must correct myself: I am a fool.

'Don't go to acid parties,' he was telling me. I was lying on my side feeling sick. I had smoked too much again. I always smoked too much around Kel. 'Acid parties are shit. Everyone gets paranoid and starts whispering about each other. E parties are great though. I was at this E party one time and this girl took three of them and chewed off her bottom lip. She chewed it right off. We looked for it on the floor, but we couldn't find it. I wanted to find it. It would have looked like a slug. There'd have been bits of carpet dirt stuck on it. I think she ate it. It was fucking amazing. It was fucking A.'

'Shut up,' I whispered, so quietly that I barely heard myself. I was staring at my hand. My fingers were shaking. How had things gotten so out of control? Kel was having fun. He started doing the chewing motion of the girl on E for me. He got really into it, sneering at me as his lip got redder and redder. He was going to break the skin. His perfect lip would burst.

'Like this,' he kept saying, poking me in the ribs for emphasis. 'Look at my face, Isolde. Isolde, you're not looking at me. Isolde. She was like this. Yum yum. Lovely lip. What's for dessert?'

'Leave me alone.'

I rolled onto my belly and buried my face in the pillow, but I could still hear him. He got up on all fours and leaned over me. 'Don't you want to play?' he was saying, making the chewing sounds right in my ear. And still doggedly poking me in the ribs, his arm going at me like the piston of a train: 'Isolde, Isolde, don't ya wanna play?' I pushed my face harder into the pillow, which just provoked him into getting louder. Jesus Christ, the man was such a freak. How had I not spotted it immediately? A strange thing started happening in my mind's eye. The picture that I had of him began to change. The face actually began to change. I got a fright, and lifted my head from the pillow to make sure that it was still him. When he saw that he had my attention again, he collapsed on top of me with a tremendous sigh. 'Ah, Isolde,' he said. 'Sweet Isolde. What should be done with a girl like you?' He lay there for a few moments, his head resting on mine, then he twisted himself around me so that we were facing each other, most of his weight still on top of me. He smiled his cut-throat smile. His teeth were level with my eyes. They were punctuated evenly by small pointed canines.

'Get off me,' I growled. 'I'm going to vomit.'

'Where is it?'

'What? I'm going to vomit!'

He tickled me under the chin as you would a baby. 'You heard me, sweet Isolde. Where is it?'

'Where is what?'

Sweet Kel became grave. He put his hand on my wrist and began bending my arm in a way that it was not supposed to bend. 'Frankly,' he said, 'I've had enough of your bullshit.'

'Get the fuck off me now!' I tried to pull away. He sat up on top of me and wrenched back my arm. I cried out in pain.

'Not until you tell me, Isolde.' *Eee zole day*. The way he pronounced it. He was mocking me.

'You're hurting me!'

'No, really? Imagine that. Do you want me to stop? Then tell me.'

I don't know where he found the knife. It was one of those box-cutting jobs. I'd never seen it before. He didn't have to reach for it. It was simply in his hands. I almost didn't believe that it was there. I twisted my head around to get a proper look. It was not a big knife. Only the tip of the blade extended from the handle. The handle was red.

Kel shoved my head down onto the pillow, sideways, so that I could just about see him over my shoulder. He held the knife like a pen, and drew with it on my neck. He drew a long line from my jaw to my shoulder. I did not understand what was happening at first. It did not hurt as much as I thought it should have. He breathed heavily as he concentrated upon the task. I wasn't breathing at all. He put his fingers on my neck to stretch out the skin. It was when he did this that I came back to my senses.

'Please,' I told him. 'I don't know where it is. But I'll try to remember. I promise.'

His drawing hand stopped. He took the knife away from my neck, and sat back to examine his work. He frowned at the line that he'd cut, as if it wasn't quite right. I did not know what he was going to do next. I waited for him to make that decision.

He climbed off me warily. I sat up and got off the bed. I heard the blade retracting into the handle as I hurried out of his room.

THIRTEEN

The girl in the mirror is unaware that she is being watched. She is depicted in a dim room, her back to the viewer. It is clear from the swing of her clothes that she has halted abruptly. Something has caught her eye. Her reflection? This is the first thing that troubles the conservator about the painting. The girl has stopped before a large gilt frame from which a young face looks out. Ostensibly, it is her reflection. The girls are similarly dressed. Their hair is golden brown. One face is tilted to its right, the other to its left. So why does the face in the frame look more like a portrait of an entirely different girl, and not like a reflection at all? The conservator removes his glasses and rubs his eyes. It is the girl in the frame's expression that unnerves him. A girl glancing at her reflection would not look so passive. Surely she would frown, or pout, or fix her hair? No woman the conservator has ever known looks at herself like this. So vaguely, so blankly, as if she doesn't recognise her own face.

The unresponsive gaze certainly does not tally with the interest shown by the figure standing in front of the gilt frame. Whatever this girl has spotted has caused her to stop in her tracks. This figure leans forward with curiosity. This figure is full of suspicion. She stares intently at the face on the wall. She is an avid little snooper. She has learned to look at everything twice. She won't make friends like that.

So why make the clothes and hair match if they are not supposed to be the same person? The painting raises too many questions. The painting is inconclusive. *Girl in the Mirror* gives the conservator a headache.

And where is the girl supposed to be anyway? It is all highly irregular. She is seen through an archway. The archway is so dark that it is almost black. The light in the girl's room is soft and warm. It is unclear whether she is in her dressing room, or has simply paused before her reflection in a hall or a drawing room. If it is a reflection. There are no personal effects in the room. In fact, there is nothing in the room at all. Just a wall with a mirror on it. A pretty, if somewhat dour, face in the mirror. If it is a mirror. The image draws on the late-medieval tradition of representations of *superbia,* pride, yet there is little of the characteristic symbolism of that tradition. There is nothing to remind the viewer that vanity is a sin, that the flesh is mortal, that the flesh will ultimately decay. There are no skulls, ravens, pieces of rotten fruit. No carcasses, coffins, urns, or ashes. Not even a diehard rat. Maybe the mirror is not a symbol of vanity at all. Maybe it is intended as a symbol of truth. The conservator shakes his head. It is rare to come across a canvas so bare. Perhaps this is what prompts him to take a closer look.

He stands at the head of the painting. It is laid out flat on his desk. He sometimes finds it productive to look at canvasses upside down. That way, he can disengage from the subject matter. He can perceive the works purely as aggregations of paint. He hunkers down so that the canvas is at eye-level. He examines the paintwork in relief. The bitter brown-blacks of the paint on the archway are not uniformly smooth. There is a difference in texture on the right-hand side. The paint in this area has been more thickly applied. The conservator runs his fingertips over the impasto. Something has been covered up.

The infra-red light confirms the presence of a form beneath. The conservator works at the painting under a microscope. He uses a scalpel. The pigment that he removes is old. It is almost as old as *Girl in the Mirror* herself. But not quite as old. It was added some years after the rest of the canvas was complete. The paint underneath rises up in four ridges. The conservator steps back and frowns. Knuckles. The four ridges form knuckles. There is a hand on the arch. A male hand, splayed and tense. Someone is watching the girl in the mirror. Someone has been following her through the chambers and antechambers of her life. But the girl in the mirror is unaware that she is being watched. She is too busy looking in the wrong place. The girl in the mirror should learn to be more careful.

❧

'She's gone.'

'Gone? Where did she go? What did you do to her?'

'What the fuck is that supposed to mean? I didn't fucking touch her. You know what she's like. She's out of her tiny head. She'll be back, though. I'll call you.'

'Fucking right you'll call me.'

'I'll call you.'

The line that Kel had drawn started beneath my ear, and curved around my neck towards the centre of my back. I was surprised that he had such a steady hand. It was only a surface cut. It would not scar. I covered it up with my hair. I wanted to kill him, so I ran away from him instead. I took the money out of the hotel safe. It was still wrapped up in Isolde's face. Black and white bricks. There was plenty of it left. At least three-quarters. I packed it into one of the rectangular shopping bags and off I went. I didn't check out of the hotel. I was in credit to them. They had mentioned one afternoon that I might like to pay in advance for Kel too, and I had. I heaped inches of cash onto their marble counter, and they retrieved it, discreetly.

A hot dry wind raged outside. Car alarms rang out all over the city. There was dust in the air. I had to keep blinking it out of my eyes. I did not know where I was going, nor did I care. The thing was to keep moving until it was okay to stop, and it was not okay to stop for some time. My body was wet with sweat, and my head thumped. I put my hands on my knees and leaned over to catch my breath. The dirt on the surface of the street was cracked up and desiccated. The rank tang of it hit the back of my throat. The city's detritus skittered about my feet in the wind; beer cans and cigarette butts, plastic bags and newspapers, the usual crud that follows humanity around.

I needed it to rain then. It suddenly seemed horrific that it should not. I began to panic for the second time that night. It seemed the whole planet would crack and splinter if dark humid water did not immediately sluice down on it. I needed to be standing in such a deluge right at that moment. I needed to have the rain fall on my face in exactly the same way as it would fall on the pavements and roads around me. I needed the rain to find no difference between me and the brute matter around me. I needed it to subsume me into that brute matter. I would have weathered it as stone would have weathered it. I would have let go of something had it fallen upon me: my humanity, my sensibility; it would have ebbed away. The relief would have been profound.

But it did not rain on me, and I did not feel like stone. I could not have felt less like stone. I still wanted to kill Kel. As much as I ever had. It was no passing impulse. It was a real desire. It was a very real desire, almost a physical pain, and one from which I could not get relief.

There was an all-night café across the road. I took myself inside and ordered coffee. It was 3 a.m. according to the clock, though it was still 3 a.m. when I looked up later. I sat in the seat nearest the door, and stared at my reflection in the window. My face in that window looked like Isolde's. Cold, small, black and white. Not even black and white – it was just grey. A grey moon of a face. I looked just like her when I had murder on my mind. The next thing I knew, I was crying.

The other diners watched me dispassionately as they chewed their food. It was probably a common sight at that hour of the night. I bundled myself off to the toilets, catching my reflection in the large mirror behind the food counter. My head had turned purple. It felt like it was going to explode.

I stood quietly in the women's toilets and splashed water on my face. The pressure in my head was quite something. My neck creaked when I turned it. The pain itself was a distraction for which I was almost grateful. I turned off the tap and slumped down on the floor. The ceiling was peeling off in parts. The water tank must have burst above it. Dead flies lay on their backs inside the light fitting, their transparent wings seared into the glass. Six or seven of them, toasted and hollow, their legs crossed over themselves beatifically. They cast little dirty shadows on the walls. It was a desolate oubliette, that tiny room. There was this stupid picture on the wall. I remember it clearly. It was a picture of the stars, stuck onto a yellow cardboard frame. I think it was a postcard. It gave life to the word incongruous. It wasn't centred on the wall. It wasn't even straight. I don't know what had possessed anyone to put it there, but it spoke to me. I saw my whole plight in it. Yes, everything reminded me of myself back then. Everything revolved around my predicament, and was there to enlighten or mock me. I had to take that postcard with me.

I dragged in a chair from the dining room. The staff watched me expressionlessly from behind their counter, as though there was nothing I could do that would surprise them. I put the chair under the postcard and climbed up to it. It was pinned up with thumbtacks. I pulled it down and found that, like so many things in life, it had been put there just to cover up a hole. I put my hand into the hole. It had given me an idea.

The street outside was stunning. The air smelled just so. The clubs and late-night venues were closing, and people were spilling out onto the street. They were dressed up like dragonflies. A car drove by, throbbing with dance music. Two men stood on the corner punching each other, while a woman screamed at them, imploring them to stop. A crazy man was begging for money. He took one look at me, and didn't bother asking. No, I'm lying: he took one look at me, and gave a nod of sympathy. I stepped into the puddle of a blocked drain, and got an electric shock. All of it seemed to be happening simultaneously. And then, most unexpectedly of all, I stumbled around a corner and there it was in front of me, looming out of the 4 a.m. dawn, the Grand Plaza Hotel. I had been going around in a circle.

All was quiet when I stepped into the lobby. There was just the smooth airy sound of the revolving door easing to a stop behind me. My feet were silent on the thick carpet. The night porter nodded to me and looked away, his face theatrically shadowed by the desk lamp.

I walked over to the doorway of the breakfast room. Kel was there. He said nothing when he saw me. The lights were off in the room. He was sketched dimly by the advancing grey daylight. He was coming forward into existence like a statue out of stone. I stepped into the room and rested my hands on the back of one of the chairs. There was a mountain of cigarette butts in the ashtray in front of him. He sat in the same seat by the same window in which he'd sat the first time I'd seen him, which was not the first time, no. He had arranged his long limbs in the same pose, the same world-weary couldn't-give-a-fuck pose as he had done that very first time, which was not, of course, the very first time at all. The same smile, the same gaze. The same wily invitation. Except that nothing was really the same anymore. I looked at Kel, and it was like all the sheen had worn off him. He was no longer a column of light, but a shadow of a human being. The only bit of him that lit up was the tip of his cigarette when he drew on it, and the grey smoke that he inhaled extinguished him further.

The longer I stood there, the more I knew that I didn't want to kill him, but the thought came to me tinged with regret, as though I already had killed him, as though I already had taken that irreversible course of action. It was a strange presentiment, peculiarly vivid. My life felt like a set of preordained steps leading down towards damnation, as was Kel's life.

A wave of remorse washed over me then, and the remorse took my anger away. When I saw Kel quiet and broken down like that, he took the heart right out of me, and I knew that this was a craving from which I would never awaken, and from which I did not want to awaken. At least I had the decency, as I stood there looking at him, to feel pity for him, and for myself.

He stood up and wandered over to me through the miles and miles of greyness that filled the breakfast room. I stood there for ever and watched him approach. He walked and he walked, and his step was tender, as though his muscles ached, as though he had walked a hundred miles to get to me, though it was me who had walked all night, to get away from him. The miles that I had already walked, to get away from him. When he finally stood in front of me, that bone-weary man, I had to look away. My face fell into darkness and the darkness was soothing. I could not see Kel's expression. Aware only of the shape of his face, grey and looming as it gazed upon me. His eyes were huge in my peripheral vision. They seemed to throb. Not a sound in the air. The two of us like sea creatures at the bottom of the ocean, isolated and strange. Unbearable, every part of it.

He reached out and touched my arm again, just like the first time, that time when he had declared that he knew me from somewhere. He touched my arm not apologetically, but merely jadedly, and all I felt this time was that his fingers were cold.

'Do you want to go for a smoke?' he asked. The revolving door started up in the lobby, and we both turned to look at it. It ground to a halt, dispatching no one.

'The wind,' the night porter pronounced carefully, unaware that we could hear him.

I turned back to Kel. 'Sure,' I said, nodding. 'We'll go for a smoke, sure,' and we went up to his room and lay on the bed, him on his back looking at the ceiling, me on my side looking at him. We didn't smoke, or talk, or even move on the bed for hours. We had never known such silence, nor such peace.

'Where were you?' he asked eventually, and then, 'It doesn't matter.' He rolled off the bed and went to the window. He lifted one of the wooden slats of the blinds and gazed out. A strip of yellow light fell across his ashen face. I knew that my whereabouts didn't matter to him – I could see it in his expression. Nothing particularly mattered to him, but I wanted it to matter. I wanted him to care, or be jealous, or angry, or whatever it was that functional human beings did. It still mattered to me.

'Why doesn't it matter to you?' I asked. 'What's wrong with your heart?' Kel turned around and stared at me in disbelief. Genuine, unfeigned disbelief, as though I was beyond the reach of sanity.

'What's wrong with *your* heart?' he asked, letting the wooden slat drop. I didn't understand what he meant by that. I understand now, but now is a lifetime away, and now doesn't count. Now is only there to let me remember then.

He'll always be a knife in my back. One that I can't reach. But if I could reach it, I'd leave it there to remind myself.

FOURTEEN

I thought of our hotel rooms last night. Not of us, just of the rooms. Some time has passed, probably less time than I think, but time enough for the dust to have settled, and despite myself, despite instructing myself not to be morbid, I caught myself thinking of those two bedrooms. Our two bedrooms. They would have been identical, were they not inverted versions of each other. Just like us, really, I told myself with grave satisfaction, as if I had hit upon a discovery that at last made sense.

I thought of our rooms not as they had been while we occupied them, but afterwards. I saw them empty of the life that we had made in them. Not ours anymore, yet still very much ours to my mind. The lights were out in my room. I stood in the corner nearest the door. It was filled with that blue neon light that the city generates. Strange, that – I never stood in the corner in the dark, yet that is how I saw the room when it drifted through my head late last night. I will never quite get it, how the mind reworks everything slightly for no apparent reason, except, of course, to bring home to itself the fact that it can never be trusted.

The bed was unmade, the covers thrown back. The sheets were creased with body shapes. The air was heavy and full of sleep. The balcony door was open. The blinds clinked gently against the glass, and the sound of traffic drifted up. I watched that open door. I half expected to see Kel appear in it, waiting for me after all this time. It made me swallow several times – the body reacts to emotional stress in the most peculiar and inadequate ways. I stood there for an age and I swallowed and swallowed. It was in *my* hotel room that I had half expected to have seen Kel, though he had never been in my room, at least not that I am aware of. No doubt he rooted through it a couple of times in my absence, had to restrain himself from breaking things and throwing them around when he didn't find what he was after, but we were never in that room together, not once. I always came to him. He only had to look my way, and I was by his side. I used to think sometimes, as I fell asleep in my own bed, that he had slipped into my room with me and was listening to me breathe. I used to wait for him all the time. But he never did come, and I am grateful to him. I am grateful for the – what is the word? Forbearance? More than that. The morality, the mercy, the dignity that he showed. I am grateful to whatever it was that kept him away from me at night. I will take it as a sign of his regard for me, though it was not his regard but his nausea that stopped him from slipping into the lift and from creeping down the corridor. The corridors were always brightly lit in that large international hotel, but I watched Kel make his journey to me through the deepest of darknesses. He would open his hotel-room door, and the lights would die down and be gone, as though the wind had snuffed them out. The hotel would sleep deeply and all in it would breathe in unison, because Kel's door had finally opened, and he had cast his spell. Into this darkness, he would take his first step. Freed, by the darkness, of his humanity, he would move the way animals move. All sheen again. Aware of himself too. Aware of the shapes his body imprinted in the night. Exquisite shapes, every last one of them. Kel would creep to me through fathoms of dead time, and not a soul would know it. Not a soul but my soul.

He would find his way to my door and stand before it. He would gaze at it for a few seconds before allowing his hand to rise up and knock. I see that part most clearly – the hand rising up and crouching into a fist, about to deliver the signal that I waited for always. Perhaps he even got that far once or twice, and froze in that gesture, his hand shaking and his knuckles white, finding that he could not do it. He simply could not make himself do it. And the lights would have shunted on again and Kel would have shrunken away. There'd be no trace that he had been there at all, and my world would have been safe, if only until nightfall. I do not know what would have happened between us had he come to me like that some stone-still night. I do not want to know. Yet I do know. I find I cannot un-know.

I wonder if they ever got those two rooms right again after we left? We made places into bombsites by just stepping into them. I wonder if they still look the same as the other hundred-odd rooms? Do they smell the same as them, maintain the same temperature? I like to think that we were not entirely erased, but hotels, by their nature, are transient things as, by our nature, were we. I worry that if I returned to that hotel, I wouldn't be able to find which rooms we stayed in. I was never any good with numbers, and have forgotten which ones were stuck onto our doors. Nobody else saw the life-and-death drama that unravelled in those spaces, only us. And in fact, only me. I cannot bear that it is all forgotten, or worse, never noticed in the first place. I was angry with myself for thinking like that. What did I want? A blue plaque? A stage? But it wasn't a stage that I wanted, nothing like. I wanted something personal from that time. Something small. Something to place beside the scrap of canvas on the dresser. I wanted a piece of Kel. I couldn't even say the word at first. My lips kept reversing over the same syllables, like it was wrong to even ask for such a thing: a moment, a momento, a momentum. I tried to say it aloud, standing there in the middle of my kitchen, the metal sky filling it up with sour grey light. I felt a sudden coldness in my stomach, and I thought I was going to get sick, but I swallowed and I frowned and I stammered, and eventually the word came out. A memento. That is all. I would like to have had a memento. But I don't. I have nothing, and there is nothing that I can do about that.

❧

'Is she back?'

'Of course she's back. Where the fuck else would she go?'

'And?'

'And what?'

'And when can I have her?'

'Tonight. As agreed. We've discussed all this. I'll call you.'

'I'll be around.'

'Whatever.'

There was the most unbelievable static in Kel's room that evening. He had brought it in from the street outside. The two of us had gone out shortly after nightfall to check on how his empire was doing, and his empire was doing well. He seemed to know a remarkable amount of people for one so recently arrived from a different country. He would say 'my man' to them, and shake their hands with both of his, and he never introduced so much as one of them to me. *Mah man,* he would say, and I can still hear his voice. *Nice shoes, mah man.*

They were young men, mostly, some not so young, and they all looked a little worn out by life. They nodded respectfully at me every so often, and I nodded back, and the displeasure that this brought out in Kel was a palpable thing. He would drag me away and tell me not to let them look at me, and I wouldn't even ask how such a feat could be achieved.

The streets were crowded with the usual evening drunks. Kel had that pimpish shimmy in his step, the one that meant trouble. I felt him swaggering beside me and I grew wary. The night used to do that to him. It gave him energy and attitude.

'There was someone following you while you were out last night,' he announced. He deliberately bumped shoulders with an oncoming night-clubber, and then turned and shouted abuse at him. *Watch where you're going, you ignorant fuck.*

'What did you say?' I pulled him away from the clubber, who was being prevented by his friends from punching Kel. I had to use all my strength to get him to back off. A dog, I thought. He is no better than a dog sometimes. And me like a smaller dog, yapping at his heels.

Kel turned and looked at me as if he had no idea what I was talking about. 'Who?' I demanded, still gripping his arm. 'Who was following me?'

'Oh that,' he said impatiently. 'I don't know. Some guy. Some man. The world is full of them.' He shook himself free of my grasp and set off through the crowds. I had to break into a jog to keep up. I followed along in the vacuum of space directly behind him. It was like tailgating an ambulance in traffic.

'What did he look like?' I called after him, my voice all shrill and tinny. If the man had been following me last night, he had probably been following me for months. He was probably right behind me as I spoke. I threw a glance over my shoulder, but didn't know who I was looking for. Some guy. Some man. The world was full of them. Kel accelerated, and though he was saying something (something that made him burst into laughter), I couldn't make out a word.

'I can't hear you!' I whined. There was a slight shadow about the size of a thumbprint just under the poll of his skull. He was hollow there. Perhaps someone had dropped him when he was a baby. I addressed myself to that thumbprint indent, like it was the underside of his face, like the edges of it would move and form words. 'Please,' I persisted. 'Was he quite tall? Did he seem quite tall to you? Did he seem quite strange? What made you think that he was after me?'

Kel didn't bother answering me this time. Didn't appear to realise that I was still there. The hopelessness of it all, the vast unlikelihood of ever getting to the bottom of it. I wanted to be back in the hotel room. I wanted to be within four walls so that I could lock myself in and lock the world out. We were getting further away from the hotel. I begged Kel to slow down, but he just got faster.

We rounded a corner and Kel stopped so abruptly that I collided into him. He stood as still as a gun dog while I bent over double and fought for breath by his side.

'I don't feel well,' I moaned. 'I need to lie down.'

No reply.

'Did you hear me?' I looked up and he was gone. I located him standing bolt upright on the kerb. He was watching something. I stared at the indent on his skull and tried to decipher his expression from it. On the street before us, a big mill of people were fighting with each other. There were at least fifty involved in it, men and women, most of them drunk and ineptly punching the air.

I came up behind Kel. 'State of them,' I said. 'Let's get out of here.' The cars on either side had been forced to stop. They had their reverse lights on, though they couldn't back away because the traffic had piled up behind. The crowd swung like ballroom dancers from side to side.

I put my hand on Kel's shoulder and tried to get his attention, but he pushed me away. 'Go back to the hotel then,' he snarled, 'if that's what you want.' He pulled off his jacket and threw it against the wall. Before I could stop him, he had launched himself into the crowd. He seemed to land down on them from a height. He began kicking and punching indiscriminately around himself.

'I'm not responsible for you!' I shouted in frustration, stooping to retrieve his jacket, and then throwing it back on the ground. My voice was drowned out by the roars of the crowd. Kel was loving every second of the fight. I could see it in his face, could see the satisfaction he felt each time the flat of his fist impacted wetly with the flesh of another man's face. He started kicking at a body on the ground. The body wasn't moving, but he kicked at it repeatedly. He kicked it like a maniac, and then turned to look for another target.

'I'm not responsible!' I shouted over and over from my sideline on the pavement. The crowd spilled onto it and I was tipped over into them. I lost my balance and fell. Someone stood on my hair and I screamed. A hand reached into me and caught me by the elbow. It hauled me out and threw me against the wall, where I gulped and flinched like a fish. Kel.

'You're fucking useless,' he was saying. 'Use your middle knuckle, this one here.' He waved his fist in front of my face. 'And aim at the windpipe. And then with your feet: groin, chin, collar.' He kicked at the air with his white pimp shoes. 'You kick the nuts, the head comes down. You knee the chin, the body falls over. So you stamp on the collarbone. Even you could do it. Just concentrate on the trajectory of your foot.' And then as an aside: 'I'd have killed him, you know, that fucker who was following you. If he'd laid so much as a finger on you, I'd have been *there*.'

We lay on the bed together and began smoking again. We smoked too much. Kel was talking. I wasn't listening. My concentration was gone.

'Your hair –' I said interrupting him.

'What?' he asked flatly. *What*. He didn't like being interrupted.

'Your hair. Was it dead straight and almost black before it was shaved?' I was finding it tremendously difficult to speak. I had to rack my brains for every word.

'Yeah. We've been over this.'

'Have we?'

'You know we have. That shit is interfering with your short-term memory.'

'Oh.'

Kel sighed heavily and settled back into whatever story he had been telling me, or telling himself. The static in the room was getting worse. I told myself to stop smoking, and still I smoked, as greedily as he did, sucking it in as if it were my last breath. I smoked until I could feel electrical currents running through me. The veins on my neck and shoulders were jumping like eels. A nerve on my eyelid fluttered. My hair was stuck to my face. I pushed it away, but it snapped back onto me like a drawn-back briar. The light bulb in the ceiling seemed to be swinging on the end of its wire. The starkness of it. The room was suddenly awful. Kel turned towards me and we looked at each other across the pitching light. His expression was inscrutable. The light whistled across his features, locating shadows and angles that I had not seen before. Then the light bulb stopped swinging and became neatly recessed into its shade once more.

'I know who you are!' he hissed. The menace in his voice! The level of bad feeling! What had I ever done to make him hate me so much?

'What did you say?' I asked, terrified. Utterly terrified. My heart thumped. Kel gazed at me mildly.

'When?'

'Just now. What did you say to me just now?'

'Nothing.'

He smiled flirtatiously at me. The ever-surprising sight of his teeth. He was right, though. I knew it as soon as I had challenged him on it: he had said nothing. I had heard what I had heard, but he had not said it. I looked at him in confusion. His face unexpectedly softened.

'Come here, Isolde,' he said soothingly. 'Don't get so upset. You're just stoned. You'll be fine.' He took the joint out of my mouth and stubbed it out on the headboard. Then he lifted up his arm like a wing and I crept under it. I put my head on his chest and listened to his heart beating.

'I missed you,' I said. It just came out.

'I missed you too,' he whispered. His arm was around me. His face rested on the top of my head. His breath was warm in my hair. My mind raced. Impossible ideas.

'I mean that I missed you from before, not just last night.'

'And I missed you.'

Maybe he did miss me. I wanted him to miss me. I wanted him to find me again when I ran away from him the second or the third or the tenth time. I wanted there to be a knock on the door at dusk when I least expected it. I wanted to whirl around and look at the door in surprise, wondering who it could be at that hour, knowing already that it could be only one person. I wanted there to be just that thin piece of wood dividing us. I wanted to open the door cautiously and find him there, all wet because he'd been walking through the rain. I wanted to enjoy the emotions washing over me when he turned and met my eye.

I moaned into his chest, a big doleful bear. Kel was rubbing my head gently, saying, You're stoned, you're stoned. Don't worry about it. It happens to the best of us.

I wanted to look into his face as he looked into mine, and I wanted him to touch the scar under my eye and say, Forgive me. Just those simple words. Forgive me. I wanted to take his hand down from my eye, and kiss it, and lead him into my small house, and sit him down by the fire, and wrap myself around him, all the time whispering: Quits. We're quits. It is over.

'Half of your brain has been switched off by the dope,' he was explaining, 'and the awake bits are the really basic bits, the animal instinct bits. That's why you're frightened. It's okay.' I didn't feel like I was on the bed anymore, but that the air itself was holding me up.

'Isolde,' he said. He gave me a little shake. 'Isolde, you're asleep. Wake up. You have to go now.'

I opened my eyes. 'What? Go where?'

'Go back to your own room for a bit. Come on. Up you get.' I took my head off his chest and we both sat up. The room spun around me. His face swam into focus. He smelled like a wild animal. I couldn't take my eyes off his throat. I placed my mouth on the side of his neck and kissed it. He curved beneath my mouth, and his lips touched my neck. We kissed, like swans, and his skin was hot.

Then he was gone from my arms and trying to throw me out of the room. I sat on the bed listening to my own breathing, doing my best not to hear his voice. He was chanting to me that I had to go, had to go. Right away. Had to get the fuck out. He held up one of his jackets for me. A black hooded one. He put my hands into the sleeves and zipped me up. He pulled the hood over my head and dispatched me onto the corridor. He performed these tasks with a dexterity that dazzled me. He became a creature with six arms. I could barely keep abreast of what was happening. The door was shut firmly behind me.

The corridor seemed ominously still after the flurry of activity in the bedroom. There was only the hum of the air conditioning. I held up my arms and looked at them. The jacket was too big for me, the sleeves too long. I looked like a day-release from a mental hospital. I felt bitterly aggrieved, and I banged at Kel's door with my fists, pleading with him to let me back in. He was on the phone. I put my ear to the door and listened to him laughing and giving out his room number. I shouted at him that I could hear what he was up to, that I wasn't fucking deaf. Or fucking stupid. *The hopelessness*, I kept whispering to myself. *The hopelessness of it all!* I wanted to cry. I wanted to roll around on the floor and howl. To elicit sympathy, I suppose, was my intention. To elicit any reaction at all.

Kel ended his call and locked himself into the bathroom. I slumped down onto the carpet, and shut my eyes.

The bell of the elevator roused me after a time. I opened my eyes, unsure of whether I'd been asleep or not. I looked at the elevator in fright. I did not know what was going to come out at me from that suspended metal box. I did not know what Kel had summoned for me on the phone from his room.

Two women tumbled out, like they'd been leaning against the doors when they'd opened. Soft and fleshy women. Not like me, not skinny and rangy like me. Not skinny and rangy like Kel. They were all high heels and short skirts. Bits of gold on them here and there, like sweet wrappers. They wandered down the corridor, counting off the room numbers. I willed them to walk by Kel's room. They stopped outside it and looked at the number. Then they looked down at me. I glowered at them with all my might. Kel's room number was written in red biro on the back of the blond one's hand. She twisted her arm around to see if the numbers read any differently the other way around. They didn't. Nobody knocked, but Kel's door opened up anyway.

'Ladies!' he said to them through his smile, bowing low. His arm swung out in an arc of invitation. The two women stepped over me, but neither Kel nor I looked at them. We stared right at each other. Kel told me to fuck off and he closed the door.

'I don't get it!' I shouted, banging at the door. 'I don't fucking get it!' It was the replaceability of it that floored me. How was I so easily replaceable to him, when only he was of interest to me? There was laughter coming from inside. I put my eye to the brass keyhole. It was like spying on tropical-island life through a seafarer's telescope. Kel was on the bed with them. His nakedness was shocking. He was as I would have imagined him, only more so. More strength in his body than I would have thought, yet slim. Something classical about him, something Roman.

An eye swooped into view on the other side of the keyhole. The iris span like a spoked wheel and locked onto mine. I snatched my face away from the door. Kel's laughter rang out again. He had moved with such lightning speed that I had not seen him leave the bed. I wondered if there had been two of him all along. When I returned my eye to the keyhole, he was back with the women.

I watched all of it. I listened to every sound. They were loud. And athletic. The women earned their money. Other guests walked by me in the corridor clearing their throats. I didn't care. I didn't conceal what I was doing.

The women let themselves out after an hour or two. They stepped over me again, and I saw him through their swinging legs – obscured, unobscured, obscured. He was lying on his back, half naked on the bed. One arm was draped over the side of it, palm upward. The other hand held a joint to his mouth. He inhaled deeply. His chest rose up and froze as he let the smoke diffuse into his already polluted blood. His head sank back slightly. His throat again. Oh yeah. A fine sheen of perspiration glimmered on his skin, making him look somehow unreal.

When was that? July, maybe? A July night, late June at the earliest. I should try and hold onto some of the facts. I feel it all ebbing away from me with the slow onslaught of forgetfulness, and there seems not a thing I can do about that, except try and hold onto the barest of the details. It was July, the Grand Plaza Hotel, late at night. These things mean nothing to me though. I looked into that room and saw Kel as if he was disconnected from everything around him. And as if I was disconnected from everything around me. His eyes were green, and his skin was golden. The blood was sluicing through his veins. He was all colour, not man but creature. The open door framed him like a painting, and I chanted the same words to him over and over: *You're so, you're so*. I could not make myself stop.

He made no sign that he could hear me. He just lay there and was otherworldly. He was more than the sum of his parts that time on that bed. He was unspeakably expressive by just being there. Unspeakably moving as a physical form. And I was his beholder, nothing more. I stood up and entered the room.

'Get out,' he said, without even looking at me.

'No.' I stood over him with the black hood of his jacket hiding my face.

'Get out.'

'No.'

And then I bit him. I lunged down and bit him on the ribs. He seized me and threw me off the bed with such force that I hit the wardrobe and bounced off it. I sat there winded on the floor. When I looked up, I caught him tearing his eyes away from something, and focusing them back on me. He forced his mouth to smile.

I turned to follow the direction of his gaze, hearing him jump up behind me. I stumbled to my feet in what seemed like slow motion. He threw himself in front of me and slammed the wardrobe shut. But I had already seen the thing that he hadn't wanted me to see. My briefcase was inside.

'You are so fucking stupid,' I said, 'hiding it in there.' I tried to open the wardrobe. There was a struggle and we landed together on the bed. He was still half naked. The gleam of shoulders and chest. I had to look away.

'Can I have a photograph of you?' he asked, and I put my head in my hands. I had the totem pole of photographs slotted into the plastic cover of my passport. Her passport, Isolde's. It was in my back pocket. I took the photos out and tore one off for Kel. He examined it, and then propped it up on his bedside table. A leave-taking ceremony had started between us. I knew that as soon as the photograph left my hands. I didn't want to start saying goodbye. So I demanded the photograph back. Kel laughed and said no. I reached out to retrieve it and he threw himself in my way. Which left the path to the wardrobe clear. I jumped off the bed and ran to it. I pulled out the briefcase and threw it onto the bed.

'That's my case,' I told him, and he told me wearily, and in tones that suggested that I was very stupid indeed, that it was *his* case. I looked at it more closely and saw that, although very similar, it was not in fact my case. It had once been identical to my case, but it had followed a different route in life, and therefore had different scars, different knocks and bangs. The leather was suddenly like human skin – it was a sickening thing to look at. Why would my case have a double? I said that to Kel, holding the case up to his face. I don't understand why there's a double. Explain to me why there's a double? He looked at me blankly, offering no explanation, and I thought I was going to scream.

There were shadows flickering in the slit of light beneath the door. Someone was standing on the other side of it, out in the corridor. Someone was listening to us. Someone was waiting.

'You deserve someone to be on his hands and knees for you,' Kel said out of the blue, and then turned his back. I hated it when he turned away from me. I was losing the ability to cope. I knew that. The rage was rising in me. My hands had started to shake again. There were times when I wanted to crush his delicate skull. There were times when I wanted to pick up the heavy porcelain lamp-stand from the dressing table, and swing it at that fine-boned cranium of his.

'Who is outside?' I demanded, practically spitting on the back of his head. I hurled the case on the ground and kicked it. It skidded across the room. Kel stopped it with his foot. 'Who is standing outside?'

Kel looked at the case, and then at the door, and of course the shadows were gone. 'Nobody is standing outside,' he said, smiling his slyest smile. I ran up and slapped him. His face rotted in front of me, like fruit. 'You do whatever you need to do to make yourself feel better about this.' He spoke in measured tones.

'Fuck you.'

A heavy sigh from him as he tried to control his temper. 'You should disappear as soon as this is over,' he said eventually, carefully pronouncing each word, so that there would be no doubt as to his meaning. 'Just like you did before.'

'You knew?' He looked away. 'You knew all along that I'd disappeared off the face of the earth?' I pulled his face back to mine. 'What is my name?'

'*Eee zole day*,' he said, in a singsong voice. I slapped him again, and he gritted his teeth.

'What is my real name?' He threw his eyes up to heaven as if I was trying his patience to the limit, and then he said it.

'Anna.'

The word coming out of his mouth was a revelation. The simplicity of it, as if jeering me. I repeated it to myself, and it sounded right on my lips. My grip on Kel slackened. He regarded me speculatively for a second or two.

'Where's the painting, Anna?'

'The painting?' I repeated, staring at him as if he'd just spoken backwards. 'The *painting*? What *painting*? What are you banging on about now?' It was moving too fast again. I was still struggling with the images that had unexpectedly assailed me. Anna. Kel calling me Anna. Not just then, but ages ago. Ages and ages ago. The painting that was in the other briefcase, he was saying. The case that you fucked off with last January. Remember? And there was money too, you might recall. You can give it to me, or you can give it to my friend outside.

'What friend? You said there was no one outside.'

'Oh, for fuck's sake, would you try and cop onto the most basic of the facts? My friend is right out there. In fact, he is waiting for you. He is dying to meet you. He has been dying to meet you for some time. Believe me, he speaks of nothing else. Do you want me to introduce you to him now, or shall we leave it for later?' I looked at the slit of light beneath the door again. Still no shadows. 'Either way,' Kel continued, 'you're not leaving this room again until you tell me where I'll find the painting.' He turned the lock on the bedroom door and disappeared into the bathroom with the key. 'And the money,' he shouted over his shoulder. 'It wouldn't be like me to forget about money, now would it?' He started splashing water on his face.

'Jesus fucking Christ!' I rattled at the lock on the door. I thumped it with my fists. Would anyone in the hotel do anything if they heard me banging and shouting to get out? Probably not. They had paid me no attention when I had been banging and shouting to get in. I tried the balcony door. It too was locked. I kicked it, to no effect. It was made of plate glass. Kel stopped splashing water but remained in the bathroom. I started to panic.

'You shouldn't have run away with what was mine, Anna.' I unplugged the porcelain lamp-stand from the wall and lifted it off the dressing table. It was unexpectedly heavy. It had a square brass base. I grasped it with both hands and turned it upside down. I crept up behind Kel. He was standing in front of the mirror, examining the bite-mark I'd made on his ribs. The skin had turned purple, but there was no blood. He prodded at it as he spoke.

'It took me a long time to track you down,' he said. 'But I suppose I always knew you'd come back to me in the end. We're stuck with each other for life, me and you.' He started to turn. I swung the lamp-stand at his shaven head. I got him right under the poll, in that thumbprint indent of his. I heard the crack on the bone as if it was on my own head. I was apologising to him as soon as I made contact. No, I was apologising to him in the split second before I made contact. I was already regretting it before I did it to him. I had never wanted to hurt my beautiful Kel.

He slumped down on his hands and knees on the tiled floor. He crouched for some moments, trying to figure out what had happened. His hand reached back and touched the spot on his head where I'd hit him. The brass edge had scraped some skin away from his scalp. He was bleeding lightly. His fingers came away tipped with the blood. He held them in front of his face and they began to tremble. I could not see his expression. I was absolutely terrified of what he'd do next. He swallowed, and took a deep breath.

'Now you're going to get it,' he said. The knife was back in his hand. He seized my ankle. And the lamp-stand came down again as if it had done so itself, and Kel collapsed once more, and this time it was his teeth that I heard as they hit the tiles. He landed right on his teeth. I heard them crack. I had broken his smile. His exquisite smile. I dropped the lamp, and it split the tile on which it landed. I watched to see what he'd do next. He did nothing. He didn't move at all. I watched him not moving. The bedroom key was sticking out of his back pocket.

And then I was out in the corridor again. There was no one outside waiting for me. I needed to shriek, but I didn't make a noise. I ran up and down outside Kel's room as soundlessly and as mindlessly as an animal, and it is like a song to me now. The words drift through my mind like the lines of a song. No, not words even, but the shells of words. The hard empty shells of words that harbour rhythm, but are hollow inside. The lamp-stand came down as if it had done so itself. Kel landed on his teeth. I had broken his smile, his beautiful smile. Now you're gonna get it, he said. Now you're gonna pay.

FIFTEEN

I stood in the corridor looking at the brass number on my hotel-room door. The phone was ringing inside. I could feel my heart. I could actually feel it there within my chest, all chambers and hollows. It was the emptiness of those chambers that I felt, not the muscle around the emptiness. I examined my hands for blood and I listened to the phone with great care, as if some knowledge could be deciphered from the sound of the ring itself. It rang for about a minute and then stopped. I was going to put my key in the lock, but the phone started ringing again.

I hurried downstairs to the reception desk. I asked the night clerk whether the room beside me was vacant. He consulted his computer and informed me that it was. I took both rooms that night. I collected the briefcase from the hotel safe. In it was what was left of the money. I went back to my first room and gathered my belongings as quickly as I could, stuffing them into a shopping bag. The phone rang once more and this time I answered it.

'I am going to cut you into shreds,' Kel said. I dropped the receiver and decamped next door.

The elevator bell rang as it dispensed someone onto my floor. I listened for footsteps, but heard none. There was a knock on the door of my old room. I didn't move. Nor did the person at the door. Both of us stood there listening for each other. Then hands fumbled with the lock and my old door swung open. Someone stepped inside.

The phone in my old bedroom began ringing again. I picked up the phone in the new room and dialled Kel's extension. It was busy. So he was still in his room. I hadn't thought that it was Kel at the door. He would have kicked and screamed and demanded to be admitted. He would never have knocked. And besides, was he in any state to walk around? In what condition had I left him? I looked for blood on my clothes. I checked for splashes on my shoes. There were none.

So who was next door? The same person, no doubt, who had been standing outside the hotel room just before I'd hit Kel. The person to whom he had sold me. *When can I have her? Tonight, as agreed.* His shadow had flickered in the slit of light beneath the door, as he'd shifted his weight from foot to foot, dying to meet me.

I turned out the light and crept over to the sliding doors at the end of the room. I opened them as quietly as I could, and slipped out onto the balcony. I leaned over the wall that separated the two balconies, and peered into my old room. The blinds were closed. I had not closed them.

There was a scrabbling of long nails against glass as a hand reached for the handle of the sliding door. *Long nails!* I remembered. It was the man from the stables. They were all one, the stable man and Kel's friend who was dying to meet me. Tall. Kinda stealthy. He'd been following me around for months. We must have narrowly missed each other when I'd run out of Kel's room. Him in the lift going up, me right beside him in the one going down. He wanted the money, but there wasn't much in the briefcase anymore. Not enough to make him go away. Maybe it was the painting he was after, as Kel had said. *The painting!* Had Kel made that up too? I had no way of telling.

The man's shoes scraped against the tiled floor of the balcony. I flattened myself against the partition wall. My heart pounded so thunderously that I wondered if it was audible next door. Treacherous thing, my heart. There was some fumbling and patting of pockets, and then the man switched on a torch. Its beam swung through the sky and disappeared into the balcony. The plant pot was dragged across the tiles. It was tipped over and prodded at. I heard him digging his fingers into the wet soil like an animal, smelling it, eating it, smearing it across his face. The patio furniture was pulled around and upturned. Then there was no movement for a while, and that made me more nervous than ever.

The beam of torchlight flitted into my balcony. What made him want to look next door? How did he know I was there? The light began to excavate my corner. If I had leaned forward, I would have seen him. And he would have seen me. It was unbearable. I pressed my head against the wall and pleaded for it to be over.

The phone started ringing again in my old bedroom. The torch beam jolted, then froze. The torch was switched off and the balcony was vacated. I too left my balcony. We both ran silently through our rooms. I put my ear against the wall over the phone. The man answered it.

'Gone,' I heard him say, and he slammed down the receiver. The door of my old room swung open and slammed shut. Again, no footsteps. Where do these ghouls come from? They do not touch the ground in the same way as the rest of us touch it. They do not lurch and shuffle like I lurch and shuffle.

I waited for the shunt of the elevator as it descended with its occupant. I snatched up my bag and briefcase, and left the room.

And then I was running across the lobby, tumbling out through the revolving doors, and spilling onto the plaza. At large again. Alone for the first time in I don't know how long. Still looking for patches of blood, as if blood was rot and would show up on the surface after the damage was done. There was no blood. There was no sign of anything untoward, at a time when I expected the whole world to look different. All I could think, if you could call it thinking, was of Kel not moving anymore.

A heavy rain began to fall. The whole city crackled as the water quenched it. The rain fell vertically onto the street, absolutely vertically. It rushed in rivers along the kerbside, collecting in its momentum all manner of flotsam and detritus. It flowed down into the network of gullies and tunnels that riddled the ground for miles beneath my feet. Where I stood at street level was just the surface of things, the barest surface of a world that extended like catacombs beneath me.

I woke up slumped in a shuttered shop front. A man was nudging me with his foot, telling me, not unkindly, to move on. 'Take this,' he said when I'd stood up. He was holding out a cup of tea in a polystyrene cup. 'Take it,' he said. 'They sell it next door. I'll get another one later. Here.'

I took the cup of tea, and gathered my belongings, and transported everything to the bench up the road. The shop shutters clattered behind me as the man pushed them back. The rain had stopped and the streets looked rinsed. I sat on the bench in the lemony morning light, and clicked open the briefcase. I found the key again in the document folder. It would be only a matter of time before I remembered what it unlocked. It would also be a matter of keeping it in my possession. I took a shoelace from one of the boots in my shopping bag, and threaded the key onto it. I tied the lace around my neck and slipped it under my clothes.

I finished the tea. There was a car dealer's forecourt across the road. I crossed over to it and informed the salesman that I wanted to buy a car. He took stock of me with my straggly hair, and pointed to an aging Fiesta. 'If you fill it with petrol,' I said, 'I'll buy it.' We shook hands on the deal. He tried to entice me with a new one when I started counting out the asking price in cash, but I wasn't having any of it. So long as the thing moved, I had everything I needed. When I was a mile down the road, I tried to roll up the driver's window. It wouldn't roll up. There was no driver's window.

I had difficulty locating the stables again. I couldn't think of anywhere else to go. It was the only other place I knew, and even at that I could barely find it. It was dark by the time I got there. A huge moon was rising over the trees. I parked the car some distance away and got out.

I headed up towards Jerry's house. The grass on the lane was knee high. The garden was straining at the garden wall. Only the roof and chimneystacks were visible behind the trees. It took a bit of effort to locate the garden gate, and a few kicks and shoves to force the thing open. It had been swallowed up by the hedge.

The path to the front door was practically gone. I had to beat my way through brambles and branches. Something brushed across my face, and elastic twanged in my ears. A huge spider scuttled up its broken web in the moonlight. The web ripped off my face like a second skin.

I banged at the front door with the knocker. The house was silent. No dog came around to thump the doormat for me this time. I banged again, and tried the handle. Locked. I shouldered the door open. It didn't take much effort. The wood had gone soft with age and it came apart with a gratifying split. I flicked the light switch in the hall. The lights weren't working.

'Jerry?' I felt around for the banister and made my way upstairs. Something scrambled over my feet and I screamed. The thing thundered down the stairs and bounced out through a broken windowpane in the front room. Jerry's huge cat, the good mouser. Judging by the size of it, the place was infested with rodents.

'Jerry?' I called again when I was outside his room, though I knew he wasn't inside. Or if he was, he wasn't doing too well. He hadn't reacted to my scream, and no one had broken through that garden path in weeks. I pushed the door open and a startled bird flapped up from the corner. It flew full pelt into the window, and collapsed back into the darkness.

The brass bed was empty and unmade. The air in the room was stale. There was a glass tumbler on the nightstand with a set of false teeth in it. The moonlight fell aslant on the glass, illuminating the silty tidemarks where the water inside had evaporated. I picked it up and rattled it. I gave it a good shake. The teeth chattered foolishly and the bird came back to life. It crashed into the window once more, all beak and claws. I ran forward and threw the window open. Fresh air rushed in. The bird hurtled into the garden with a downward arc. I pulled the window closed and ran out of the house, making my way down to the stables.

'Here, girl!'

I called out to the chestnut mare as loudly as I could. My voice echoed around the courtyard. She would definitely have heard me. The stables were empty. The straw was still in each stall, just as I had left it, only a little more settled. I picked up an old head-collar, but couldn't remember which horse it had belonged to. I brushed the dust off and hung it on one of the hay-net hooks.

'Here, girl!'

I stood where I had first seen the mare, and I watched the gap in the trees. Not a sign of her. I climbed into the paddock and unwrapped the barbed wire that blocked off the gap. The woods were full of dark shapes. The wind ran through the leaves like an overhead river. I stumbled around and called her a final time. She didn't respond. The big hole that Jerry had dug was filled in.

Normally I could build up to his entrance with a stray sound. He would have knocked something down on purpose to frighten me. He would have knocked it down and stayed in the shadows, so that he could enjoy my fear as I stood alone in the dark. Kel was merciless that way, but it was worth it when he relented and offered me comfort. He'd have let me fret for a minute, and then he'd have come out to save me, arms spread wide, and I'd have seen the familiar beauty of his face once more.

There was no tell-tale sound when it happened. He was all stealthy contortions and sinewy manoeuvres. It wasn't Kel. It was the other one. The one who had held my throat. He was right there in the paddock with me. I ran, and he chased after me. I escaped from the paddock and sprinted through the courtyard. I swung the five-bar gate into him and he staggered.

I got to my car just ahead of him. He caught his arm in the door as I hauled it shut. He pulled himself out and fell over backwards. He didn't make a sound. I was the one who cried out. All I heard of him was the dull thud of his bodyweight hitting the ground and rolling.

I started the engine and threw it into gear. As the car jumped forward, I looked out through the missing window. The man was gone. Another engine started up. Headlamps shunted on a few hundred feet away.

I got myself onto the tarmac lane that led back to the main road. The other car was behind me in no time. I snatched a glance at him in the rear-view mirror, but I couldn't see his face.

It all happened quite elegantly then. I hit something, God knows what. I wasn't even looking at the road. I hit something head on, and the car lurched sideways and swung into a spin. Through the missing window, I saw shards of the shattered headlamps tumbling through the air, illuminated by their own, somehow still alight, bulbs. The shards sprinkled down like snowflakes. Some of them came in through the missing window. Like driving through a chandelier. The windscreen split into a silver web.

Then my car was upside down and the passenger compartment was caving in. I was propelled out of my seat, ending up behind it. The headlights were finally extinguished. I hit the top of my head, heard my teeth slam down hard, and everything went black, and silent.

That was when you finally entered my tale. I was halfway through it on a hiding to nothing, and had never considered the possibility of the intervention of a stranger. You told me how you had seen the whole thing from the hill, those two mad cars racing through the black countryside, one spinning violently, the other in full pursuit. Did I, careening around in the back of the driverless one, twist my head and glimpse your silhouette on the eastern horizon? Did I watch it run towards me, that jet-black shape, without knowing (yet knowing) that it was your shape? That it was you? Did I?

No. There was none of that. None at all. I have much to be grateful for. Our bond was natural. A choice, I told myself, not a fate.

IV

Your House, High Summer

SIXTEEN

I could feel the softness of a bed beneath me, entirely different to the sharp pitted surface of the road that had been pressed into my face only hours before. Another scene change that made no sense. The curtains were drawn, but it was bright outside. Daylight itself was a comfort. I had made it through the night. The world was still revolving, and carrying me with it.

The wind whistled and the curtains billowed out whitely. The room creaked and seemed to tilt. Then it righted itself once more. Am I at sea? I wondered. In a cabin on a ship at sea? The draught swept briskly through the room. It died in the corner in a flurry of dust motes. The swollen curtains deflated gently. The room fell still again. I waited. My heart raced. I held my breath.

There was another shrieking whistle of wind and I was out of the bed and bolting barefoot towards the door. My body ached all over. I was sick, not just injured, but sick. Fever, nausea, mottled vision. I had caught some disease. I threw the door open and blundered out onto the wooden floor of a corridor. No ship this, I realised, but someone's house. There were doors on either side of me and I threw them all open. Every room was empty, and the emptiness was in some way a physical representation of the nausea in my stomach. Each door made me retch – I cannot explain the connection, but it was there, and made perfect sense at the time.

I continued on down the corridor until it rounded a corner and opened onto a broad sunny room. I saw this person sitting by one of the windows, his back to me. I saw this person, this man, in a high-backed armchair, and I stopped dead behind him in surprise. His hair was blond and he was staring at something that I could not see. A book, perhaps, or looking out at his windswept garden. Or maybe he had his cat in his lap, and was scratching her chin. The chair blocked him from me, and I saw just the barest hint of his face, maybe even the upward curl of an eyelash.

All of the windows in the room were open. The wind rose again and the man's hair yielded to it like a cornfield. Something alerted him to my presence, and he began turning towards me, and I have never seen anybody turn as slowly as that man by the window turned that day, or perhaps he didn't turn slowly at all. Perhaps it was just me, open-mouthed me, making him move that way in my search for horror. I stood frozen behind him in my fluttering rags, more scarecrow than ever.

'I –' was my first word when the blond man stood up from his chair and faced me. There was another gusty whoosh in the room, as of wings, and a warm bird smell. We stood perhaps twenty feet apart, and the room took on an expectant air as it waited for my introduction. The man was a few years older than me. His feet, like mine, were bare. He inclined his head slightly, inviting me to continue. I wanted to fold up on the floor with the pain.

'I –' I said again, and then shook my head in bewilderment. My hair lifted up in the breeze, and a bird was there, invisibly before me, back-pedalling the air with its long white wings. The wings brewed up a dust cloud that made my eyes sting, and my hand came up to shade them. I stood there with my hand up like that, looking at the man as if he was drifting out to sea, though he was standing right there in the centre of his airy room. The bird was steady eyed. It was level with my face. No fear in it at all.

'I –' I tried one last time, and the sound of that useless croak almost brought me to tears. Ai, ai, ai. A wretched crow to the blond man's clear bird. That huge bird beat the air so slowly that I did not understand how it could stay airborne. I stretched out my hand to startle it off, but the bird was gone again. I wanted to turn and run away, but I stayed where I was and faced the man. And the man did the most unexpected thing. The man smiled. 'It's okay,' he said. 'Everything is okay.' And that was it, all that I remember of it, of that warm room flushed through with a sun-bleached whiteness. There is the vague recollection of the man running towards me as the bird finally knocks me over and the room falls away. I hit the ground, croaking my awful ai, ai, ai, and I don't know how much later it was before I woke up again.

There was a huge old tree outside the window of this new bedroom. The branches swept grandly up and down in the wind. I lay on my side and stared at them. There were no other houses in sight. Just fields. The fields were full of wild flowers.

'Cyclamen.'

I turned my head and there you were, sitting on the bedside chair. My wrist was in your hand. Your fingers were on my pulse. You didn't lift your gaze from your watch.

'Cyclamen,' you said again, pronouncing the word syllable by syllable. *Sick la min.* I had no idea what you meant. I thought it was the name of the disease I had caught.

You finally looked up from the watch. 'The pink flowers in the field', you explained slowly, returning my arm back to the bed, 'are called cyclamen.'

'Ah, the flowers,' I said, relieved. Only I had said 'flowerth'. There was something wrong with my tongue. It felt bigger in my mouth than it usually did. 'I thoughth you meanth –' I jerked my hand nervously, and didn't finish the sentence.

'Oh right,' you said, as if you knew exactly what I meant. I smiled and my lip stung. I licked it and tasted blood.

'And that's speedwell,' you said, pointing. 'And there near the tree: milkwort.'

'Oh really,' I said, nodding. 'They're beautiful.' I put my fingers inside my mouth. All lumpy, but the teeth were in place.

'Bit my tongue,' I explained. Bih my thongue. You made a sympathetic noise.

'Still on though, isn't it?'
'Yeah,' I said, and nodded again. 'Thill on.'

You had found me on the road and brought me to a hospital, you explained. We had gone there together in an ambulance, straight after the crash. They had released me from Accident and Emergency that same night, after a few initial tests and x-rays. A few hammers on the reflexes, torches in the eye. Count my fingers, miss. Count them yourself. She seems all right, sir. We don't need to keep her here.

You stayed with me. You stayed by my side, a source of warmth in a chill room. They told you that there was nothing wrong with me, physically at least. I remembered nothing of the hospital, nothing from the hours immediately after the crash. I only remembered the gentleness with which you handled me. You guided me through the velvet darkness that had engulfed me then. I felt your hand on my arm. When you saw that my belongings were gone, and that my car was a write-off, and that I didn't have anybody to call in case of emergency, well, you had to take pity. Your heart was kind. Your heart was compassionate. I had you trapped. A small part of me, for only small parts of me were capable of feeling anything then, a small part of me felt sorry for you, felt sorry for this man who was a slave to human decency and who had therefore found himself, through no fault of his own, unexpectedly lumbered with me. The authorities would have picked me up or I'd have run to ground again, and this time I would not have been cushioned by a case with cash. This time I would have been empty handed. It would have ended badly. Had you not taken me home.

Home. How easily that slipped out.

After that, there were days. Many days, and it began coming back to me, drip by drip. I remembered bits of the journey to your house. We were already out of the city by the time my surroundings eased themselves into my awareness. It was a long trip. I sat belted into the passenger seat of your jeep, gazing out the window. The broad flat landscape gushed by, the fields scorched yellow and tan with drought. I was picking road grit out of the heel of my hand. I turned my head, and there you were, this man, this you. No, not yet you. Just this man who gradually became you.

You kept glancing across at me while you drove, checking to see if I was still upright, still breathing. So long as the jeep was moving, I was satisfied. You might have chatted a bit. The traffic's not bad today. Nice weather we're having. Driest summer on record, did you hear? I didn't hear. I wasn't listening. I was thinking about that man in the stables. That horrific man. The more distance I put between myself and him, the better. I couldn't even begin to think about Kel.

I didn't notice any road signs or town names. I barely registered your house when we pulled into the driveway. You opened the front door and I walked through it. You could have led me through the whole house and back out the front door again, and I would not have questioned you. You could have opened the door to the mouth of hell and I'd have stepped inside. I was following the path of least resistance. Because at least it was a path.

You led me to a bright bedroom. You'd have carried my things in from the jeep and put them on the bed for me, only I had no things. You went out to the kitchen and came back with a hot-water bottle. Why does the recollection of that in particular make me want to cry? I am so soft these days, so shapeless and soft. You helped me into the bed. How awkward you were, how shy. You handed over the hot-water bottle, wrapped in a towel so that I would not burn myself. 'For the shock,' you said. I held it to my stomach. A small, black cat came in to watch our ceremony, her tail wrapped demurely around her feet.

You didn't dare remove my clothes, though they were filthy, and the bed was clean. I had lived and nearly died in those clothes for days. You didn't even try to remove Kel's black hooded jacket. It was far too big for me, and hung around my shoulders like a cloak, but you didn't so much as attempt to unzip it. You seemed to consider doing so, but changed your mind. You kept hesitating, then blustering on, chatting away to me though I was as good as deaf. So reluctant to touch me. Apologising even for having to lean over me to fix the covers of the bed.

'Here. I've made you tea. Look. I've made you tea. Here, drink it.' I took the handle of the cup. My hands were bruised and scratched. I couldn't put any weight on my left little finger. I held the cup to my lips and it shook. I sipped at the tea. It made my tongue sting. You peered into my face.

'Are you okay?' you asked. I smiled and shook my head. You nodded. 'That's to be expected. You'll feel better when you drink the tea.'

You drew the curtains and closed the door on me. It was still bright outside. I hadn't gone to bed during daylight hours since childhood, but I had never felt less like a child in my life. And then I began to sleep. I'm not sure how long I slept for. The next time I saw you, that time when I was delirious and thought the room was full of birds, maybe two or twenty-two hours later, I had no idea who you were.

'So,' you said. 'How's the patient today?'

'The patient's great, Doc. The patient's as good as new.'

'And the patient's tongue?'

'Shipshape.'

'Glad to hear it. The patient is lucky to have come out of that crash alive, you know.' We were sitting at the kitchen table. I had been in your home for just over a week, and had only recently begun getting out of bed.

'Thank you for everything that you've done.'

'That's okay.'

'No, really, thank you for going to the hospital with me. Thank you for putting me up in your house. It was very generous of you.'

'Ah, it was nothing. Anyone would have done the same.'

I laughed sceptically at the unlikelihood of that. You smiled politely at your knees.

'I like your place,' I offered after a while. 'I like the way it's so open plan.'

You glanced around the room as if you'd never really noticed it before. 'Yeah,' you said thoughtfully. 'It's a nice enough place to recuperate in, I suppose.'

'Oh, it's perfect!' I said. 'It's been just perfect. Really, it couldn't have been better!' The words had come out too fervently. Embarrassed, I stared at my fingernails, what was left of them. 'Anyway,' I told you, 'I'll be on my way soon. I was just wondering about my car.'

'Jesus,' you said, shaking your head. 'You've no real notion of what happened, do you?'

'Is it wrecked, yeah?'

'Oh yeah.'

I nodded.

'Total write-off.'

'Oh. What about my stuff?'

'Same as the car,' you said. 'Gone.'

I scratched at my temple with my blunt fingertips. I distinctly remembered having the briefcase after the crash. I distinctly remembered having it prised out of my hands. By a doctor, I had assumed. Someone with strong fingers. They had been rough with me. My fingers were still bruised and sore.

'Did I not have a briefcase with me when I was lying on the road?'

'Oh yeah, you did. It wasn't destroyed in the crash.'

'Well, where is it then?'

'It was stolen.'

'Stolen?'

'Yeah.'

'Who stole it?' I was horrified. 'Who in the name of God would have stolen my case?'

'Well, I don't know. I didn't steal it.'

'I didn't say you stole it. Why would I say that you stole it?'

'There was this man who showed up at the crash,' you said suddenly.

'What! Why didn't you tell me this before? Jesus Christ!'

'I'm sorry. Maybe I should have told you before. But you were, you know. You were laid up in bed. I dragged you out of the car and this man had –' you gestured into the air and raised your eyebrows '– just materialised.'

'What!'

'I shouted at him to get help, but he seemed more interested in the case. He said that it was his case. I couldn't believe what he was saying. I would have hit him right there, but I was so worried about you.'

'What did he look like?'

You stared at the ground, your face strained with concentration, and then you looked with great significance at me. I thought, fucking hell, he's going to tell me that the man looked like me.

You shook your head and shrugged helplessly. 'I don't know what he looked like.'

'What do you mean, you don't know what he looked like?'

'I mean just that. I have no idea what the man looked like.'

'Think!' I demanded, rising a few inches from my chair. And then: 'Oh God, I'm so sorry. Look, I didn't mean to raise my voice. It's just – this is really important. It's really, really important. I need to know all that I can about this man.'

'Of course you do. I fully understand, and I'll help you in any way that I can. I just don't think I'm going to be of much use. I didn't get a proper look at him. He was all bent over. It was a dark country road.'

'What were you doing on a dark country road?'

'I was out hill-walking.'

'In the middle of the night?'

'It wasn't the middle of the night. It wasn't that late at all. I was making my way back to the jeep. I know those hills backwards. It didn't bother me that it was dark, and the night was a clear one because of the full moon. The man got there soon after I reached you. He must have been driving the other car that was chasing you.'

'You saw the car chase!' This was incredible news. I had at last a witness. A witness, that is, to the chase, and not just to the messy aftermath. I already had many witnesses to my messy aftermaths. 'What did you see? Tell me exactly.'

'Well, I was up on the hill and I saw these two cars come shooting out of a side road. They followed each other for a while, but then the one in front swerved into a spin. The other one skidded to avoid it, and came off the road on the far side from me. Its lights went out and I couldn't see it anymore. The spinning car began to tumble. There was glass breaking and metal crunching, so I rang for an ambulance on my mobile phone. I started running towards the crash and –' You paused and gave a small shrug. 'And then I came upon you.'

I took a deep breath. 'Okay,' I said, as calmly as I could manage. 'What did you see then?'

'I ran up to your car and dragged you out through the back seat. You were holding onto your briefcase even though you were unconscious. Then the man came up. I thought he was helping. You presume when someone is hurt that everyone is going to help. He seemed to know what to do, and that was good, because I sure as hell didn't. He reached for you with such authority that I thought he was a doctor. He didn't say anything. We dragged you away from the car. It looked like it was going to topple over. The man went to take the case out of your hands. I don't know how you held onto it, because you were still out cold. I wasn't really watching him. I was leaning over you to see if you were breathing. Then I realised that the guy wasn't taking the case for medical reasons. He was a scavenger, or something. I tried to stop him. He said it was his case. I tried to push him away. He didn't even look at me. I shouted at him, and he elbowed me in the face. I fell over backwards and rolled into the ditch. That's when I hurt my arm.'

You pulled back your sleeve and showed me your forearm. It was badly bruised. Shades of yellow and black.

'God almighty,' I said. 'That looks like it could be fractured. Did you get it checked out when we were at the hospital?'

'Yeah, they said it's fine. It looks worse than it is. Anyway, I climbed out of the ditch, yelling at this guy. He was literally dragging you around by the case. You were still unconscious, but you didn't let go. Anna, your grip on that handle was like iron. You have no idea. I thought, Jesus Christ, rigor mortis. I ran after the two of you. He had his car waiting, the engine running. It looked like he was going to take both you and the case, and separate the two of you later. Then the ambulance arrived. It drove right up to him. The medics ran out. You finally released the case and flopped out flat on the road, right on your face. The man climbed into his car with the case and drove off. The horrible thing is, he very nearly got you as well.'

I had ended up face down on the road immediately after the crash. It was pitch dark. I had managed to get myself halfway out through the shattered back-seat window. I remembered that much. The tarmac was embedded into my cheeks like shrapnel. It was warm, the tarmac, warmer than my face was. I could smell it. And I could smell petrol. The engine was still running in my car. It sounded raw and hoarse. It was chugging in little leaps. I lay there with my hands above my head, as if preparing to dive into the road. Both hands held onto the handle of the case. I couldn't move. Then the engine of my car died and I thought I was next. Here it is, I thought: the distillation of everything that I am. Here, embedded into the surface of a road, is the logical conclusion of all that falling.

Then I heard them, drifting through the air. Most unexpected. The words just hung there in the dark background. Full of regret. More remorse in them than even I could have mustered. I did not know the voice of the speaker.

'I never meant,' the words said, addressing themselves to the back of my head. 'I never meant.'

SEVENTEEN

With a most extraordinary and merciful case of mind over matter, I stopped thinking about Kel. Perhaps it was a re-enactment on a miniature scale of the loss of my memory. Once more, the safety valve kicked in. Thoughts of Kel were just too much and I tidied him away into one of the cupboards of my head. Shut the door tightly and bolted him in. Yes, somewhere in the back of my mind (or my throat, actually, for I could feel the metallic taste of him occasionally rising up my throat) he was always *there,* but not as an actual formed thought. He existed only as a mute source of anxiety and guilt, one that could generally be deflected by a distraction of some sort. And that distraction was generally you.

It was evening time when your jeep pulled up. I had been fidgeting in the corner for a few hours, trying to find the right words to say something that was in all likelihood going to upset the equilibrium. I wasn't sure how to phrase my question, and half of a line of a song kept coming out. *Oh, my love, I wish that we could* . . . something something.

As soon as I heard your key in the door, I tucked myself in beside the bookcase, pressing my head against the wall. Everything was excruciating. My heart started to thud. You opened the door and dropped your keys on the telephone seat. You were only about ten feet away, but you didn't seem to notice me.

You set down your bags of groceries, came into the living room, and placed yourself on the rug with your back to the fireplace as if warming yourself. Still you did not notice me, though I was staring at you. I wanted to shake my head, but I didn't dare move. I just watched you. I watched you closely. I liked you. I had liked you from the moment I'd set eyes on you, sitting there in your old armchair. I had liked you even more when you'd smiled and told me that everything was okay. You were one of those people who often sang or whistled to yourself, and you whistled as you stood there in the evening sunlight. There should have been a flurry of leaves in your wake, or petals, even. Yes, that seems more appropriate – a scattering of petals. Too feminine though. I must think of something else. It is so important to get it – to get you – right. It is critical to decipher who you are. The devil, they say, is in the detail. Dandelion seeds, then, or whatever they are, those breezy white things that float through the late summer air. Dandelion seeds should have drifted behind you. Your hair lit up in a golden glow. What is it about blond hair that it can look so, well, defenceless?

You whistled and looked about yourself, in your jeans and T-shirt, and then you yawned. *Oh, my love,* I sang silently, *I wish that we could* . . . something something. You moved about the room, making minor adjustments here and there. When you saw your cat, you stooped down and scratched her under the chin.

'Wonderful egg,' you told her, and she stretched out her front paws and squeezed her eyes shut. You sifted through the things that I had discarded on the sofa: an old newspaper; an empty cup (the contents of which you sniffed); a crumpled biscuit packet; and three cushions. You rearranged the cushions and scanned the page of the paper that I'd left open. Can't remember what page it was, but I'll call it the OBITUARIES. I noticed for the first time that one of your fingers was damaged. The very tip of the middle finger on your left hand seemed to be missing. The fingernail hooked over it protectively.

I couldn't bear to wait any longer. I tiptoed up behind you and covered your eyes with my hands. 'Guess who?'

You sighed. 'Would it be the mentler who has taken up residence in my house, by any chance?' You took my hands down from your face and turned around. 'Well, imagine that – I was right.' A bit of a smirk at me, then you collapsed on the sofa, clasping your hands behind your head. I stayed standing. I had trouble with my question. I suddenly felt shy. I gave a tiny laugh.

'What's funny?'

'Nothing.'

'Tell me, Anna. Doctor's orders.' Your eyes darted all over my face, as if you would find a small door concealed in it that would admit you into my head.

'Really, it's nothing.'

'Okay then.'

Silence. I realised that I didn't want you to stop pursuing your line of questioning.

'It's just that,' I started, and put my fingers to my chin. 'It's just a question that I have, but it's stupid.'

'I'm sure it's not stupid. Ask me.'

'But it's stupid!' I held onto the tip of my chin with forefinger and thumb, almost scared of what would come gushing out of my mouth before I could slam it shut. The last thing I needed was to make an arse of myself again.

'I won't laugh. I promise. Trust me.' Trust you? I wanted to.

'Well, it's just –' I took a breath and frowned and scratched my head. 'It's just –' I had to stop repeating the same words. I dropped my hands and looked you in the eye. 'Do I know you from somewhere?'

You laughed. 'I was right. You are mental.'

'You said you wouldn't laugh.'

'Jesus, Anna, it's hard not to.'

'But do I?'

'Do you what?'

'Know you from somewhere?'

'I can't answer that. Do you?'

'I don't know. Do I? Do *you* know me? Have we come across each other before?'

A fraught moment as you weighed up your answer. Then you jumped up and grabbed me. You seized me by the waist and thrust me up into the air. 'You should learn to fly a plane,

Anna! You should learn to soar through the sky so that all kinds of things come flooding through your head. Then you'll remember whether you know me or not.' You swooped me around, and swung me down onto the couch.

'By the way,' you added, your face bent over mine, 'don't you think I'd remember it if I'd met you before?'

You were gone before I could respond. I sat there blinking on the couch. You got the grocery bags from the hall. Then you set about cooking dinner. I heard the clink of the frying pan being placed on the stove. I heard the chopping board coming down on the counter. And there was the fridge opening and closing, and the sound of something landing in the pan with an enthusiastic hiss and sizzle. I listened to those kitchen sounds with great care. I studied them, in fact, as if they were a code of some sort. I listened to them with the notion that if I could crack that code, I would break through into, I don't know, there must be a word. Safety, perhaps, though that is not quite it. Something inaccessible that I will call safety. A black line on which I could stand, and which would finally put a stop to my fall. The thought made me chew at the stubs of my nails. And then the first waft of whatever it was, something salty and flavoursome, drifted out to me from the kitchen, and my exhilaration was complete. I found the possibility of salvation in the smell of something frying, and I felt like singing. You would have known for sure that I was mad had you heard me from the kitchen. I wanted to belt it out as loudly as I could, in my awful croaking voice: *Oh, my love, I wish that we could.*

'He's gone now,' you said the next morning over breakfast. I nearly choked on my toast.

'Who is gone?' I demanded. I had instantly thought of Kel. He had slammed back into my mind just like that, with a mere word, a male pronoun, at a time when I'd thought I was safe from him.

'The man at the crash. He's gone. He has the case. That's all he wanted. So it's over. Whatever it was . . .' Your voice trailed off, inviting me to fill in the blanks. I didn't open my mouth. I considered your words in silence. It didn't feel over. You reached into your pocket.

'Here. This is for you.' A thin glinting amulet hovered above the table, casting flashes of light about the breakfast dishes. The cat jumped up and snatched at it. You tossed it into my hands, where it immediately became mundane.

'It's the key to the front door. Now you can come and go to your heart's content. The town is down the road. Turn right when you leave the driveway. I'll see you after work.'

I sat on the steps of the monument in the centre of the village. It was a stunning day. Crowds of people were stumbling out of the dark doorway of the church into the hot blinding sunshine. The clergyman shook their hands. Children were running around. It must be Sunday, I thought. I took out the postcards that I'd bought in the craft shop, and began to scribble on them. I filled them in with descriptions of the village, and descriptions of how much I was enjoying myself there. I squeezed in afterthoughts in tiny and barely decipherable writing that ran up the sides of the cards and around the fake addresses. I asked to have my regards sent to people who did not exist, by people who did not exist. I signed myself off as Isolde.

And then I went looking to buy stamps. My postcards with their fake addresses and addressees needed stamps. A post-office sign jutted out over the shop across the road.

The shop was open, but was empty inside. I wandered up and down the aisles. They were stacked up in no apparent order with those hardware and gardening implements that other people seemed automatically to know how to use. At the back, double doors led out to a sunny yard full of plants.

A young man came out from the door behind the counter, and asked if he could help me.

'The post office?' I enquired.

'It's closed on weekends.'

'Oh.'

The man smiled apologetically. I thanked him and made for the door. Behind me, a machine came alive. I stopped and turned. The man was holding a key to a grinder. He manoeuvred it along the wheel of the machine. He squinted at the original key and turned back to the copy that he was making from it. I stepped up to watch. He didn't notice my approach. The noise of the grinder masked it. I found myself looking not at the key in his hands, but at the man's face. His mouth puckered up in concentration, as though about to say a word. His long hair was tucked behind his ears. I didn't know him, but I could have grown up with someone just like him. There was no reason why not. He was about the same age as me and spoke the same language. My accent did not sound foreign to him, nor did his to me. For an instant, it didn't seem impossible that there was some level of shared experience between us.

He glanced up at me over his work.

'Still here?' he said with another smile. My hands jumped up and pulled out the key that hung from the shoelace around my neck. The key that I had found in the briefcase, that is. I dangled it in front of him, just as you had earlier dangled the key to the front door in front of me.

He turned off the machine and put his hand out. I pulled the cord over my head and dropped the key into his palm. He turned it over in his hands and pressed a thumb to it.

'It's warm,' he said.

'Do you think you could tell me what it would unlock?'

He squinted at the key and ran his finger along the edge. He tossed it up and down in his hand, mentally weighing it. I, meanwhile, examined him. I could have been just like him. There was no reason why not.

He handed back the key, shaking his head. A lock of hair fell into his face. 'I've never seen one like it before,' he said, pushing the hair back behind his ears.

'What does that mean?'

'This key is not for anything –' he grasped for a suitable word '– domestic.'

I saw it in his face, just as I had seen it in yours: a face that told me that it wanted to help, but didn't know how. I had been mistaken. There was no level of common experience between me and the key-cutting guy. I thanked him and left his shop.

The bell rang out in the belfry when I set off for your house. Cars were arriving for the second sitting in the church. Sunday, I thought again. Why had you gone to work on a Sunday?

EIGHTEEN

I loved it that you were an archaeologist. You left the house in the morning and prised lids from wooden boxes that had the word 'Fragile' stencilled onto their sides. The boxes came to you from all around the world, as if they had heard tell of a man who could fix them. Sometimes you picked up splinters on your fingers, but they were easily removed. The wood was so coarse that the splinters were large and visible. Everything was straightforward and reparable. I thought of you in air-conditioned rooms, momentarily contemplating those boxes before reaching into them and divesting them of their treasures. You held those treasures up to the light with fingers that showed them infinite respect. We never really discussed your work, did we? Isn't that a shame?

Nor did you ever tell me in which area you specialised, but I decided that it was in ceramics from antiquity. A broad area that I knew nothing about, but in which I quickly became emotionally involved. I saw all those urns and ampullae that had been restored by your hands standing safely in temperature-controlled glass cases. I felt the calm that settled in the display rooms when the lights were switched out at night. It was the same calm that I saw in your face.

But more clearly than that, and more gratifyingly, I saw those vases when they first came out of their pine boxes in as many as a thousand blunted and chalky pieces. The patterns on their sides were not yet patterns. Their shapes were not yet shapes. I thought of your quiet hands on them, coaxing a form out of them. Slowly they grew back to their original state. They were rarely complete, but you never forced them. You accepted that the pieces were missing and you didn't try to conceal the gaps, or replace the pieces, or guess at what had probably been there. You left clear perspex mouldings where the fragments were missing. If the fragments were subsequently discovered, you were there to guide them into the right place. You gently reconstructed the past without distorting the relics from which you worked.

It was only a matter of time before you started to pick through my own handful of fragments. I think, though your face didn't betray it, you had been waiting to do so for some time.

I stood behind you in the garden, clutching the wooden handle of the little shovel that you had optimistically thrust into my hand. 'Tobacco,' you were telling me, poking at the velvety flowers on the ground. The eaves of the house contracted as the day's heat faded. The sprinkler had released the scents of the flowers and lawn. Lilies and lavatera. Violas and valerian. Windflowers, meadowsweets, and snapdragons. I smelled many things on the air that night. 'I put down tobacco plants because someone once told me how great they smelled. At first I put down woodbine, because I thought it was all the same. And the woodbine smelled good, but tobacco's the one with that particular scent. Here, come closer. Lean forward. Do you smell that? Yes, I thought you might like it. There's lavender out there too. And jasmine somewhere, though I don't think it flowered this year. Or if it did, I must have missed it.' You stabbed your garden fork into the soil. 'You hungry?'

'Yeah,' I said. 'I'm always hungry.'

'Me too.' You stood up and headed for the back door. I threw my shovel down beside your garden fork. The sprinkler caught you as you made your way up the garden path. The water made your shirt translucent.

I seem to remember a fire in the hearth that evening, though it was too hot to have lit one. A candle then. You were a great fan of those big square candles that had four wicks and burned for nights on end. A candle flickered in the fireplace, and I placed myself in front of it. You were across in the kitchen, banging pots.

'Anna,' you asked, 'do you mind me asking what you were doing before you ended up here?'

I shrugged and glanced at you over my shoulder. 'I was working in these stables.'

'Oh really? Horses?'

'Yeah.' I smiled. 'One of the horses was mine.'

'That's nice. Where is it now?'

'Dead.'

'Oh.'

This is the point at which the conversation should have ended. I took a book down from the bookshelf and propped it up on the mantelpiece. *Encyclopaedia of Flowers and Plants*. Steam started rising out of one of the pots. You stirred it and took a box of spices down from the cupboard.

'What did your horse die of?'

I looked up from the index of the book. 'Nothing.'

'How could it have died of nothing?'

'She was put down.'

'Oh. Why?'

'Because I wouldn't mind her anymore.'

'So you put it down?' You unscrewed the lid of one of the jars of spice and squinted in at the contents.

'The old guy who owned the stables did it after I left.' You considered this information with a slow nod.

'Why did you leave?'

'A number of reasons.'

'Give me one.' You sprinkled a spoon of something red into the pot. What was I supposed to say to you? That a man had seized my throat in the night and scared all hell out of me?

'I felt like a change.'

'That's hardly a good enough reason to put down a horse.'

I scowled at you. You were too busy with your spices to register my scowl. 'I told you: I didn't put her down.'

'The old guy did.'

'Right.' This is the wrong conversation, I wanted to say. None of this matters anymore. We should be talking about other things. Page 176. *Nicotiana. Tobacco plants. They bloom for long periods during summer and autumn. Some open only to give off their scent in the evening. The flowers offer a range of harmonious colours, and are excellent for bedding.*

'Are you sure he put it down?'

I slammed the encyclopaedia shut and returned it to its shelf. 'Quite sure.'

'Did you see him doing it?' Another teaspoon of spice. Yellow this time. You stirred it in, with your usual maddening deftness, then scrutinised the contents of the pot. I hadn't once seen you taste the sauce. It seemed to be more about getting the colour right.

'No, of course I didn't see him doing it. Do you think I'd have stood by and watched?' I scratched my head. It itched all over. The midges in the garden must have gotten at my scalp.

'Then, how can you be sure he did it?'

'I saw where she was buried.'

'So?'

'What do you mean, so?'

'Just because you see a grave, Anna, doesn't mean there's anything in it.'

'Maybe on your planet.'

'Hey, I'm not the mentler. Here.' You placed a glass vase full of water on the counter. 'Put those flowers in that.'

You pointed at the kitchen table. On it were flowers cut from the garden. Yellow flowers. I picked them up and inserted their stems into the narrow neck. They fanned out on top like a peacock's tail. 'They look really nice,' I said, holding the vase up to the window.

'They do.'

'Why don't I leave them here so we can both see them?' I placed them on the table.

'Lovely,' you said absentmindedly. I came up behind you and peered into the pot. Something with tomatoes.

Something red and bubbling. 'Smells good,' I said, and hooshed myself up onto the counter. 'Smells almost as good as the flowers.'

'Here: how does it look? More chilli? What do you think?'

'I think that your shirt is wet from the sprinkler and you should think about removing it.'

You looked at me in a far-off way, as if considering an abstract problem. Then you added more chilli to the pot. You watched with satisfaction as the sauce deepened to russet. I watched you watching it. You frowned.

'This horse,' you began again. 'Did you have it long?'

I rolled my eyes to heaven and slid off the counter. 'Her. She was a mare. No, I didn't have her long. Only as long as I was working in the stables.'

'And how long was that?'

I shrugged again. 'I'm not sure, to be honest.'

'Are we talking months or years?'

'Months, I suppose. Maybe two months. I really don't know.'

'And what were you doing before the stables?'

Here we go. 'I don't know what I was doing before the stables.'

Silence. You packed away the spices into the box. You put the box in the cupboard, and closed the cupboard door. Then asked softly: 'Anna, why don't you know?'

'I don't know why I don't know.' I suddenly felt terribly sad. The doctor–patient relationship was coming to an end. I could see that clearly, and was sorry to watch it go. Pick me up again, I wanted to say. Pick me up and run around the room holding me up in the air. Tell me that I should learn how to fly. You just stared at me, stirring your pot.

'Tell me about that scar,' you said.

I hadn't thought about the scar in weeks. I raised my fingers and touched it. One time when I had done so, my fingers had come away smeared in blood.

'What's with all the questions?'

'I need to know about you, Anna, is all. You seem to be living in my home.'

'I'll go then.'

'If that's what you want.'

'Fine. I'll leave.'

But I didn't. Why would I? The yellow flowers were on my dressing table that night.

You spent a lot of time smirking at me after that. 'She's not talking to us,' you told the cat. 'Do you hear her not talking to us?' The cat got up and left. Doors were slammed. Meals were eaten in silence. I should have gone. I should have left you in peace. But I didn't, and the days were long, and the evenings were endless. And the heat of the summer became humid and the humidity became volatile, and it was everywhere then, that tension.

But one night you squared yourself in front of me. Yeah, I remember now: you stared at my neck. I put a protective hand to my throat.

'What?' I asked.

'Nothing.' You reached out. I stepped back.

'What!'

'Nothing.' Another step towards me. I banged into the wall.

'Don't touch me.'

Wearily: 'I wouldn't dream of it.'

Without making contact with my skin, you took a hold of the black shoelace that was still around my neck. You hitched it up on your hooked fingernail, and gave it a pull. The key slid up my chest and materialised into the room.

'What does this unlock?'

'I don't know.'

'Give it to me and I'll find out.'

'No.'

'Give it to me.'

'No, it's mine! I'll find out myself.'

'We will find out together what it unlocks.' The way that you said it sounded like a threat.

I decided that night that it was time to leave. I told myself that I had relied on your hospitality for far too long, and that you were beginning to get a little weird. I got out of bed and dressed in the dark, working out the words to a polite thank-you note in my head (never was one for doing things the brave way). I pulled on the hooded jacket that Kel had thrown over me on our last night together. I hadn't worn it since my arrival in your home. It was still torn from the crash, but it was black and it hid me. I opened my bedroom door as quietly as I could, and when I stepped out onto the corridor, there you were. The fright you gave me, lurking in the hall like that! Standing with the lights out, fully dressed. Looking right into my face though the hood was drawn over it.

'I'm going to the airport,' I announced.

'I'll drive you there,' you replied with a gentleman's bow.

We should never have left the safety of your home. I knew that as soon as we were in the jeep. We had made a disastrous mistake. We hurtled through the night in our tiny steel capsule. I wish that I could say that we travelled in silence, but you were still full of questions.

'Were you alone at the hotel?'

'When did I tell you about the hotel?'

'The doctors told me. They said that you'd told them you'd been living in a hotel, but that you weren't going back to it.'

'I told them that?'

'That's what they said. The hospital asked for your address, and you said you didn't have one. Why else do you think I took you in? I don't ordinarily bring home strange girls. So were you alone there?'

'In the hospital?'

'In the hotel, of course.'

'Yes. No.'

'Who were you with?'
'A guy.'
'What guy?'
'I don't know. Just some guy. The world is full of them.'
'What guy, Anna?'
'Some guy. There was this guy at the hotel.'
'Was he your boyfriend?'
'No!'
'A friend?'
'Not really. Just another guest at the hotel, I suppose.'
'What was he doing there?'
'Not a whole lot, as far as I could see. Just passing through, like myself.'
'What was his name?'
'I never asked.'
'You never asked?'
'Are you going deaf or something? I never asked him his name.'
'How old was he?'
'You're driving too close to the car in front.'
'How old was he, Anna?'
'I don't know. Please slow down a little. You're making me nervous.'
'Take a guess at his age.'
'I would guess that he was my age.'
'Twenties?'
'Yeah. Maybe a little more. I think he might have had a couple of years on me.'
'What did he look like?'
'I don't know.'
'Take another guess.'
'He was tall and skinny.'
'And was he green-eyed, with a big mouth?'
'Yeah.'
'Just like you, really.'
I hesitated. 'Yeah, a little, I suppose.'

'Oh, Anna!' Your voice filled the car and your voice was sad. I didn't understand then. I thought you were jealous.

We drove in by the ring roads. We followed all the blue airport signs and we reached the place in the early hours of the next day. You stood in the car park and waited for me to do something. So I led you to the departures floor. Even at five o'clock in the morning, the place was busy. People wandering about looking gaunt. We joined their number.

'What are you looking for, Anna?'

'Baggage lockers.'

'I don't think there are baggage lockers in airports anymore.'

'Don't be ridiculous. Where would people leave their luggage?'

I marched up to the information desk. You were right. The woman behind the desk informed me that there were no lockers.

'What about in the car parks?' I persisted.

'There are no lockers in any part of the airport,' she said. 'There are shelves. You get a docket.'

'But I have a key! Look.' I pulled out the key and waved it in her face.

The woman shook her head, smiling politely. She didn't even look at the key. 'I'm sorry, madam. That key is not from here.'

'Yes it is!'

The woman blinked.

'Anna, come on. There haven't been lockers in airports for years.'

'Well, what's it from then?' I demanded of the woman.

'I have no idea, madam.'

'Yes you do!'

'Anna!' You dragged me away from the desk and made me sit on a plastic bench.

'The bitch!' I said. 'The silly bitch!' I knew that if I was not careful, I was going to burst into tears. I put my key back under my clothes.

'Maybe it's from a train-station locker,' you offered.

'Maybe.' I wanted a cigarette. There were people smoking just beyond the glass exit doors. I got up and set off towards them.

'Now what are you going to do?'

'What do you think I'm going to do? I'm in a bloody airport. I'm going to catch a bloody plane.'

'Have you any money?'

'Some.'

'Enough to buy a ticket?'

'Maybe.' I hadn't enough to get myself on a bus.

'You don't have much money, do you?'

'Not really.'

'You can't buy a ticket then.'

'I know that.'

'So what are you going to do?'

'I don't know.'

I stopped walking, and I said it again: I don't know. Jesus. We could have become strangers then. No one would have noticed you turning away from me in a crowded place like that. Such things get swallowed up in the small dramas that go on in airports and train stations. You could have walked away without even saying goodbye, and it would have been okay. It would have looked like you were going to get yourself a coffee. We'd have kept an eye out for each other's faces in crowds and in café windows, the usual sort of things that people do to torment themselves. We'd have caught our breath every so often in false alarms. We might even have put our hands to our hearts at the first such alarm.

But we didn't. I said that I was sorry about shouting at the woman behind the desk. It happens, you shrugged. We all get upset sometimes. I told you that I was sorry about the key. You said that it was okay. I said that I was sorry about dragging you out to the airport when you should have been in bed. You said that that was okay too. I said that it was not okay. None of it was okay. 'Sometimes,' I told you, 'it feels like I'm walking around just waiting for the next ton of bricks to land on my head.'

'Come here, you freak,' you said, pulling me into a hug. I rested my head on your shoulder and you stroked my hair. 'You have to learn not to take things so seriously, okay? Do you hear me? Okay, Anna?'

'Okay, Doctor,' I mumbled into your jumper.

We walked back to the jeep and began the return journey to your home. We went through the city this time, and I banged at the passenger window and told you to stop.

'Look!' I said. 'It's the hotel that I stayed in!'

'You stayed in the Grand Plaza?' There was incredulity in your voice.

'Yeah,' I said, my suspicions roused by your tone. 'So?'

'So someone got killed in there a month or so back. It was all over the news. Didn't you hear?'

'No.'

'It was around the time that you said you were staying there.'

'Oh.'

'And they never caught anyone for the murder.' The traffic lights went amber, then red. Then they turned green again, but the traffic didn't move. The junction up ahead was blocked by a truck. I felt a sudden urge to jump out of the jeep. Disappear down a side street. Never be seen again.

'So who was killed?' I eventually asked.

'Some guy.'

'What guy?'

'I don't remember. Just some guy. A young guy. Young enough. Around thirty, as I recall.'

'What was his name?'

'I don't know the details. It was in the papers. I can look them up for you.'

'Would you?'

'Of course.'

'That would be nice.'

I already saw that corpse in the hotel room. Kel's corpse. I saw it quite clearly in my mind's eye. He was slumped under the sink in the bathroom, just where I'd left him. The tiles were awash with his blood. He lay on his stomach, his face resting on its side. His skin was lavender. His lips were blue. Something tiny and white was on the ground beside him. It was as sharp as could be – his tooth. The tip of his eye tooth.

I was there too. My reflection hovered over him in the bathroom mirror. The porcelain lamp-stand was still in my hand. I saw it in the mirror before I knew that I was holding it. I dropped it yet again onto the tiles, and it shattered in the pool of blood. A droplet of the blood splashed onto my face. I put my fingers to my cheekbone and I smeared that blood across it. This time it would not have been blood from my scar. But it would have tasted just the same.

NINETEEN

I read in the papers that *Girl in the Mirror* will be ready to go on display again in the new year. I had no idea that these things moved so quickly. Perhaps Kel and I did not do as much damage as it seemed at the time. I know that we were amateurs. Kel seemed to know even less than I did. I know that we rolled the painting the wrong way around. I know that we should never have detached it from its stretcher frame. Should never have detached it from its rightful owners, either.

'The task of restoring *Girl in the Mirror* was particularly slow and delicate,' the article reads. 'Much of the work was carried out mechanically, that is by using surgical scalpels rather than chemical solvents to gradually lift away the crude overpainting. Most of this was done with the aid of powerful microscopes.'

There is no mention of the conservator himself, but these words could have come directly from his mouth. That is how the conservator would speak. Precisely and clearly. The conservator is too busy for obfuscation. Perhaps they did come directly from his mouth. Perhaps he was interviewed by journalists, but I don't think that would have been the case. It is more likely that he prepared a few sentences to be included in the gallery's press release. The conservator is a private man. He prefers to be left alone with his work, or so I imagine. What do I know about the conservator?

The article also mentions that the painting is to be presented to the National Gallery on permanent loan. This must be great news for all concerned. The conservator, in particular, must be well pleased. He will be able to give *Girl in the Mirror* her own catalogue number. She will be assigned a little patch on the wall. The other paintings will be told to shove up and make room for her. It has turned out tremendously well for everyone. Except, that is, for me and Kel.

What would happen if I turned up at the gallery to visit the painting when she's on show once more? For some reason, I feel that I've more right to see her than the public. The mess that I have made of my life for her! Surely that earns me a front-row seat? 'She will hang with her counterparts in the Flemish rooms,' the article concludes. *Girl in the Mirror* is Dutch. It must be a misprint in the paper.

Would anyone stop me if I tried to get through the door? Would anyone even know who I was? Thousands of people must pass through every day. All I'd have to do is wear heavy-framed glasses to cover the scar. I've already found a pair that will do just the job, though I can't see much through them, the lenses are so thick. They must have belonged to the little old lady who lived in my cottage, though they look more like the property of a man. They're about the only item in the entire cottage that could have belonged to a man. I'll have clear glass fitted to them. I wouldn't even have to put on a wig for my visit. My hair is all cut off and dyed, though the roots have long since begun to show. I considered getting a perm, but made a bolt for the salon door at the last minute. I decided that I wasn't that desperate to conceal my identity. The conservator would know me, but he wouldn't see me. He would be up in his glassy eyrie, bent over some other broken and cracked-up thing.

Will he visit *Girl in the Mirror* when she has left his studio? His relationship with the painting is so very intimate. We have much in common, the conservator and I, though it is unlikely he would see it that way. It is the painting's irreplaceability that astonishes me. It is the idea of her irreplaceability, over and beyond what she actually is, that I find impossible to grasp. But it is *Girl in the Mirror*'s physical genius that moves the conservator. That something as simple as the application of pigment can create such an evocative form takes his breath away. Maybe he perceives it as proof of something – that man has a soul, that there is a god. I don't know what, if anything, it would prove to the conservator. It didn't, in fairness, prove a whole lot to me. I don't know what kind of value system the man has, only that art is right at the top of it. Will the conservator miss *Girl in the Mirror* like I miss her? Will he miss being allowed to touch her, to tilt her, to contemplate her under light? Will the conservator resent it when she is out of his custody? Or will he immediately replace her with another project? The conservator has worked on Rembrandts and Caravaggios. Where will poor, lost *Girl in the Mirror* fit in to company like that? Will she be just another plaudit on his résumé? And in such world-class company, a comparatively minor one? How possessive a man is the conservator? As possessive as I am? Perhaps he will come downstairs every so often, just to stand and gaze at her the way I wish I could. Imagine if he looked up one day and I was right there beside him! Regarding the painting from an entirely different perspective. Do we even see the same thing when we look at her? I don't see how that is possible. Would the conservator's heart stop when he realised that it was me? Would he be able to react in time to prevent my escape? I would want him to do something. I would want him to shout for Security, or hurl abuse at me. What would he say? How dare you come here, after all that you have done? How dare you pretend that you care about art! Oh, he'd say far worse than that. He'd reduce me to a snivelling heap. The conservator could produce a fairly toxic insult if he put his mind to it.

But I don't think that the conservator would say a word. I don't think that the conservator would even blink if he saw me. I believe that if I did appear at his side, he would turn away stonily, making it clear that I was beneath his disdain.

❧

It had not been necessary to return to your house via the city. We should have used the ring roads that we had arrived by, but we didn't. Instead we had gotten ourselves ensnared in the morning's rush of cars, and had moved barely a mile during the hour between eight and nine. It had taken at least fifteen minutes to creep by the Grand Plaza itself. It stood there whitely to the left of us, glaring in the sunshine. Like a gravestone, it was. Like a big skull and crossbones. You had driven me past that hotel on purpose.

'This is for you.'

We were back in your house. It was the day after the airport debacle. I was sitting on the kitchen table, swinging my legs. My feet were bare. Head thrown back, no doubt. Nonchalant that evening, or at least affecting it. I knew I was in trouble, I suppose. I knew that you were on to me. You were just in from work. You were the same height as me when I sat on the table. Our faces were level.

'What is it?' I asked, sitting forward to receive the package.

'It's a present.'

'Duh – I can see that. What's in it?'

'Duh – open it and find out.'

I sat the thing on my lap and stared at it. A shiny green box tied with a gold ribbon. I untied the ribbon and removed the lid. There were shoes inside, wrapped in violet tissue paper. Stiletto-heeled shoes, the toes of which were fashioned out of silver mesh. There were blue and amber and red stones entwined in the mesh. I ran my finger along the heel.

'Spiky,' I said, 'like me.'

'Foxy, Anna, like you.'

You cupped the heel of my foot in the palm of your hand and held it up, so that my leg was straight. You ran the fingers of your other hand from my knee to my toes, and I shuddered. The shoe slid on with ease. The gemstones sparkled. You didn't release my foot, just held it and gazed at it, tilted it under the light. Then you stooped over and placed your lips on it. Your mouth was warm and smooth. 'Don't.' My lips formed the word, but no sound came out. Something was softening in me. Something was giving way. I covered my mouth with my hand. You didn't take your lips away. I didn't move. The blood pounded in my head. You kissed my foot and then pressed the side of your face into it.

'I don't know anymore,' you said quietly. 'I just don't know anymore.' You shut your eyes tightly as if enduring pain. A deep breath, then you swallowed and spoke my name. My foot was released. It swung to the floor. You straightened up and reached into your pocket and held something out to me.

'I got you this as well. I dug it out at work.' There was a piece of paper in your hand. It was folded in four. The gift had come with thorns attached. 'This is the guy that we were talking about. The one who got killed.'

I unfolded the page and there he was again. The lovely Kel. It was shockingly wrong that he had found his way into the room with us.

It was a photocopy of a newspaper article. He had long hair in the picture. He looked like Isolde had looked when I had magnified her. The same cavernous smudged eyes, the same cruel downward smear of a mouth. Everything that was black about his face was twice as black in the photocopy.

He was looking away in the picture, and his mouth was slightly open. His lips were forming words, or demands, or orders. His eyes were narrowed and he was addressing himself to someone to his left. I could almost hear him. *Do this, do that, no, that's wrong. You are an idiot. I'll do it myself. No I won't.*

FOUND DEAD, it said under his picture, IN THE GRAND PLAZA HOTEL. I folded the page up again without passing comment and handed it back to you. I hadn't recognised him without the hair when I had first seen him in the hotel, in just the same way that I hadn't recognised myself in Isolde's passport. My brain has pot-holes. Things fall into them. Things disappear.

'Did you know him?'

'I never knew him.'

'Don't lie.'

You replaced the folded page in your pocket and we both looked at the glimmering shoe again. You slid the other one onto my right foot. I twisted my ankles this way and that, so the gemstones would catch the light. My feet were not on the ground.

'Do you know a woman called Isolde Chevron?'

I continued playing with my shoes. 'No.'

'Anna,' you said angrily. I corrected myself.

'I don't know her. I know of her. Why?'

Another newspaper cutting exchanged hands. My face, her name underneath it. No scar. She was looking to her right. I think, perhaps, that if you had put my photograph beside Kel's, and jogged the two of them up and down a little, you could have made a whole conversation out of it.

'That's me in the photograph,' I said to you in a matter-of-fact tone. I handed it back. 'Don't tell the police.'

'Why does it have this name under your face?'

'I was travelling under an assumed name.'

'Oh,' you said simply. *Oh*. How tongue-tied you were that evening. (And how gentle.)

'Did you find out his full name?' I asked after a while, hoping to sound casual.

'Whose full name?'

'The dead guy's.'

'No. Apparently he too was travelling under an assumed name.'

'And they didn't manage to identify his corpse?'

'No,' you said, and I immediately thought of an anonymous headstone. I knew right then that Kel would never leave me alone.

'Did you know about this?' You unfolded a third newspaper cutting.

'Oh Jesus fucking Christ, do we have to do this now?'

'Yes we do, Anna. I need to know who or what is living

with me in my own home. So tell me again: did you know about this?' You dropped the clipping onto my lap. VALUABLE CACHE OF PAINTINGS STOLEN, ran the headline, FROM THE PIOTR LUDOWSKI COLLECTION. 'And what about this?' You threw another clipping down. TWO OF THE LUDOWSKI PAINTINGS RECOVERED FOR SIX-FIGURE RANSOM, ONE STILL MISSING. 'Do you know anything about that, Anna, do you?'

'Why are you being like this?'

'Because you're lying to me. I know that you are lying. Look at the painting, Anna. It's still missing, and you're not telling me something.'

'Stop bullying me. I swear I'm not lying. I don't know about any bloody painting.'

You covered your eyes with the heels of your hands. 'I want to believe you, Anna, I really do. But the fact of the matter is, I can't.'

I waited until I heard you leaving for work the next morning before I left my room. I hadn't slept that night. I wandered around the house for a while, picking up things and putting them down again, before finally settling at the kitchen table. I poured salt into the sugar bowl. It was a beautiful morning. Another beautiful morning. By then, Kel had been dead for well over a month. His flesh would have decomposed. The blood would no longer be red, but black. The photocopy that you'd produced the evening before was probably an accurate depiction of how his rotted face looked. No more of the beauty that had fascinated me so. Sometimes, when we had looked at each other, I had wanted him so much. And he had wanted me. I was sure of it. I had seen it in his face. It was like looking in a mirror. I said that to myself a few times as I played with the sugary salt. It was like looking in a mirror. Yes, that was exactly it.

I'll have to tell it from your point of view, because I can't even begin to think of it from mine. You were driving home from work, and you were thinking about not driving home at all. You had a gun with you, just in case. An old rifle. I believe that you did not intend to use it. You left it in the boot of the jeep.

You drew up to the house. All the curtains were closed, though it was still bright. Was I gone? you wondered. You scoured the building for clues of my absence. What sort of thing were you looking for when you tracked me? Cloven footprints in the flowerbeds? Tiny headless birds? Most ominously of all, you found nothing.

You stepped into the house and called my name: Anna! Anna! I did not answer. There was nothing unusual in itself about that, though that day seemed different, or at least it did in retrospect. The mind adds these subtle changes later.

You checked the kitchen first, which is where you would normally have found me. The kitchen, however, was empty. You threw back the curtains, and the evening sunlight streamed in. There was something spread out all over the surface of the table. Something white. White grains. There was a face picked out in the grains. You stuck your finger into some of the stray ones and tasted them – salt, no, sugar. Both. You looked at the face again. You crossed to the other end of the table to view it the right way up. Cavernous eyes. Dark lips. Slight smile. It was Isolde Chevron.

Wrong. It was supposed to be Kel's face. I can see how you made the mistake though.

So: did the hairs crawl on the back of your neck? I heard the front door open again, and you took something out of the jeep. The rifle. You slammed down the boot and came in. You worked your way through the rest of the house calling my name. Your tone of voice fluctuated between anger and concern. I followed your progress in my mind's eye. I saw you standing in the corridor outside each room, gingerly pushing the door open with your fingertips, so that the room was revealed to you without you having to step inside. The rooms were empty. All of the rooms along the corridor were empty.

Finally, you came to the bathroom. It was the only room left. The door was locked from the inside. You had me.

You knocked. There was no answer. You called my name again. I did not respond. You instructed me to open up. I did not obey. You sounded miles away from me, though we were barely three feet apart. I heard you cursing me, more in fear than in anger. Open the door, Anna! Open the motherfucking door! You started throwing your weight against it. On my side it throbbed rhythmically with your efforts like a great white heart. There was a splitting of wood as the bolt broke off. You came bursting in.

You found me on the floor beside the toilet where I had been retching all day. Ah Jesus, Anna, you said, scooping me up. My body was slack. That is what I remember – an inability to move. And the taste of vomit. I'm sorry, I kept saying to you. I'm really sorry. You closed the seat of the toilet and flushed it and sat me down on it. You filled up the sink with warm water and you washed away the tears and the sick from my face with a soapy cloth. You tied back my hair. You washed my hands and my wrists. You dried me with a fresh towel and then you wrapped your arms around me. Your hand was in my hair. It caressed my temple first and then it buried itself in my hair. Cradled the back of my head as though I was a baby. Talked to me as if I was a child. 'Look,' you said, pointing at my feet, 'you're still wearing your pretty new shoes.'

Later – how much later? I don't know, hours perhaps; not quite night outside, but getting there – later, you led me back to the kitchen and sat me down at the table in front of the salt and sugar face. You made me a cup of tea and you lit the fire for the first time since I had arrived. Yes, there was definitely a fire that night, not that it made any difference. It was just something for you to do with your hands, and somewhere for me to direct my gaze. A simple act in the middle of a complicated mess. You peered into my face.

'Do you want to tell me what happened?' you finally asked.

'I know who he is. Was. The man at the hotel. I know who he was.'

You looked at the face picked out in white grains on the table. You picked up my hand and rubbed it.

'So who was he?'

I had been waiting to say the words all day, but when they finally came out, I still stumbled on them.

'He was my brother,' I said.

Fratricide. There's a word. See here, the thin scar under my left eye: the mark of Cain.

TWENTY

Kel was never his name. I should say these things now lest I forget to correct myself and my version becomes the official one. Kel was never his name. It became his name to me until the mere sound of it was enough to make me clench my fists. I have no desire to speak his real name, so in my mind I started indexing him as Kel. A kel was the glint of a knife's blade catching the light. A kel was an indecipherable letter from a dead alphabet. It was a unit of energy, or the scientific abbreviation for some base element. Cl. Zn. Kel. I will look the word up one day, if indeed it is a word. I will research the matter thoroughly. I will have time for all of that. I could've just initialled him, delineated him as K, but it wasn't appropriate. Too familiar. Too intimate. Too indicative of the need for secrecy that he induced in me. So instead I just called him Kel, until he became Kel. Kel. Cull. Kill.

And then there is you, the problem of you. Whatever shall I call you, what with protection of identity and all of that? Your name was a good one, sort of old-fashioned and strong. I liked saying it and missed not saying it, but I had to change it too. Again, as with Kel, I did so after you were gone. Unlike Kel, I had to think and think. Amazing, the difficulty it caused me. Ewan, I said to myself, and tilted my head ruminatively. I tried the shape of it out on my tongue a few times, using different intonations. It wasn't quite right, but it was almost right. Ewan or Eugene or Eustace. Euclid, even, can you imagine! I was halfway there, I knew that much. And then for short: you. I suppose I got stuck there, though stuck is not the word. You. I had again made the sound that sounded right.

Outside, your once so carefully tended garden ran riot. Your cat started bringing in carcasses to us. Sparrows that she had pierced in the belly with her white needle teeth. Mice that she had decapitated. Three or four of these little broken bodies a day, placed on their backs, their wings and limbs askew. She left them on the kitchen table and in our beds. I even found one in my new shoe. The jeep mysteriously rolled into the pond. The house alarm was triggered. Or was it the smoke alarm? Did we even turn it off? I think the battery ran out. The wind chimes chimed when there was no wind. You stopped going to work. How could you have gone? – I wouldn't let go of your wrist. You didn't attempt to disengage yourself. I moaned horribly and showed no signs of recovery. I showed no signs of sanity. You said nothing. The questions that you must have had for me, but you still said nothing.

You cooked for me. You ran baths for me. You held onto me as if you thought my body would come apart if you released it. You listened to all of my awful noises, but you didn't let go. 'He was the most beautiful thing that I had ever seen,' I tried to explain. 'I couldn't get beyond the fact of his beauty.'

'Sometimes,' you said simply, 'it is a tragedy to have eyes.'

I got up one night and went down to the kitchen. I opened the drawers by the sink and went through them in the dark. They weren't there. I went out into the hall and rooted through the papers by the telephone seat.

'What are you looking for?'

I gasped out in fright. You were standing at the end of the corridor. You switched on the light and I shielded my eyes.

'What are you looking for, Anna? Perhaps I can help?'

'The newspapers. The bits of newspapers that you had the other day.'

'You mean the clippings? They're in my case. Beside you.' I looked down and there was your case, leaning against the wall. I opened it and found the clippings in the storage folder. LUDOWSKI COLLECTION. GIRL IN THE MIRROR STILL MISSING. I examined the photograph above the caption.

'I've seen this painting before.'

'Have you?'

'Yes.' I squinted at the photograph. The face was so pale that it seemed no more than a thickening of the air. I chewed my nail and put the clipping back in your case.

'It is hidden somewhere. I hid it. Ages ago.' I could barely believe what I was saying.

'Where did you hide it?'

'I don't know.'

'Think!'

'I can't think!'

'Has your key anything to do with it?'

I pulled the shoelace over my head and stared at the key in the palm of my hand.

'Oh Jesus Christ,' I whispered. The key had everything to do with it.

The next day, we were loading up the jeep with all sorts of things. It took us for ever to dig the damn thing out of the pond. We had left it there for so long that it had started to sink into the mud. Up to the doors, it was. The carpet inside was ruined. It took you the whole morning to get the engine going. We were off to find the painting. It's very valuable, you know, I had told you, and you had nodded gravely. We weren't sure what to bring, so we brought everything that we could think of bringing. We loaded it all up and said goodbye to the house with a level of solemnity that implied we had doubts over our return. What did we do about your cat? I don't know. Could we possibly have abandoned her? It seems quite feasible that we forgot about her altogether. How shocking. I am surprised, if not at myself, then at you. It was not the kind of thing that you would normally have done. We climbed into the front of the jeep and drove to the end of the driveway. The two of us sat there looking at the T-junction ahead, and neither of us knew which way to turn.

'Back to the city, I suppose,' I shrugged.

You turned the jeep out onto the open road and I must catch my breath for a second, because it is ending in my head all over again and I can hardly bear to go through with it, even in retrospect.

❧

December! The first day, and it is a remarkably beautiful day. Beautiful days are few and far between on the island. Sometimes the light breaks through the thick blanket of clouds, but it never lasts. The sun, if you get to see it, straddles the horizon from east to west and barely rouses itself from the ground. But I will not let that detract from the fact that the first day of December was a wonderful thing. In no time it will be May again. That is what I thought when I turned the calendar page. Ah, December! December is good because it is that bit closer to May than November was. Not for itself is December lovely.

The air is so cold that sounds are carried on it with the speed of light. The countryside is more immediate than usual. The sun, though it will last little more than a few hours, is sharp and bright. It comes at my face from an unexpected angle, that low winter light, and it burnishes the trees, or what is left of trees at this time of the year.

I went out for a walk earlier and the land was frozen. Crystals of ice sparkled all over it. I pulled on my hat and scarf, and out I went, and the mud on the moors had frozen into little footprints. Hoof prints mostly. The island is full of wild ponies. You hear them galloping past in herds every so often, running away from God knows what. Shaggy mud-caked bear-like animals. I don't know what they find to live on. Certainly not on grass alone, there is so little of it here. Their foals grow taller and more awkward with each passing week.

I might try to catch one some day. Try to break it in, teach it to be good. Get myself lynched by its owner. The locals will swim them over to the mainland in spring and sell them at auctions, or so I've been told. I should not play at tour guide. I should not attempt to speak with authority. They are stocky, truculent little creatures, and their deep narrow hoof marks pattern the land everywhere. And this morning, each little hoof print was filled with ice. The land looked like it was pocked by a thousand tiny volcanoes, and I was a giant, thundering upon them. Like a child, for a few hours. I behaved like a child. The hoof prints cracked and split under me like glass. I shattered as many of them as I could find. I enjoyed myself hugely. Destruction without the consequences. It'll all freeze over again tonight.

Eventually it got too cold for me and I had to come in. It is still bright now, though the strength of the sun is dying. The white walls around me are turning grey. This day is not like that day with you. The two are a million miles away from each other, yet I lived them both. I cannot fathom the disparity between them. It is irreconcilable in my head. Today is not like that day when you and I drove through a sunlight that lit up the world like a match to a flare. No, now is not at all like then. Nothing is like then. Nothing is like your face looking across at me from the other side of the jeep. Throwing glances at me while you were supposed to be concentrating on the road. The colours in your skin, your blond hair, your clear blue eyes.

'Once we get this thing done,' you promised, 'we'll go away somewhere nice together. We could maybe go to Arizona. Or to Tuscany. Or to Umbria or Cumbria. Or to Vienna or Siena. New York or Cork. We could go anywhere at all. Where would you like to go, Anna?'

'Perhaps we can go somewhere where the seas are warm.'

'Yes, that's an excellent idea. We'll go somewhere like that,' you said, smiling across, 'once this thing is over.'

'Okay, Doc,' I said, and sat there quietly, an inert lump of panic and sweat. All I could see were the brick walls ahead.

'I can't do this!' I blurted out suddenly. 'Please let me out!' I scrabbled at my seatbelt. The jeep slowed and bumped as you pulled up onto the side of the road. I had the door open before you had come to a halt. The wind gushed in and you called my name and

I should finish the tale, get it over with, but suddenly I feel so tired.

TWENTY-ONE

It is all just light, really, what is left of it. I cast my mind whirring backwards through the air like a hook on a line, but when I wind it in, all it catches is the light, spilling through my fingers like water. I comprehend that light as though it were my blood. The quality of the light, the colour of the light, the temperature, the way it felt on my skin – the taste, even, of the light – this is what my mind returns to me. The light that tasted of salt and of metal and sometimes of an indefinable flavour that I will call burnt sugar, though it was not burnt sugar. Just some childhood taste that I'll never manage to put my finger on. The light of those days spent with you and the way it made my mouth water. I understand it intimately. I understand it until I want to cry. But the figures on the landscape, what of them? The two people standing by the side of the road – they are barely visible. The jeep beside them is more clearly defined, seems to hold onto the ground more firmly than they. The farmhouse to the left of them is, no doubt, still there to this day. As is the water tower beside it. Will be there for years. Just the two people then. They're the only unverifiable part of the recollection. The two lost strangers, the man and the woman who are gazing down the road with their hands in their pockets, they are *unverifiable.*

The man takes something out of his pocket and stares at it in his hand. He tosses it up and down in his palm and it glints in the sunlight – it is his set of keys. He is considering his next move. His blond hair is alight. The girl standing in front of him is despondent. She is not making eye contact with him. Her expression, what little can be seen of it, is dour. The jeep is navy, almost black, and the two people are practically translucent beside it. They're not quite in the picture anymore, not really. They are just human shapes that displace the light, tall fraught zones of non-light, standing there like half-developed Polaroids. They are all that is left in my mind of us.

They are vanishing steadily, those aimless figures on the road. We are evanescing gradually, like print fading in the sun. A wave of nausea in my belly and we are gone altogether. Might as well never have happened. There seems to be not a thing that I can do about it. Two nothings by the jeep. Two nothings in that house. Two nothings staring across a kitchen table at the two empty chairs in which they weightlessly sit. And Kel with his gravestone that doesn't say Kel; he is the biggest nothing of them all. Who will remember him? It is too much. The shadows are barely beneath us anymore in my memory of us on the road, as though the sun had gone in, though it blazed all day like an inferno that summer. Shone right through us though. This is it. This is what is left. My expired world, overflowing with empty light.

The insurmountable difficulty of continuing. It is almost entertaining. The painting, I told you, is in a safety deposit box in a bank. You put your fingers under my chin and said encouraging things. Your thumb on my cheekbone made my face feel small. I listened to your words with care, nodding and trying to smile. After a time, I got back into the jeep, and we headed yet again for the city. I missed you suddenly, though you were right there beside me. I leaned against the passenger window. My eyes were shut tight. Do these details matter? I don't know. I'm sure that I'm concentrating on the details that don't matter, and neglecting to mention the ones that do. At least, not neglecting to mention them, so much as not noticing them in the first place. I did not notice the important details. The murder weapon was under my nose. I chose not to see it there. I chose not to catch the smell of gunpowder on the air. We still had to go through *this thing*, you and I. The painting, wherever it was. We had to get it back.

The fields outside turned slowly blue, then black. The blackness eventually gave way to the burnt-orange glow of streetlights. We drove straight to the financial district. It didn't take long to locate the right bank. I knew it as soon as I saw it. We sat in the jeep and regarded the building in the darkness. The security guard on the graveyard shift examined us in dismay. We drove on.

It was late. Well after midnight. The financial district was dead. I couldn't bear to stay in another hotel, I told you. Oh fuck it, I sighed, let's just stay up. What, all night? you asked. Yes, all night. Okay, Anna. Whatever you want. We drove back across the river, and kept driving until we found an all-night café. We sat ourselves down in the booth by the door, and slumped there like unmanned puppets. There was something floating in my coffee. I eyed it mournfully.

The clock on the wall told us that the bank was due to open in seven and a half hours. And in the bank, in the smallest vault of the bank, concealed deeply within it like a mutinous cell that would rot the whole place from the inside out, was the painting, letting time wash over it.

'I'm going for a walk,' I announced, after we'd sat in silence for a full half hour. You came to life again and read out the standard objections – that I wouldn't be safe on my own at that hour of the night, that others wouldn't be safe from me, that I'd get lost, disappear, scuttle away on all fours.

'I should come with you,' you insisted, placing your hand on mine. The hand with the hooked fingernail. 'You should let me come along, Anna. I really mean that.'

'I'll meet you back here when I'm done,' I said, pulling my hand out from yours.

It was a warm night. It was that arid, city kind of warmth – caused more by the trapped air between the buildings than by the weather overhead. The streets were busy, even at that hour. Lots of people were wandering around. There was a homeless man shouting at them at the top of his voice. He had his blanket laid out flat on the pavement, carefully placed so that it was in everybody's path, and he was standing behind it roaring through cupped hands: 'Don't walk on me blanket! Don't walk on me fucken blanket, cause it's not just a blanket. It's me fucken home!'

Further up, an unofficial market was in full swing. People had their wares spread out along the pavement. Clothes mostly, and some books and broken-looking electrical appliances. Kel used to lie on the hotel bed, his hands clasped behind his head, telling me about such markets. Outbursts of enthusiasm for a culture in which he recognised himself. Like a kid he was sometimes, for all his wiles. A perfect child with all his fingers and toes.

I pulled up my hood. I was still wearing his jacket. Stitched and repaired, though not by me. I walked until the crowd thinned out. Soon the streets were empty, and I did not recognise them. Warehouses mainly, with the occasional shuttered shop. The signs above those shops were missing letters. There were bags of rubbish stacked up in heaps at every corner. The area was poorly lit. Everything either dangerously black or the draining amber of the streetlamps. The predatory colours of a tiger. I knew, suddenly, that I was being watched.

'Isolde!'

I had been pulling my hood up when I heard the voice. The waterproof nylon fabric had brushed over my ears at just the wrong moment for me to hear it clearly enough to recognise it. I asked myself if I had imagined it, but even at my most paranoid, I knew that I could not conjure up a human voice. A whisper perhaps. Yes, I could make myself hear whispers where there were none: the wind skittering along through dead leaves and crisp packets, the rustle of the branches of a tree; all of them were words to me, all of them were urgent warnings. I had even, when stoned, heard Kel hiss. But I could never have constructed an entire voice: deep, peremptory, male:

'Isolde.'

I turned, saw no one. Kel was the only person who ever called me by that name. But he was dead. The other one then? The one who had chased me at the stables? I turned around and around, stumbling on the kerb, but whoever had called out the name was gone.

A police car crawled by at the intersection, the two dark faces inside gazing out at me. I started to walk towards them. The car rolled on. The bin bags shuddered and squealed. There were rats writhing around them.

When the police were out of sight, I began to run, hands stuffed into my pockets and head down. No one followed me; at least, not that I could see. People were still haggling with each other when I got back to the market. I passed through them hurriedly, searching for the café.

'Miss! Hey, miss! You with the black hoodie.' I looked around and saw only blank faces.

'Miss! Do you want to buy a pair of runners? Look: your size, miss.' I stopped and looked around again. There was a man standing beside me. Right up beside me. I was sure that he hadn't been there the first time I'd looked, but my eyes play tricks on me. They are always at their games. He was wearing a snorkel parka that was zipped up over his head. All I could see was the fur of the lining, and no face looking out from within. He couldn't have seen much more of me. I don't know how he knew that I was even female.

We stared at each other through our hoods. I could hear him chewing gum at a ferocious pace. In his hands, he was holding out a pair of white runners. Same size, different make. I looked at the fur-lined hole, and then at the runners. The runners that find a match for themselves. The discarded runners that out of nowhere, out of the swell and ebb of the city, find their equal size and opposite foot despite all that mitigates against such a thing happening, and I thought, that's like us! That's how we were, me and Kel, nowhere near as good as a new pair, but we'd brazen it out anyway, because we sort of made sense when we were paired off, and it was either that or be thrown away altogether. The man backed off uncertainly, and I let him go. I wanted him to run away from me. I wanted him to escape, reeking of possibility, leaking it out into the city night. I wanted that possibility to breed more possibility, and then more, and then more. I stood there almost shaking, and I was in the hotel room, and I was dead, and Kel was alive, and I was alive, and it had never happened. And everything was okay, and our paths had never crossed, and I had never crossed Kel, and he had never crossed me, and it went on for ever, that rush to the brain.

And then when I finally did get back to the café, you were gone! Your seat was empty. I ran over to it, looking for some remnant of your presence. A moment. A momento. A memento of you.

Your seat was cold.

But I found your face again. You had moved across the café so that you could keep an eye out on the street for me. You stood up and came towards me, and I saw that, though you were furious with me for disappearing just as you'd said I would, above all you were relieved to see me return.

And not just relieved. You were plenty more.

Those dark shadows under the eyes. I do not understand the people who try to conceal them. I never saw those dark shadows as anything other than beautiful. I want to reach up and touch that translucent skin, trace over the tilt of the eye socket, and follow the sweep of the cheekbone to where the light falls. Those shadows lend the eye a steady candour. As though you have pushed the face so far into living that what you are seeing is somehow the essence. I can never get enough of them, because that's how we were when the morning light came, you and I, sitting across a littered table, staring at each other in silence. Your hair seemed blonder than usual. Your skin was lustrous, though it was more of an afterglow than a glow. And your eyes were huge. I couldn't look away from them.

Couldn't even blink. Those dark shadows on the skin speak to me. They say, I have seen things. They say, I have lived. They say, listen carefully to me, and pull your seat towards the fire. Make yourself comfortable, for I have a story to tell.

TWENTY-TWO

I wonder how the conservator's Nordic assistant is getting on these days? They're attracted to art and the like, those frail white females who drape themselves around the place like they're auditioning to be muses. I know her game. I know how it works. I bet her Nordic hair is as soft as silk. And her complexion is flawless. Her neck and throat are whiter than those of the marble statues in the display rooms below. Her long thin arms entwine themselves everywhere. Her arms are climbing roses. They have lain across every desk. They have rested against every wall. Embraced every painting that the conservator has brought her. Those arms have embowered the studio. The conservator watches them stretch into the late afternoon air, and the clock eases off. Her charm bracelet slips towards her elbow with a jangle. Her charm bracelet makes music all day. Can the conservator see the lavender veins on her inner wrists from where he sits? Perhaps he will buy a charm for the Nordic assistant on her birthday. A little gold picture frame, or a tiny easel. No, he won't want to embarrass the girl. She wouldn't know what to say. She is young. She is terribly young, the Nordic assistant. Much younger than I am. Far too young to be alone in a foreign country. Her mother, she tells him with a shake of the head that makes her flaxen hair fall over her face, her mother cannot visit her. Her mother is afraid of aeroplanes. *Air-oh-planes*. The Nordic assistant pronounces every syllable with equal emphasis. She has not seen her mother for such a very long time. She adjusts the bracelet and examines one of the charms. Some of the charms are yellow, and some of them have a rosy hue, depending on the vintage and provenance of the gold. The bracelet has been some years in the collecting. Perhaps there is a ferry, the conservator suggests. The Nordic assistant nods thoughtfully, still examining the charm. Perhaps, yes, there is a ferry. But oh, she will have to think about all this tomorrow. She is too weary now. She wilts, she yawns, she throws back her head. She elongates herself, and then contracts into a girl once more. The evening light settles around them. It settles so stealthily that the conservator forgets to turn on his desk lamp. The two of them sit in the dusk, thinking of the girl's mother crossing icy waters. And then just thinking of icy waters. Of the sea frozen into a motionless white. Beneath the ice, there is movement. Ice fish and ice urchins. Ice coral and ice caverns. On the glittering surface of the ice sheet burns the midnight sun. Streamers of light on the northern horizon. Auras and auroras – how can the conservator keep his eyes off this girl? There is always one. If I have learned anything, it is that there is always one creature in the background so extraordinary that you cannot think. Is the Nordic assistant the conservator's madness? (Was I yours?) Does she call the conservator by his first name, or does she always say 'Mister'? Or maybe even 'Doctor'? I hadn't thought of that. *Dok-a-tor*. Her voice, like her bracelet, is melodic and light. I have no idea how she addresses the man. I have no idea what the conservator's correct title is. I want to believe that she doesn't use his first name. *Meester*, she'll say solemnly when she raises her head from her work, a little serious frown on her little serious face. *Shall I reline this canvas, Meester? Dok-a-tor, I reline this canvas now, yes?* Oh yes, my love, reline the canvas now! *Like this, yes? I make like this?* Precisely, dear girl, just so. Could I ever have spoken to you the way the Nordic assistant speaks to her conservator? Could I in a million years make myself sound like she sounds? Does the conservator melt when she speaks through those Nordic lips? Does he close his eyes when her mouth forms those words? Does the conservator trust her? Even though he knows he shouldn't? Oh, I'll bet he taught her everything she knows.

❧

We sat in the jeep in the clean bright light of the morning. It was mid-September, and the leaves on the trees had not even thought about turning. It was surely the longest summer on record. Nine a.m. We had been parked there for an hour. The day's heat had begun to build up.

Across the road was the bank. It hadn't yet opened. There seemed to be a delay of some kind. A few customers already stood in line on the steps. We watched them through the criss-crossing cars. Then the queue of people turned towards the bank doors, alerted by some noise that was inaudible to us. A security man unlocked the doors and drew them back. The people crowded in. We jumped out of the jeep and jogged through the four lanes of traffic.

It was agreed. You were to wait in the bank. I was to check the security deposit box. We stood in the foyer and looked at each other.

'Tell me that my life is going to be okay,' I said.

'Your life is going to be okay, Anna. Your life is going to be great.'

'Liar.'

You smiled and sat down. I was scared. It is now so close, I whispered as I turned away. It is now so close that I can feel it throb.

The journey to the information desk was a thousand miles long. I knew that your eyes were on me all the way. And when I disappeared from view, I knew that you would watch the space in which you'd last seen me. It was now so close that it was terrifying. My heart was in my mouth. My warm and bloody heart.

Things began to seem illusory. The staff that I dealt with were just people pretending to be bank clerks. Which is essentially what bank clerks are, I suppose. It is now so close, I told myself, that it is no longer real.

I was sent up to an office on the second floor. The clerk

asked for my six-digit identification number, and I rattled off a series of numbers without even thinking. He typed them into his computer.

'Have you the key with you?' he asked.

'I do.'

'Sign this please.'

Isolde Chevron, I wrote. A plunge on the 'v' that swept back up to the 'r'.

He accompanied me in the lift to the underground levels. We conducted our descent in silence. He guided me through a maze of corridors, through gates that he unlocked and relocked. He opened a door that was indistinguishable from all of the other doors. There wasn't even a number on it. There was a table and chair inside. Nothing else. Everything, including the floor, was painted pale grey. On the wall was a bank of metal lockers. The clerk selected one of the lockers, and inserted his key. The box slid out horizontally, like a corpse from a mortuary fridge. It was long and slim and much smaller than I had expected. The clerk extracted it from the wall and placed it on the metal table.

'Please leave the key in the lock if you are finished with it,' he instructed me. 'Knock when you are ready to go.'

I thanked him and he closed the door. A spring-loaded lock clicked behind him. I checked the door, and found that I was locked in. Is this it? I wondered. Have I been caught? Is the clerk notifying the police at this exact point in time? It began feeling real again, the whole thing, worryingly real.

I sat down at the metal table. The air conditioner pumped unpleasantly cold air down the back of my neck. I looked at the front panel of the box. There it was: the tiny mechanical gap in the universe for which I had been searching. I recognised that keyhole instantly, if not the box around it. My key slid into it with robotic precision. I felt the most peculiar urge to laugh.

There were two things inside: a metal canister, about two feet long, and another passport. I opened the passport and found my face inside. It was an older photograph than that on Isolde's passport, yet somehow this was indisputably my face while the other one indisputably wasn't. There was no scar under the eye of this photograph either. Pre-Cain, pre-Fall. I read the name. Anna Hunt. Hunt! I snorted aloud. I closed the passport and put it in my back pocket.

I tried to screw the lid off the metal canister, but it was stuck tight. I ran my finger along the lip of the lid, and discovered that it had been soldered shut. I wanted to beat it off using the box as my hammer, but the bank didn't strike me as the right place for such an activity. So I zipped the canister up inside my jacket and double-checked my passport. I am Anna Hunt, and no one else. At last, the proof. At last, finally, the proof.

I closed the deposit box and left my key in the lock, as instructed. I paused when I was halfway to the door. I hated leaving my key behind like that. I hated stripping myself of my few artefacts. Everything else was already gone – the money, the briefcase, the first passport, Kel. I sat back down again and quickly untied the frayed shoelace from the key, and tied it back keyless around my neck. You found it around my neck later that night, and you ran your fingers over it, lost in thought. Around and around your fingertips went, and I tilted my head back for you. I touched it too, that worn cord, and my fingers still find their way to it, from time to time, though it is barely a thread now. I do not know what my fingers hope to find. I'm not sure what your fingers had hoped to find either. It is just a shoelace.

You jumped up in your seat when I resurfaced in the foyer.

'I have it!' I whispered, and you ushered me out. I thought perhaps that we should have started cheering, but the appropriate moment never arose. You held me by the elbow and guided me to the jeep. We drove off with a skid and the parking ticket on your windscreen flapped like a startled bird. Eventually it blew off.

'Show it to me,' you said when we were out in the suburbs. Excitement in your voice. Our side of the road was clear. The other side was plugged with mile-long traffic jams. It was like turning the car around on a whim on the way to work. I held up the canister for your inspection.

'Open it,' you said.

'It's soldered shut.'

'Shake it,' you said, 'but not too roughly.' I shook it. Something smooth rattled inside.

'It sounds right,' you said, and we exchanged a conspiratorial smile. It was done. We had done it. You and I.

How did we get the canister open? You rooted around in the garden shed, and returned with a selection of blunt instruments. You laid them out on the table and I picked them up and examined them one by one. I think it was the hammer and chisel that did it in the end. The lid sprang off and bounced across the kitchen floor. We both frowned at the noise. You stuck your fingers into the mouth of the canister and tried to pick the innards out. Your fingers were too big. Let me try, I said, but you didn't seem to hear me. You shook the canister like a ketchup bottle. A rolled canvas slithered out onto the table. I glanced at you in excitement. You reached out and unfurled it. We both stood back in shock.

'Oh,' I eventually managed to say, 'it's a landscape.'

TWENTY-THREE

It is another watery day. The sun fires darts of weak light through the rain clouds, and my small room lights up and dies down again like a struggling flame. The shadows of leaves dance on the walls, though there are no leaves outside my cottage. There are only the moors; the low, dark, tightly entwined moors. And the moors fall away to the sea, and there is no beach in between, just sheer rock, and nothing could stand up to the wind that comes off that sea, least of all a tree. Least of all the leaves of such a tree.

I told myself today that I would make Kel again. I would get myself a great block of white marble and I would make him once more. I would sit in front of that pale rock and I would feel him inside it, resting there calmly, cooler and more impassive than even the stone surrounding him. Unmoved. That is how he was in life and that, I told myself, was how I would remake him. Unmoved and unmoving, shaped out of milky stone. I would lay my fingertips upon him and bring him forth as he was, only more so. I would strip him of flesh and blood, and he would be colder and more perfect than I had ever known him to be. I would sketch the reflection of Isolde in each of his pupils. A tiny signature, one that only I would see. His mark of Abel to mine of Cain. I would bring forth the sheen of his cheekbones, and the malice of his smile, and, of course, the beauty. I would bring forth all that dead beauty. I would drown him in an ocean of his own dead beauty.

It seems, however, that I have only succeeded in drowning myself in his dead beauty. I am the one who has become the cold form. I am the one who has ground to a halt, suspended as still as stone in this watery room, my determination to remake him falling steadily away. I am transfixed by the panorama of the land and the sea, having tricked myself into thinking that it is all just sea. It is all just shapeless angry grey sea. I can taste my panic; cannot rid myself of that taste.

Typical Dutch landscape with church spire and high sky.
Oil on canvas. 58cm x 82cm. Mid-seventeenth century in style.
Unsigned, undated.

I replaced the index card on your desk. From a distance, the painting, which was positioned portrait-wise on your desk, looked like a fat blue vertical stripe with a thin greenish-brown stripe running parallel along the left-hand side of it. The land was brindled and mossy like the bark of an old tree. The sky, which took up two-thirds of the canvas, seethed and boiled. Clouds rose upon it like heat bubbles. I reached for a blister that swelled up in the middle.

'Don't touch it!'

I hadn't noticed you entering the room. You inserted yourself between the painting and me.

'What do you mean, don't touch it? I'll do what I like to it. It's mine.'

'Ha!' you laughed. 'Not anymore.' I was ushered out of the room.

There was a bottle of champagne in the fridge. It hadn't been there the last time I'd looked. After over an hour of waiting, I brought the bottle and two glasses to your study. The door was shut. Your cat was mewing at it.

I put my ear to the wood. There was a scratching sound coming from inside. A rhythmic scratching noise. The cat kneaded my feet with her paws and implored to be admitted. Shh, I whispered to her, and listened to the scratching a little longer. I transferred the glasses and the neck of the bottle to one hand,

and knocked. The scratching stopped and I heard you curse. There was a pause as you determined whether you could get away with just ignoring me. I knocked again. Another curse, then your chair creaked and rolled back. The door opened a few inches. You were wearing glasses. I had never seen you wearing glasses before. You looked quite different in them. Older. More serious. In your hand was a scalpel.

'What?' you demanded.

'What do you mean, what?'

'What do you want?'

'I want to come in.'

Eyes thrown to heaven and then I was admitted. The cat trotted in after me, purring ecstatically. The painting was face down on the desk. A strong lamp was angled onto it. A layer of canvas was half peeled away, revealing another older canvas beneath it.

'What are you doing?'

'Working.'

'Are you sure you should be touching the painting?'

'I'm not touching the painting. I'm touching the back of the painting. There's a big difference.'

'Oh.' I peered at the old canvas. In amongst the glue residue were barely decipherable words. 'There are words there.'

'I know.'

'Can you read them?'

'Not yet.'

'Oh,' I said again.

You folded your arms over your chest. I looked around for somewhere to sit, but there was only the one seat in the room. 'I found the champagne,' I said hopefully, holding the bottle up.

'So I see.'

'Will we open it now?' I went to place the glasses on your desk.

'Not near the painting!' The cat jumped up onto your chair and you snatched her up. 'And I don't want your paw prints either. Here.' You thrust the cat onto my free arm. 'Bring your friend with you as you go.' The cat, whose policy was that any attention was better than no attention, continued to purr.

I went back to the living room and sat on the sofa. I ripped the gold foil off the bottle and popped the champagne open.

❧

I'm losing interest in the telling. It doesn't seem as important anymore. It doesn't seem as urgent. It's the background details that draw my tormented eye. How did I miss the background details? Like us? How did I miss us? It was a complicated dance that we wove around each other through the interconnecting rooms of your home. There were moments though. Accidental splinters of moments. A pain runs through the heart of me even now. I must try to breathe deeply and count to ten. I am full of inadequate ways of coping. Here it is: I caught you looking at me once. That should not cause such uproar, but it does. I can't remember what we'd been doing. Talking, probably, or maybe you were cooking. That's it. You were cooking, with your back to me, and you had a big knife in your hand. It was probably just a wooden spoon, but I will call it a big knife. And I will say that you were slicing meat with great enthusiasm. Red bloody meat, though it was probably an onion.

I was behind you somewhere. I was standing in a part of the room that was darker than the rest of it. I don't remember any alcoves in the kitchen, yet I seemed to have found myself a shaded little nook to lurk in that evening. The wall engulfed me like an alcove, and I fidgeted in it, standing on one foot, being mindless.

I was trailing my finger along the wood-grain of the table when I noticed that the chopping had stopped. I looked up. You were staring at me. You had turned around to face me full on. I too stopped moving and stood there, caught in the glare of the headlamps.

You took a step towards me. I shrank back into the ochres and the peaty browns of my alcove, which was doubtlessly not an alcove at all, but something I installed afterwards with the dour paintbrush of my mind. The fridge rumbled and shut down. Then you were standing over me. You put your hand on my shoulder and the whole room was suddenly quivering and bruised. The whole room ached softly with my grief, which was not grief at all, but just a sort of, I don't know, a sort of raw tenderness. I was overwhelmed by a tenderness that made me weak.

'It is not easy, you know,' I finally managed to say.

'No,' you commented, shaking your head. 'It is not easy.'

You didn't remove your hand from my shoulder. The unexpected intimacy. I was unprepared. I looked out at the falling evening in an effort to distract myself. The sky was turning from mauve to navy, as though pockets of dark ink were bleeding into it. I bit my lip. You leaned over and touched my face and said it to me again. 'I know it's not easy, Anna. Nothing is easy. But it will get easier. I promise you that.'

The fruit in the fruit bowl was over-ripening behind our backs. Beneath its leathery skin, the flesh of the melon was softening. At any moment, the first apple would have fallen from its tree, had there been such an apple tree in your garden. The dull thud would have made me turn my head, and I would have seen what was happening. I would have understood that the summer was ending. But I was not paying attention to the tell-tale signs. I was oblivious to the onslaught of winter. I did not understand that our season would end. Did not understand that it was just a season. I have made so many mistakes.

I had emptied the bottle of champagne by the time the door of your study opened.

'Did you miss me?' I asked.

'Voor myn liefste Elsbeth,' you replied.

Dear God, I realised: I am extremely drunk.

You looked at the champagne bottle, now on its side on the floor. *'Voor myn liefste Elsbeth,'* you repeated loudly, as if I had a hearing problem. 'It's the inscription on the reverse of the painting.' (*I reline this canvas now, ja, Dok-a-tor?* How can other races love so hard, when we can barely speak?) I tossed back my hair and tried to look sober.

'What does it mean?'

'It means, Anna, that this is precisely the painting we've been looking for.'

And then we were back in the jeep again, and it felt like we'd hardly been out of it, which, I suppose, was the fact of the matter. I held onto the elbow rest and tried not to puke. We were going to pay a visit to where you worked, you informed me. You hadn't been there in several weeks, and now we were going to show up in the middle of the day. I had forgotten that you even had a place of work. I thought I was your full-time occupation.

'I don't want to go with you,' I moaned.

'Oh, I'll bet you don't,' you replied with alarming conviction, starting the engine and reversing up the driveway with speed. 'I'll bet you don't, Miss Hunt.'

I had presumed that you worked in one of the national museums. I had never given any consideration to the fact that there were no national museums within commuting distance of your house. After about half an hour, you turned off the main road onto a country lane that was too narrow for two cars to pass each other. You drove me to this cattle shed. That is what it looked like from outside. An abandoned cattle shed.

'You can't be serious,' I said, and you laughed heartily, as if I'd cracked a great joke. I don't think I'd ever seen you in such good spirits before. We got out, and I followed you around to the boot of the jeep.

'I mean it,' I insisted. 'You can't be serious.'

'Well, Anna, I'm extremely serious. Here, hold this, and keep it flat.' You handed me what looked like a large wooden pizza box. 'It's in a very delicate state, so don't shake or drop it.'

I stood in the yard with my huge pizza, listening to distant farm noises while you fumbled with the padlock on the door of the shed. It was a tall green corrugated iron door, maybe fifteen feet high. Weeds were growing all over the yard. The trees were full of ravens. They festooned the branches like torn rags. The lock snapped open and you pushed the door back. It did not open inwards, but screeched along sideways on a rusty track. It took all of your strength to push it across. I did not offer my help.

'Hold it flat!' you bellowed when you had the door open. I looked at you blankly.

'Jesus, Anna, the box! Hold it flat!'

'I am!'

You came marching over. 'You're not. Like this.' The lurch of the flat wooden plane as you straightened it up made me gag.

'Oh for God's sake, sober up! And why in the name of Jesus are you wearing those shoes?' I looked down at my feet. They were in the jewelled stilettos. 'Go on,' you said, directing me into the shed. In I went, feeling black-hearted. You pushed the door back into place and shut us into darkness. I stood in that darkness, sensing that there were a lot of things beside me. You struggled in the background with the padlock, cursing all the time under your breath. I wondered why it was necessary to lock us in.

You reappeared by the wall when the lights came on. They jolted on in segments, revealing the vast length of a building that was mostly bare.

'Is this where you work?' I asked incredulously.

'Sometimes.'

You took the box and led me towards the back of the building. Our footsteps on the concrete floor echoed around the roof, mine spiky, yours soft. There were small dark birds nesting in the rafters. Or perhaps they were bats. Metal corrals and troughs flanked the walls. Excavated runways ran down into the ground and back up again. It was indeed a cattle shed, or worse, some class of an abattoir. Just for a second, I got a fright. Here, I wondered, in the middle of nowhere? Without even daylight to count away my failing hours? It was not how I had pictured the end.

We reached the back of the building. You started pulling canvas covers off machines. I was relieved to see that there were machines. I was scared that there would be nothing. Just four concrete walls, and hoses for washing down whatever might spill on the floor. Gullies and drains to secret away that spillage. You flicked on all the sockets and an electric hum started up.

'What's all this?'

'Stuff from work.'

The care with which you treated the painting was astonishing. I was almost jealous. You prised open the lid of the box and placed the canvas horizontally onto a tall steel rack. You lined it up with a machine that was on the floor beneath it. The process of lining up took some time. I didn't look at the machine or at the painting. I stood there looking stupidly at you. You had the most beautiful forearms. I had never noticed them before. Your shirtsleeves were rolled up, and in my drunken state, I wanted to draw the shape between elbow and wrist. They tapered off like fish.

'This,' I said, stepping forward and running my fingers along your inner arm, 'this is my favourite part of a man's body.'

'Now there's a lie, if ever I heard one. Go stand over there.'

We stood behind a large screen on the other side of the shed. You pressed buttons and twisted dials. I was too drunk to be able to concentrate on what was happening. Your voice was rattling away in the background, trying to explain things to me step by step. Telling me about roentgens and x-rays and the higher lead content of seventeenth-century paint. I wasn't listening. If only I had listened to you, right from the start. I might have put two and two together a little bit sooner than I did. 'You're right,' I agreed. 'I *was* lying. My favourite part of a man's body is this bit here.' I put my hand on your neck and slid it under your shirt to where it met your shoulder.

'Jesus, Anna!' you cried. 'Your hands are freezing!'

Over to the darkroom then. You made me wait outside, and promise not to interfere with any of the equipment while you were occupied. I kicked at the floor and hugged myself for warmth. The door opened up after a time, and out you came waving this plastic sheet around.

'Anna,' you said like a visionary. 'She's back.' You held the x-ray up to the light and there it was, the ghostly image of a woman in black and white, horrifically familiar. She hovered delicately like a hologram, breaking through the clouds in the sky. It was the painting from the newspaper article. 'You need to turn the painting around in your head,' you explained. 'She goes that way, so the landscape is vertical. The landscape was painted over it when the canvas was on its side. There's a layer of monochrome paint separating the two images, so there shouldn't be too much damage to the original. Isn't she beautiful, though? Isn't she the most beautiful thing you've ever seen? See here, where the shadows creep in on her face. The lighter paint is applied on top of the dark, not the other way around, as is more usual. It's the light paint that hits the retina first. Look how focused some parts of the portrait are. Look at the hair and the left eye, how sharp they are, how clear and lucid. But the other eye, look at it. It is soft and muted. All in the one face. Isn't that something?'

'Art gives me the hump,' I said. I couldn't make out much on the black and white plastic. It kept reflecting the lights of the ceiling back at me. I had no idea how you could discern such detail. You kept waving the x-ray around, discussing the techniques for removing new paint from old. I still wasn't listening. I was taking a deep breath. I was preparing to make a little speech of my own.

'I killed him, you know.'

Your disquisition stopped abruptly. The sound of your last syllable reverberated around the tin roof. I glanced at that roof with a frown. The place suddenly reminded me of a church, and I shivered.

'I killed my brother.'

You didn't seem to know what to do. I didn't want to do anything at all. A heightened sensation of sobriety washed over me, as if I'd been drenched by a bucket of freezing water. The world was stark and overly real. My eyes started to hurt. We stood there in that slaughterhouse and contemplated our different fates in silence. There had been days and there had been nights when I had come padding out to you from my corner, my hair stuck to my damp brow. Without asking, I had clamped my head against your chest. Here, I had said to you without words, you take the weight of it for a while. I've had enough of it. And you would take my head and smooth my tangled hair, and then hold onto me with both arms, whispering kind things in my ear. All I understood at that point in time was that those days between us were over.

'Hold me?' I asked. How small my voice sounded in that vast building! You looked up distractedly.

'Anna,' you whispered in a slightly astonished voice, as if you hadn't seen me in months.

'Hold me?' I asked again, but you didn't move. 'Please?'

You swallowed, and then slowly unfolded your arms. I stepped up to you and rested my head in the curve of your neck. We swayed gently. We swayed to the same subconscious tune. The shed was pervaded by its melancholy lilt, though neither of us hummed or sang, not even quietly. We both heard it though, and listened to it attentively. I looked up at your face. Your eyes were tightly closed, just as they had been when you had kissed my foot, knowing that the picture of Kel was folded in your pocket and that you were going to have to ask me some difficult questions. Here it comes again, I thought. He knows he's about to hear something awful. He knows he's going to get it right between the eyes. I tilted my mouth towards your ear. My lips touched your skin as I spoke.

'His lips turned lavender,' I told you, and watched you wince a little harder. 'His eyes went red. All the veins in him burst. There was blood everywhere. It pumped out of his head like a bubbling spring.'

You cupped the back of my head and pushed it into the crook of your neck. My face was pressed tightly against your throat, preventing me from continuing with my confession. I wanted to bare my teeth against your skin, illustrate for you in detail how monstrous I was. You held me tighter and ever tighter, as you swung me around to the dance. Your voice rumbled in your throat. I couldn't hear what you had said because your hand was covering my ear. I pulled my face away to look at you.

'What did you say?' I asked. Your eyes were still closed. Your voice was failing you. It took you a moment to speak again.

'I said: there was no blood.'

I stopped swaying and stepped back. You stood there with your eyes closed and your arms still cradling the space in which I had stood. You said it again, more quietly this time.

'There was no blood.'

'What do you mean!' I had seen the blood. I had seen it everywhere. I had tasted the blood and smeared it across my scar.

'He was strangled to death,' you said. 'With large hands. Not yours. You barely even grazed him, Anna. You barely even scratched his skin.'

TWENTY-FOUR

Thought I saw you out on the beach this morning. Hours ago now. Have I already mentioned that? No, of course I haven't. Forgot about it as soon as it happened. Until now, that is, halfway through the night, and I cannot say what prompted it. Thought I saw you standing on the white strand, your back to the wind. The rain had stopped and there was a brisk clarity in the air. You watched me over your left shoulder, head tucked in coyly. Seabirds flying low in the sky, and the grey-green waves at your foot. A whole panorama thrown up behind you.

I was on the coast road coming back from the shops. I stopped walking once I caught sight of you. You were wearing a reefer jacket with the collar turned up against the weather. It might have been navy, but it looked black in the distance. As did your trousers. As did your shoes. All of you was black except for your face and hair. You wore no hat. Everyone here – even me now – we all wear hats. Woollen ones that don't blow off. We pull them down over our ears. Never once saw you in winter clothes, yet there you were, as clear as day for a whole moment. Only your eyes were visible above the upturned collar. Your hair was in your eyes. You watched me through those pale strands. And I watched you. Intently.

The man from down the road drove by in his faded red car. He was going the other way, so he didn't offer a lift. He just waved. I waved back. And then I turned to you again, and we looked at each other a little longer. Very calm. Heart barely shifted. Too far away to see your features. No matter. There was salt on your face. Sea salt. It was in your hair. It was on your mouth. It was all over you, as though you gazed at me through ice. And it was all over me. It tingled on my skin.

After a time I moved off, and you broke into two. You realigned yourself into driftwood and stone. I came inside and lit a fire. Sat in front of it and watched it burn. The window fogged up as my clothes and hair dried out. That was hours ago. The fire is nearly gone. But I can still taste the salt on my lips. It is a dry and stinging substance and it is everywhere now. It has touched everything that is left. Coated every surface with its sparkling silt.

I will always be thirsty.

❧

You drove too fast on the way back to the house. The countryside rushed by in a blur. This was worrying. This was not what you would normally have done. I had, since I had known you (had I ever really known you?), been able to count on you doing things in a normal way. I turned my head and found myself in the jeep with a stranger.

And then I must have drifted off, because it was dark outside all of a sudden. Not like me to fall asleep with ease, but then, neither one of us was ourselves that day, were we? I was jolted awake by what sounded like an animal screeching. It could have been anything. You had the stereo on full blast. *Fever, when you touch me.* It was not the version of the song that I was used to.

'How long have I been asleep?' I shouted over the music.

'Ten minutes,' you shouted back. Impossible. I had slept through dusk, and dusk lasted at least half an hour. *I light up when you call my name. Fever all through the day.*

There was something big on the road up ahead. You slowed down to get around it. It was a car. It was an upside-down car, just sitting there.

'Should we not stop?' I asked. 'Someone could be hurt.'

'We're not stopping.'

A dark shape further up the verge caught my eye. You accelerated. The whoosh of the jeep made the thing come alive. Black clothes fluttered. A white bony hand extended onto the tarmac. The face was hooded. For a split second, I thought it was Kel.

'There's a man on the road!' I shouted, banging at my window.

'There's no one on the road,' you shouted back, still accelerating.

'There's a man on the fucking road,' I screamed.

'There's no one on the fucking road!' you screamed back. 'It's a fucking bin bag!' You thumped the roof of the jeep with your fist, and we veered towards the ditch. I clutched the dashboard in fright as you struggled to get the jeep under control again. You got us off the verge, but you didn't reduce your speed. We are going to be killed, I thought. This is it. In the midst of mad music and darkness and this sudden hatred of each other, we are going to come undone.

Then something touched my skin. It was under my clothes. I shrieked and started writhing around in my seat.

'What the fuck are you doing?' you shouted.

'Let me out of the jeep! There's something crawling on me! Let me out of the fucking jeep!'

I pulled my jumper off and started swatting at my skin. I expected to see lots of tiny black things. Ants, or ticks. But I couldn't see anything at all. You turned the music up even louder. *Fever* (drums). *I'm afire. Fever, yeah, I burn forsooth.*

Whatever had been crawling on me stopped crawling. We were thundering along at breakneck speed. I was thrown from side to side when you took the corners. We were barely making contact with the road. Animal eyes lit up in the hedgerows. Winged insects burst against the windscreen. Out of nowhere, and swerving to avoid us, shot an ambulance, its siren blaring. It flashed blue light into the darkness, and sounded its horn on top of the siren. It *had* been a crash that we had passed. Then there was something in my hair. It was digging into my scalp. I started screaming again and tore at my head with my nails. You screamed at me to shut the fuck up and I screamed at you to shut the fuck up. We were definitely going to crash. The ambulance would find us on its way back from the other crash. I scrabbled at the door handle. You reached out and grabbed me. You threw me back into the seat and told me to stop fucking moving, that we were nearly fucking home, and that another fucking word and I'd be *sorry*.

I ran the thumb and index finger of my right hand up and down the bone of the little finger on my left hand. Picture it: I want you to understand what gave you away. You were still driving like a madman. The music was deafening. The engine roared and the brakes screeched. I, however, had fallen quiet. I was examining my little finger. My little finger, unless I was mistaken, had always been straight. There was no reason for it to have been otherwise. However, it was no longer straight. I looked at it and touched it and finally acknowledged that it was crooked, and that it was not going to miraculously come right. It was as crooked as a knotted tree branch. And it had been crooked for weeks. It had been sending shards of pain through my hand. Those shards were a warning that I had chosen to ignore for some time, a warning that I had chosen to ignore from the second it had begun, insistent though it was. That finger had been troubling me since the day I had arrived in your house.

I kept running the fingers of my good hand along the length of that knobbled bone, up and down, up and down, like a blind woman reading Braille. And I *was* reading it. I was reading all kinds of things into it. I read it, and I was flat out on the road again in the aftermath of my car crash. The middle of the night. My body had given up on me. I could smell the petrol fumes of my little choking car, which was valiantly trying to stay alive behind me somewhere. Poor little car with its missing driver's window. What had it ever done to deserve the treatment it got from me? My hands were above my head, as if preparing to dive. I remembered all that, and remembered suspecting that someone was standing over me. But at that stage I did not care. I eased in and out of an unconsciousness that I did not fight. Small stones pierced the skin on my cheekbones, but I did not lift my head. I could not lift my head. In my hands was a leather handle. That of the briefcase. And coming down on my hands, with cruel and mechanical determination, was a foot. It was a large foot, a shod foot. The pain was unbelievable. But I couldn't release the handle. I no longer cared about the case, yet I could not get rid of it. Nothing in my body did what I asked of it.

The foot came down on my hand one last time, and I felt my finger-bone crack. My fingers were cleared away by another set of fingers. They were cleared away like the cracked shell of a walnut. The handle of the case was removed like the nut itself. And then there was nothing for a while, and I was pleased to be left to rest, or to die, until I was jolted back to life again by those most unexpected words:

'I never meant,' they said. 'I never meant.'

I sat there in the passenger seat of your jeep, running my fingertips along the buckled bone, and I thought about how strange it was that the doctors had never detected the fracture in the hospital, especially since, as you'd told me, you'd specifically requested that they x-ray both hands. How strange that they'd never set the bone. How strange it was that they had left me mangled like that. It was my hand, for God's sake. It was not as if it was something that I would not need. I tried thinking back to the journey in the ambulance with you by my side, solicitously mopping my forehead, praying that this stranger would pull through. How awful it is to be presented with the almost embarrassing spectacle of someone else's blood. I vaguely remembered being scraped off the tarmac and scooped into warm dark arms, but no flashing blue lights invaded this darkness. No men in white coats. Nothing invaded this darkness at all, except your tenderness. The memory of your tenderness. All I remembered with clarity was the return journey in the jeep with you. Daylight, by then. Turning my head slowly, my neck feeling like pulverised meat, and seeing you. And then looking away, indifferent. Just so long as you were not him, not the other one, the one with the long nails. And that was all that I could remember. No nurses, no sharp lights, no asking of my name for the file. Just you.

And then it came to me. It came to me and I could barely breathe. It came to me as steadily as the night clears to make way for the day: *that I had never been brought to any hospital*. Which meant. Which meant.

That you had lied.

TWENTY-FIVE

The conservator will have bad dreams tonight. *Girl in the Mirror* will move. At first he will think that he has imagined it. He will stop what he is doing and watch the painting. The dark figure with her back to him will be motionless. The face in the picture frame will be as remote as it ever is. The conservator's heart will settle down. But then the dark figure will begin to turn. Slowly, inexorably, like a clockwork doll. Her movement will be accompanied by the creak of stretched rope. One face will be obscured from view as the other face reveals itself. The girl and the conservator will be full of dread at that moment before they meet each other's eyes.

❧

We drew up to your house. I wore your jacket, because I was still convinced that there was something alive in my jumper. There was a thread coming loose on the cuff. I wrapped and unwrapped it around my crooked finger. Not a word when the engine was turned off. Just this angry breathing to my right, a noise that would have frightened me had it come from anybody else. You sat there, staring ahead and fuming, or maybe you were trying to calm down. I didn't dare look at you. Any sudden motion, any careless word from either of us, risked producing disastrous consequences.

You climbed out of your seat and slammed the door. You took the painting from the boot. I wanted desperately to be left on my own. I'd have spent the night in the jeep if you'd let me. My door was pulled open and I was bundled out. Your nails dug into my arm.

You lifted the lid of the wooden box to make sure that the painting was still inside. It was. I was all out of tricks. You unlocked the front door and we stepped into the hall.

'Here.'

You handed me the box. I felt around in the dark and put it on the table by the phone. Your hand glided along the wall, looking for the light switch.

'You never brought me to the hospital the night I crashed, did you?'

Your hand stopped moving and your head dropped. 'No.'

'Look at my hand. It is broken and bent.'

You reached for me and tried to take hold of my crooked hand. I pushed you away as hard as I could. You fell backwards over something. The umbrella stand, or the cat. I didn't know what it was in the dark. A hand reached up from the floor with lizard speed and grabbed my wrist, a hand that was tipped with long nails, and yet was not tipped with long nails. It was my mind that was tipped with long nails. The hand pulled me down to him, to you.

'I never meant,' came the words, full of remorse and regret. You took my hand in yours and stroked my twisted finger and addressed yourself to it. 'I never meant.'

'You!' I couldn't stop saying it. Still can't. 'You!' I tried to pull away, but your hand tightened around my wrist. There had been no one standing on the horizon, witnessing my crash and speeding down a hillside to rescue me. There had only been you, witnessing the crash from behind the wheel of the jeep that had caused it. The bruise on your arm from when you'd caught it in the slamming door of my car, and you telling me that you'd hurt yourself falling into a ditch. And me like a halfwit, believing you! What a fool you must have thought me when I didn't piece it together. How did you not laugh out loud? He who had stood over my bed in the stables at night and grabbed my throat. He who had ransacked my hotel room, made the chestnut mare rear in fright, stolen my case from the crash, and whispered Isolde's name in the dead of night as I had walked the empty streets. He who had waited so patiently outside Kel's room, shifting his weight from foot to foot, dying to meet me. He who had scraped me off the road and driven me straight to his home as fast as wheels could go. He was you.

I pulled myself free and staggered backwards. I couldn't get enough air into my lungs. It was as if there was a hole in the bottom of them, through which all the oxygen was escaping. The front door was still open and I held onto the door frame, wheezing and huffing at the cool night air. It was raining outside. I hadn't noticed it starting. First time I'd seen it rain since the night of Kel's death. They were big swollen drops and it looked like there were enough of them to drown the world.

It was the painting that you wanted, you began to explain. You had restored it once already. Six or seven years ago.

What do you mean? I demanded. I don't understand. Why would an archaeologist restore a painting?

I'm not an archaeologist. This said so quietly that I had to strain my ears to hear you. As if to compensate, I found myself shouting.

You're *not* an archaeologist! But you said. You told me. And you were working. I saw you leaving the house every day!

No response. I paced around the hall in the dark.

So what are you?

A conservator.

That threw me. I had never heard the word before. I swung my arm out and pointed at the door, knowing that it was nonsensical to point at the door. A conservator! I bellowed. What in the name of fuck is a conservator? No, I won't sit down. Stop telling me what to do! For once, stop telling me what to do! I *am* calm! Oh God! Oh God, oh God, I wailed. Why else would you have followed me around all summer? Why else would you have kept me safe all this time in your home? It was the painting that you wanted. And me like an idiot thinking that it was because.

I slumped down on the telephone seat and put my head in my hands. They were shaking so hard that I wanted to rip them off and hurl them across the room.

It *was* because, you said. You tried to pull my hands down from my face.

Leave me alone! I moaned, slapping you off. For God's sake, why can't you just leave me alone?

Because, you said again. You reached forward and put your hand on my throat, just as you'd done the first night I'd seen you. The movement was sudden. I caught my breath. This time, there was no fear. This time, it was like peace. We stared at each other. Your thumb stroked the nape of my neck. Outside, the rain kept raining. It grew heavier for a time, and then began to wane. Of course it had been you. Picking me up off the road, placing me safely in the passenger seat of your car. Anyone with sense would have left me there. Your other hand began to undo my jacket. Your jacket. I was still wearing your jacket, but it was coming off me. The silver zip sank slowly. It glimmered in the dark like a fish. I didn't move, just kept staring. You looked so strange in the dark. I was amazed by how strange you looked. I wanted to ask you again what a conservator was, but knew I wouldn't get the sentence out in one go. It didn't really matter anyway. I didn't really care. 'The jasmine must have bloomed after all,' you said absentmindedly. 'I can smell it even here.' You angled my face towards yours, just as you had done the first time you'd touched me. You had a good look at my scar, then you kissed me. I kissed you back. You released my throat. The jacket fell to the ground. You stooped down. I held your head in my hands. Blond hair is soft. It is softer than dark. So soft I thought I would cry.

'Are you still drunk?' you asked.

I shook my head. 'No.'

'Good.'

You ran your fingers down my sides and we gazed at each other for a very long time. 'Look at you,' you whispered, then pressed your face into me. Your eyes were closed again. 'Anna,' you said hoarsely, 'I have waited so long.'

In my stiletto heels, I was nearly as tall as my barefoot you. I rose from the telephone seat and you rose with me. I put my hand on your throat. Softly, softly, I pushed your head back. 'Good girl,' you whispered as I leaned my weight against yours. 'That's very, very good.' I ran my fingers over your mouth. The way your teeth reflected the dim light. Like jewels underwater. If I could just swim down deep enough. 'Yes,' I agreed, 'it is very, very good.' I listened to my words. I barely knew myself. The way I sounded. For all the world like Kel.

So when exactly did the final realisation occur? The nights had grown longer by then. Late September. Dawn didn't arrive until after six at that time of the year, and it was still dark when I made my discovery. All around the house, droplets of rain were falling at ever-decreasing intervals from the eaves of the roof to the sodden garden below. The rain had hours before exhausted itself. As had you. You had fallen asleep on the rug beside me, but I was wide awake. My mind was sifting through the odds and ends with which it is obsessed. The last night that I'd spent in the Grand Plaza Hotel was the first night I'd heard your voice. I smiled at you in the dark and kissed your chest. How frightening you had been to me back then. You, of all people. You, who made everything better. It was straight after I had hit Kel that I first heard you speak. The phone had been ringing on the other side of the partition wall in the hotel, and we were both running towards it through our different rooms. 'Gone,' you had said, and the word had terrified me. This was the voice of my tracker. This was the definitive confirmation that there was a third party involved. Before, I had wondered if it was just another thing that Kel had dreamt up to torment me. *There was someone following you while you were out last night*, followed by the malicious smile. 'Gone,' you said coldly and slammed down the phone. You withdrew from the hotel room. I listened for your footfall and heard only the bell of the elevator. Once it had descended, I gathered up my belongings and escaped.

Was I even still in the building when you encountered Kel? It is almost certain that I had already fled. I don't know why the timing is important to me, but it is. I want to work it out. I want to have a clear picture in my mind. Where was he when you found him? Was he expecting you? Was he standing before you when the elevator doors opened? Or was he still in his hotel room, sizing up the bruise that I'd made on the back of his head? I see him quite clearly on one of the corridors, for some reason. I see him there in one of the many narrow tunnels that bored through the hotel. Some part of the building that I will never be able to pinpoint. He is lurching his way along in the direction of my room. You turn a corner and come upon him there, trapped in his fox run. No room to turn around. You are cold with fury. He writhes before you with plans of revenge. He is all spinal now, and appears to have grown himself a little tail. He squirms about in a delirium of murderous intent, and obviously thinks that you share in it.

Who spoke first? Was it you? *She's gone, you stupid fuck. You couldn't even get that much right*. But no, I think Kel was the one who would have opened his big mouth. Kel had problems keeping it shut. Looking at you sidelong, his lips itching with spite. Leaning forward and confiding in you gleefully: *now she's gonna get it. Now she's gonna pay*. The knife with the red handle is back in his hand. The little tail twitches and he leers. But something is wrong. There is no response from you. After a moment, the smile on his face perishes.

It was you who killed him. Of course. Who else would have bothered? Who else even knew who he was?

In death he is beautiful again. The sneer falls away from his mouth. The tight wire that strung his features together relaxes at last, and he looks the way he looked as a boy.

*

You remained asleep while I gathered up my clothes and dressed. Dawn at last. The painting was still on the phone table. Your scalpel was in the cup full of biros beside it. I sliced off a piece from the corner of the tacking edge. A piece about the size of the heart of a daisy. I thought about taking the painting itself, but didn't. I'd had enough of it, of everything. I took the keys to the jeep, though. I staggered out onto the gravel driveway, and was dazzled by the morning light. The sun was burning off the night's rain. It rose up in steam around me. The place smoked like a bombsite. I had a full-blown hangover by then. My head was all bruised membrane.

I kept a hand on the wall of your house to guide myself. Gradually I got used to the light, and began to see the world in minute and intricate detail. I could no longer face the big picture, so I focused instead on all of the little ones. All of the millions of little pictures with which the world suddenly distracted me. A mesh of droplets on a spider's web. An earwig lurking in the cup of two leaves. A long black slug with a ridged back, its horns straining forward like a pony's ears. Something burst under my foot. A snail. There were scores of them all over the place. Tiny slender snails that were dragging their soft underbellies along the gravel and up the walls. The rising steam left a white silt behind on the driveway pebbles. I picked up one of them and examined it. It was pale blue in colour. I put it to my tongue. It tasted of the sea.

'Anna.'

I turned around. You had been quietly following me. As was your wont. I took the pebble out of my mouth.

'It was you, wasn't it? Who killed him?' No response, so I said it again. 'It was you who killed my brother?' I was still half hoping that there was another explanation. The reply that I got was like a slap on the face.

'You should be glad.'

'Glad?' I took a step back. 'Are you fucking insane?'

'You should be glad that you didn't kill him. That someone else had to do it for you. He wasn't your friend, Anna.'

'No, you're right. He wasn't my friend. He was my flesh and blood.'

The sunlight was truly appalling. My brain felt like it was wrapped in hot fibreglass.

'Now is not the time to be righteous,' you said quietly.

'Oh fuck you!' I cried. I threw my pebble at you and missed. It bounced off the window. I picked up a fistful of pebbles and they skimmed across the driveway like a meteorite shower. You averted your face. 'You were going to kill me as well, weren't you? That night in the stables when you nearly strangled me? You'd have killed me as well, only I hadn't yet led you to the painting.'

'It is precisely because I didn't want you killed that your brother is dead.'

'There is no defence!'

'He was going to cut you to shreds. You wouldn't even have been his first victim. Two days before his death, he'd cut up some junkie who didn't pay him on time. You were next.'

'You make me sick,' I said.

'Don't give me that crap.'

'His only problem was that he scared people like you.'

'You'd stolen all his money and then beaten him on the head. He was going to shred you. Look at your sliced-up eye, Anna. He used to boast about what he'd do to you. He swore that he'd someday kill you.'

Whatever way you pronounced them, the words conjured up Kel's voice. *I think that I will someday kill her*. I shivered and examined the sky. Perfectly still and clear, but monochrome and remote, as if distancing itself from our ugly scene. My eyes hurt so much. 'This isn't fair,' I wanted to say. 'He'd never have found me,' I said instead.

'You know that's not true. If I thought you were halfway capable of taking care of yourself, I wouldn't have touched him. But you were a lamb to the slaughter.'

'So you decided to kill him first.'

'I never *decided* to kill him. But I did kill him, yes.'

'Because it was the painting that you wanted. If he had killed me, the painting would never have been found.'

'If he'd killed you, the painting would have been found a whole lot sooner. All that was needed was the key. The police could've identified it and matched it with the security box. It's not exactly rocket science. There was more to keeping you alive than just the painting, Anna.'

I covered my eyes with my hands. 'Sweet fucking Jesus.'

'Do you know how much you cost me?'

I lowered my hands. 'Do I what?'

'Do you know how much your brother charged for you?'

I rolled my eyes to heaven. 'I don't believe this.'

'Fifteen thousand pounds, Anna.'

I laughed at that. You had to admire Kel. Never one to let an opportunity slip.

'You were ripped off.' Fifteen thousand pounds. What surprised me most was that he hadn't extracted more. He must have been down on his luck that day.

'I don't know about that, Anna. Felt like the bargain of a lifetime to me.'

I swayed there on the gravel, and started to sob. Hot tears ran down my face. I rubbed them with my sleeve and saw that it was your sleeve. I pulled your jacket off and threw it in a crumpled heap on the grass. I gave it a kick and it landed in the pond. You were following me up the driveway telling me – I don't know what you were telling me. I made my way in a shell-shocked fashion to the jeep.

I opened up the boot and pulled out my jumper. I shook it out in daylight, knowing already that there'd never been anything crawling in it. Something caught my eye as I swung the door closed. I opened it again and saw the rifle. I took it out and brandished it.

'Fuck off!' I shouted at you, and waved the rifle about, as though that concluded the argument. What strikes me most in retrospect is how matter-of-fact it all was. The cows in the meadow across the road lined up along the hedgerow and gazed at us, chewing sedately. I slammed the boot and crossed over to the driver's side.

'Fuck off!' I shouted again, and fired a bullet upwards. The loudness of it gave me a fright. The cows galloped away, if you could have called it a gallop. More of a swerve and a swagger. It hadn't occurred to me that the rifle would have been loaded. Loaded by your hand. I was shocked.

'I kept your horse for you.'

'My horse?' I lowered the rifle.

'She's down the road.'

'Down the road?' I repeated stupidly.

'Yes.'

I looked down the road, half expecting to see the chestnut mare standing there. Nothing seemed unlikely anymore. Nothing could have surprised me.

'I heard you promise her that someone would come for her, and they did.'

'You were there that night?'

'I was there every night. You weren't hard to find. I can take you to your horse now, Anna. I can drive you there right now. If you want me to. You just have to say.'

'Oh, what bullshit this is!' I threw the rifle into the jeep and climbed in after it. I slammed the door shut before you could get your arm stuck in it again. You pressed your hands against the window.

'Don't go now, Anna. We can sort this out.'

I thought that maybe if I pointed the rifle at you, you might back off, so I grabbed it from the passenger seat and tried to aim it at you, but the barrel was too long and I couldn't turn it around in the jeep. 'Oh, for fuck's sake!' I threw it into the back seat. Your mobile phone was on the dashboard. I picked it up and dialled. I started the engine and rolled the window down an inch so that you could hear me.

'Police,' I said, staring at you.

You banged the window. 'I could've left you believing you'd killed him, Anna. I could've left you stewing for ever in your own guilt.' That was true. That was what I'd probably have done. There was mercy in you. Well, mercy for me. You stuck your fingers through the gap in the window. I dropped the handbrake and the jeep rolled forward.

'Yes, hello? I'm ringing about a murder that took place this summer. Yes. In the Grand Plaza Hotel.'

'Anna, don't.'

I pushed the jeep into gear and pulled off down the road. You held onto the top of the window and ran alongside for a bit. I shouted at you to let go, but you didn't. So I jammed down hard on the accelerator. I did not expect what happened next. Your body was lifted clean off the ground, and you trailed from the jeep like a piece of caught clothing. I braked in shock and you went crashing forward. You tumbled into the hedgerow. There was a crack of finger bones as your hands parted from the window.

I wanted to run out to you and see if you were okay. But I didn't. The little monster in my head assured me that you had merely got what you deserved. I waited, the engine still running. After a few seconds you got to your knees. 'The things that I have done for you!' you roared. I moved off, glancing at you in the rear-view mirror. You stumbled out into the middle of the road. I pushed the mobile phone out through the gap in the window. It skidded along the tarmac and ended up in the ditch.

V

The Island Again, the End of the Year

TWENTY-SIX

The conservator is bent over his desk. The studio has been quiet for some time. It is always quiet at this time of the year. It is the eve of Christmas Eve. A Monday.

Downstairs, the majority of visitors who had turned up that morning were middle-aged men, parked there in their jumpers and anoraks while their wives got on with the Christmas shopping. They wandered around the display rooms with the air of the greatly put upon. Some of them made no effort at all, and headed straight for the café, newspapers rolled up and tucked under their arms like weapons. There were a lot of waist-high children about the place too, probably in the care of the men. They ran around in packs, noisy and overexcited because of the time of year.

At half-past twelve it was announced over the intercom that the gallery would be presently shutting its doors. It was requested that all visitors make their way to the exit. The greater number vacated the place at speed, grateful that the ordeal was at last over, but one woman burst into tears when the security guards blocked her entrance to the gallery shop, informing her that it was closed. She pleaded to be allowed in, wailing that nobody had told her it was shutting early that day. Nobody ever told her *anything*. Her voice could be heard as far away as the Dargan Wing. The mortified guards gave her ten minutes, and she came out perfectly composed again, a mound of books and calendars under her arm, wishing a Merry Christmas to all around.

It was a quarter past one before the staff finally had the place cleared. The display rooms were closed up for the holidays. Sealed off like a time capsule. There are doors upon doors, and locks upon locks in the gallery. The building is shut for four days over Christmas. The temperature will not fluctuate by more than a fraction of a degree during this time, no matter what the weather brings. No draught shall sweep through the corridors and display rooms. The humidity will remain constant. The only movement will be the rhythmic flash of the red light on the alarm system that monitors every room. Are the paintings left in darkness when the gallery is closed? I don't know. I image they must be. I would not like to be locked up with them when the lights are out.

There were Christmas drinks in the staffroom when everything was done. Mulled wine and hot port. Mince pies and Christmas cake. Everyone put on paper hats and pulled crackers for a laugh. Someone had brought in a statue of Michelangelo's *David* in a Santa suit. He swivelled his hips to *Jingle Bells* when he was switched on. By half-past three, the gallery staff had dispersed. It was like the last day of school. But you didn't immediately go home, did you? The conservator said he had some paperwork that he needed to finish off, though by that stage he was noticeably drunk. His tie was loose and his hair was untidy. He was in royally good form, and he kissed everyone goodbye, even the men; the earnest, greying, unmarried men who perform their duties in the gallery with such meticulous care. Posterity is a quietly spoken but unforgiving master. The Nordic assistant announced that she too had to stay back. The conservator tried to send her home. Don't be ridiculous, he argued, pointing a finger at all the people departing, but the girl was determined to stay. She isn't returning to Oslo for the holidays. The conservator hasn't asked where she intends spending Christmas. He presumes she's found herself a local boyfriend, something like that. Or maybe her mother finally steeled herself and made the trip over, hands frozen onto the rail of a ship as she squints into the blustery southern distance, discerning only more waves. Is the Nordic assistant in fact from Oslo, or does she come from the really remote bit at the top that doesn't have any towns big enough to make it onto a map? It's within the Arctic Circle, that part, isn't it? Population density of God knows what. Apart from the conservator and his assistant, and a couple of security men four floors down, the gallery is empty. Just them and the paintings. But this does not explain the weight of the silence that descends upon the studio at four o'clock that afternoon.

The conservator pauses from his work at ten-past four. Not *Girl in the Mirror* anymore. He is long finished with that now. The conservator has moved on to greater things. The light in the studio, he realises, has turned grey. The dying year light is always tired and drained, but this light is different. This light is thick and oppressive. The conservator is engulfed by a sensation of hollowness, followed by a feeling of dread. The air is too heavy to inhale. He puts down his pen and presses a hand against his chest. The studio has an underwater appearance. He glances up at the glass ceiling. He can no longer see through it. It is snowing outside. And he is drunk. That is all. Hence the muted silence and the muffled light and sudden inability to breathe. Alcohol and snowfall. The conservator is relieved.

His next thought is that the Nordic assistant will be pleased with this development. She has been wishing all week for snow. The conservator calls her name. He will draw her into the centre of the room when she appears. Look, he will say, and point at the veiled ceiling. Look at that. Especially for you. Like being in an igloo, what? (No! For God's sake don't say that to her: wrong bloody country. She'll think you're an idiot. Just wish her Happy Christmas.) But the conservator does not have to worry about what to say. The Nordic assistant is not around.

The conservator goes down to the mezzanine floor. The Nordic assistant is not in the office either. This is unusual. What is the girl up to? Maybe she has gone out to look at the snow. She knew it was going to start soon. The conservator had heard her mentioning to one of the archivists at the party earlier that she'd seen snow clouds on her way to work. The girl can read the winter skies. The box hedges flanking the gallery doors will be capped in white. The rose bushes will look stark and forlorn. The girl's prints on the avenue will be small and halting. Snowflakes will have gathered in her hair, and it won't look so white anymore. She'll make sense in the context of the snow, just as tigers make sense in Indian forests, no matter how exotic they seem in European zoos. In the snow, the Nordic assistant will no longer look like something that fell out of the sky. In the snow, she will be just right.

The conservator will come down the steps and stop dead. The mulled wine will still be warm in his blood, despite the frozen air that turns his breath white. He'll take a moment to look at the girl. And another moment to stop looking at her. A sensation of well-being will sweep through him at this point. He'll bend down and scoop up a snowball. He'll throw it in her direction, deliberately missing. The Nordic assistant will turn around in surprise. At first, she will be unsure how to respond. Then she'll laugh, and throw a snowball back. The conservator will let it knock him down. He will collapse with drama onto his back, throwing his legs up in the air. He doesn't mind making a fool of himself – at least, not when there's no one around to see it. Not when it's to make the Nordic assistant laugh. She has a wonderful laugh. She is full of youth and happiness. He'll stay on his back, pretending to be dead. Perhaps she will pick up one of his hands and pull him to his feet. The conservator will come to life again before she starts feeling awkward.

But the conservator will not make it as far as the avenue. There will be no snowballs, not today. He will be distracted while on his way down to the ground floor. As he's about to enter the lift, he will hear something. He'll stop and listen. He will ascertain that the noise comes from the women's toilets. He will ascertain that it is the sound of a girl crying. It must be the Nordic assistant. She's the only woman left in the building. She had printed, one afternoon for a joke, in her geometrical handwriting, a sign saying 'VAN LOO', and stuck it to the door. And now she is crying behind that door. The conservator will be uncertain as to how to proceed. He will clear his throat to indicate his presence, and then he'll knock. The weeping will stop. There will be a brief flurry inside, followed by silence.

'You've been in there a long time,' the conservator will say. He'll try to sound gentle, in case she thinks he intends it as a criticism of her work. 'Is everything okay?'

The girl will mumble something, he won't be sure what. The doors of the lift will clamp shut behind him, and the lift will descend, almost petulant in its decision that it has waited long enough. The conservator will knock again. 'Perhaps I can help?' he will suggest. Not a word out of her. He'll wait tensely, shifting his weight from foot to foot. Perhaps the Nordic assistant will look down and see his shadow, flickering in the slit of light beneath the door. 'May I come in?' the conservator will ask. Another incomprehensible mumble from her. The lift shunts up again, and a security man steps out. He greets the conservator warmly, informs him it's snowing outside. 'Is it really?' the conservator exclaims. He enquires after the hours the guard has to work over the holidays, and sympathises when he hears that he's on duty Christmas Day. 'Could be worse,' the guard is saying. 'Could have to work New Year's, like last time.' The conservator keeps nodding. His mind is not on the conversation. He is wondering whether it's obvious he's been hovering outside the women's toilets. If the Nordic assistant walks out now, it is going to look bad. The conservator relocates himself to the centre of the room. He picks up a sheaf of papers from the Nordic assistant's desk and frowns at them brusquely. If the guard has detected anything untoward, he makes no comment. He laughs at whatever offhand joke the conservator makes, and makes a joke of his own. Then he continues on his rounds. The conservator waits until he's out of earshot before dropping the sheaf of papers and renewing his campaign on the toilet door.

'Look,' he will say to the door, 'I could hear you crying from outside. If you're not coming out, I'm coming in.' He'll say this loudly enough so that the girl will hear him, and quietly enough so that the guard will not. He'll knock one last time, and then turn the handle. He will push the door open slowly, giving the girl plenty of time to organise herself. The Nordic assistant will be standing before the mirror, her hands grasping the sink. She will avert her face from the conservator.

'*Dok-a-tor*,' she will whisper apologetically, stealing my name for you. She will be embarrassed to be seen in this state. Her face will be tear-stained and her skin will be flushed. She will straighten her clothing, and push back her hair. She will still look dishevelled. *Dok-a-tor, Meester. Myn liefste Elsbeth.* The sounds that these creatures can make! Something in the conservator will hear her, and yield.

'Nerine,' he will say soothingly, though that is not her name. He will stand before her and fill up the whole of the door. He will open his arms to her. 'Nerine, my little nereid, I command you not to cry.'

One finger is all it takes to wipe away a sea nymph's tears. The things you had to do for me, when she requires so little. Those northern waters are much clearer than ours. They freeze up and thaw out again, freeze up and thaw out. You and I didn't last the summer. I am jealous of a girl who doesn't exist. Look up at your glass ceiling and you will see me stretched across it, watching you through the hole that I've made in the snow: web-fingered, amphibious, stricken.

Gull Cottage,
December 23rd

Dear Sir, dear Mr Conservator,
Happy Christmas. I hope that the New Year will bring you peace.
Anna.

TWENTY-SEVEN

Peculiar, the morning I left you. As with all things. Everything peculiar all of a sudden, as if a switch had been flicked. A few miles down the road, I came across the up-ended car we had driven past the night before. It looked much smaller in the daylight. I think it was another Fiesta. It was even the same colour as the one I had crashed a few months earlier. Someone had pushed it to the side so that it no longer intruded upon the road. It lay on its roof like an up-ended beetle, its insides crackling and drying out in the sun.

I experienced a blast of euphoria when I crossed the bridge. Well, that's that then, I told myself with certitude, as if I could ever trust another word that came out of my mouth. Something clenched up in my chest. I gripped the wheel so hard that I could no longer steer properly. I was just swerving and bouncing along these tiny country roads. My arms no longer felt like parts of my body, but prosthetics that fastened me to the steering wheel. I knew that I was going too fast. It wasn't a voluntary response. On the worst of the bumps and on the many hump-backed bridges, I left the road altogether. Thankfully, it was too early for traffic. I knew that I risked crashing, but I didn't care. The laws of physics had changed. The whole world had changed. There were birds everywhere, a little secret population of them that I'd never properly noticed before. I'd only ever seen them in ones and twos when they'd lost control of flight and collided with my world, yet here they all were that morning, ten of them in a tree, a further fifty in a field, a whole city of egg-sized brown ones rustling around in the hedgerows. All of them furiously pre-occupied with their own affairs. You could almost see them frown. How could something so small and transitory be so serious when nothing mattered to me? I shouldn't have laughed, but I did.

I never made that call to the police, as you've probably gathered by now. Didn't even switch on the phone. I hope you didn't spend too much time waiting for a knock on the door. I don't think that Kel's murder will be solved. Or if it is, they'll pull me up on it. Do they close unsolved cases automatically after a number of years? You must be studiously steering clear of Kel's murder investigation, while at the same time helping the police in their attempts to catch their art thief. I'll say one thing for you: you can't have told them much, because I'm still here. They'd have found me by now if they knew who they were looking for. I'm not exactly a million miles away. What a position you are in, my poor murderous conservator! Running with the fox and the hounds. It'll never work. These things rarely do. Someday, one or both of us will be caught out.

I wonder how you explained the appearance at your home of *Girl in the Mirror*? You have an extraordinary talent for stringing out lies, it has to be said. You must have put in the performance of a lifetime. I wish I'd been there to see it. What was it that the priest said to me the day he showed up on my doorstep? That *Girl* had turned up in a bank? Did you slip her back into her deposit box, you wily thing? God knows where the rifle ended up. In a field somewhere in the midlands. I just hurled it out the window, didn't even pull over to do so. Stupid move on my part. The thing was probably licensed in your name. More explaining to the police if anyone handed it in. But no doubt you came up with another watertight explanation.

I drove to the car ferry, though I had no intention of boarding it. Sold everything that I could remove from the jeep – your camera, your toolbox, the car stereo and CDs, even your sunglasses (which, I noted, were a pretty fancy make – dear Mr Conservator, I'd never have thought of you as vain!). I'd have sold the tyres too if I could have wrenched them off. God knows, but I did try. The spare tyre, you will note, is gone. I needed the bit of money to get myself started. There was some class of a market on the side of the road, and I went up to the man with the biggest stand. He had a moustache and a green anorak, and he didn't think much of my wares. I considered selling the jeep itself, but figured that might land me in trouble. I'm sure you immediately had it registered as stolen. I checked around the frame of the passenger window for a dent, or for blood, or even for a scraping of skin, but there was nothing. There was no sign at all of the damage done. For your broken fingers, I am sorry. I hope that you are not too badly hurt. I hope that you will be able to pick up your cat. I hope that you will still be able to use your scalpels and your swabs and your magic potions. I hope that your hands will be as beautiful as they were before you ever laid eyes on me.

The film that was in the camera, should you be wondering, is under the carpet in the boot. I did my best not to expose it to light while trying to fish it out, but I was never much good with picky little things.

What else? It was a strange day. Clear and bright, and tremendously unreal, as if I'd walked out of a fatal crash, understanding that I was dead. The smell of the sea was on the air. Beside the pier was a small marina, and the masts of the yachts clattered eerily, though there was no wind. I suppose it was the heave of the sea that made them jangle. No sign at all of the rain of the night before. It was like the downpour had never happened.

I want to tell you all about the little place I had lunch in. I wanted to tell you at the time. I wanted to say: look there out the window, isn't that just the happiest dog you've ever seen? It was a big soft vanilla-coloured Labrador with a fat wrinkled scalp, and it was ambling down the sunny side of the street, wagging its tail at the world. I wanted to say: have you ever seen anything like this cutlery in your life? (Since I left you, I have encountered the most extraordinary cutlery in the world. Really, I should have stolen a few pieces to remind me of my trip. And the toilets in these places! They have so much personality.) I wanted to ask if you too perceived a change in the weather. Did you reckon that autumn was finally stealing in? What was the quickest way to get to the west? How much would it cost? Would I have difficulty finding somewhere to stay? Would I hate it? Be lonely? Would the locals think me a bit odd? Would they be a bit odd themselves? All through my lasagne and salad ('salad' is a synonym for coleslaw once you leave the city), I conducted a conversation with you. And then I remembered what you had done to Kel.

I presented myself at the local hairdresser's and got my hair chopped off. 'I love this bit!' the stylist, who was a girl of about sixteen, told me as she cut away a foot and a half of hair. Nearly died when I looked down and saw part of myself in a sorry heap on the floor, but I swallowed and breathed deeply and the girl hurriedly shoved a cup of tea at me. I got up, grabbed a hairbrush, and ran over to the windowsill, and crushed the wasp that had been bothering me since the moment I'd set foot in the salon. I couldn't bear to watch it in its death throes any longer. I pulverised it with the heel of the brush, and the creature separated into its component parts. Legs like snapped eyelashes, torso indented like a beer can. They don't burst and spurt liquid the way flies do. 'This,' I said to the girl, replacing the brush on the shelf, 'this is no country in which to be alone.' The girl's smile faltered, and then she beamed at me from ear to ear. 'Your colour will be done by now,' she said brightly. 'Why don't you come over to the sink?' I don't think I'll tell you what colour I ended up. You wouldn't like it. I certainly don't.

I took off and bought myself a horrible yellow windcheater in the shop two doors down. Choose something that you would never have chosen, I told myself, and there it was in the shop window, in amongst the maroon polo necks and the elasticated trousers and the rubber-soled nun shoes with the roundy toes. The yellow looked unbelievably bad with my sickly hair. It really did. I was something to behold. Then I backtracked up the country roads again, humbled by my appearance. I don't know why I'm telling you all this. I don't know why I think you might want to retrace my steps. All I know is that I hope that you will.

I hitched a ride in a truck. Sat juddering in the cabin, gazing at town names and road signs. 'Soft Margin.' 'Hard Shoulder.' Several big billboards with just the word 'Danger'. I don't think I said a word to the driver for the whole trip. The driver didn't say anything to me either, bar: you can catch a bus from there, love. I caught a bus. Overnighted in a pub on the coast, ran into the man with the dirty teeth who fixed me up with his great-aunt's cottage. Then caught a boat very early the next morning. A small one that smelled of fish. The cabin was jammed with green lobster pots, orange fishing buoys and blue nylon rope, so myself and my yellow windcheater had to travel outside. The skipper put me in the bow of the boat and rigged a tarpaulin over me. 'Not many tourists this time of year,' he apologised.

It was still early when I arrived on the island. I walked inland, shedding selves behind me with every step. They fell away from my skin like silk stockings. They drifted down to the beach and dissolved in the water. The gulls were suddenly raucous in the sky, warning the island of what was coming onshore. The rusty clock that hung from the sign over the pub told me that a full twenty-four hours had passed since I'd last seen you.

The summer broke that night. Late September. It snapped like a chicken's neck. It snapped, and it felt like I'd snapped it with my own two hands. At first, it was just rain, warm heavy rain, and then it was cold heavy rain, and then it seemed to be neither raining nor not raining, but simply wet, and cold and dark.

I think of you sometimes. That is a lie. I think of you often. All of the time. At first I kept seeing you being driven back from the gallery in a taxi. This time, you were me. Did you think of it that way? This time, you were the passenger, the shell-shocked patient, being driven numbly into the heart of the countryside, wondering if you could possibly have imagined all of what had just happened. And just like me, you had broken fingers. Amazing, aren't they, these little coincidences? Only, unlike me, your fingers were properly splinted. And unlike me, several of them were broken.

I thought of you pulling into the driveway of your home, and seeing it through new eyes. Just like when you drove me to it the first time. How strange it will be to find yourself in a practically identical position to me, yet in such different circumstances. And to find that the second time makes even less sense than the first. To find that even in a pattern, there is no pattern.

It is a Friday evening. You have been absent from your cottage for the entire working week. You have been staying in your apartment in town. I have concluded that you must have an apartment in town. How else could you work in the gallery? Impossible. The gallery is a three-hour drive from your home. If it is your home. That house is probably just a holiday cottage. That's why there were so few clues there as to who you were. The phone on the phone seat wasn't connected. Your jeep had a city reg. You never got post. No one knocked on the door while we were there, not once. The real world just left us to our own devices. And devices they were. The real world had no input into our lives. How did I not notice the gaping hole where normality should have been? The apartment is where you actually live, I suppose. The city apartment is full of who you are. Was I born this stupid, or did it happen when I lost my memory? Did I forget, along with everything else, how to be smart? I notice, by the way, that you didn't bring me to your city pad that night we spent together in the city. Dear Sir, dear Mr Conservator, I declare that I am hurt!

I think of you parked in the taxi on the gravel driveway of your house, trying to climb out of the passenger seat. The driver has to get out and open the door for you. You can't do it yourself. He stands there holding it ajar, but you can't even release the bloody seatbelt from its catch. So the driver has to lean over you and release it himself, a situation that both of you find excruciating.

'Do you want me to . . .?' the man asks, nodding at the house.

'No,' you say, as you heave yourself out of the car. 'I'll manage.' You raise one of your big bandaged hands to him in thanks and farewell as he reverses up the driveway. (I have done my sums and decided that it is more likely that both of your hands got hurt. You look like a boxer wearing white boxing gloves. You look like a bear with sore paws.) And then you are alone for the first time in, God, how long is it, *months*. Same as myself, really. By this time, I have been settled in my island cottage for four days, living off the tinned food that the great-aunt has left behind in the cupboards, still quite convinced that none of the locals have spotted me.

You stand on the driveway, looking around. I think of you noticing for the first time how wild your garden has become. How tangled it all is, and how impossible a feat it would be in your state to even think about pulling it into a shape again. Did you really plant that garden, or did you pay someone to do it for you? Those stories about the tobacco plants and the cyclamen – are they real, or did you just read about them in the estate agent's brochure? The tobacco plants and the cyclamen and the late-blooming jasmine. The lilies and lavatera. The violas and valerian. Were they just things that I wanted to hear? That little pond in the middle, the one that now has your jacket submerged in the mud, did you dig it yourself, or did it come with the cottage? Sometimes I think that the only thing that is real about you is the missing tip of your middle finger. Like my scar, it is the one thing that can never be concealed. Like my scar, it indicates that . . . That what? I don't know. Many things. That you are not perfect. That you are damaged goods. That you have also been through the wars.

Your little black cat will come prowling out to you from some dark corner, a small panther, all shoulders and darting eyes. She too, like your garden, will have grown into a feral version of herself. She'll be furious that she wasn't brought with you to your apartment. She'll be furious that she's been left on her own for almost a week, feeding on mice and birds and whatever else she could find. You'll crouch down to her, but she'll pace right by you in recrimination, slowing down, if you're lucky, to sniff disdainfully at your bandages. You can't even stroke her with your broken hands. She won't let you anyway – she'll make that much clear as she stalks off, her ears flattened and her tail twitching. She'll never come right again. It has gone too far. Perhaps that will be the moment of recognition for you, seeing her like that, fragile little thing that she is. *The damage,* you will whisper to yourself, as though those words sum the whole thing up. *The damage*. You will perceive imprints of that damage everywhere, and feel yourself reeling. You won't know what to do for a second, and you'll delay there on the gravel, bent and swaying. You'll notice that the police have dropped back your jeep. One of the lads investigating the painting told you he'd take care of it, and there it is. The man was as good as his word. What did you tell them about the jeep's theft? Did they not think it odd that it was taken the night *Girl in the Mirror* reappeared? Perhaps you told them it had been stolen from the village. Perhaps you told them it had been stolen the night before. Perhaps you didn't tell them it was stolen at all, and they contacted you because it was reported as abandoned on a pier. So your friend from the force helps you out. Or maybe he doesn't. I am getting sick of all the guessing. The dried-in slime from the night it spent in the pond is gone. The police have washed it for you. Or maybe they haven't. Maybe I washed it. It is your turn to guess.

You go over and place your broken hand on the bonnet. The days of the paintwork being hot from the sun are over.

Well, for six or seven months, at least. Not that you would feel the heat through the white muslin and plaster. The leaves have finally started falling from the trees. They are piled up on the windscreen like snow. Something occurs to you. You unlock the door of the jeep and climb in. The interior is dark from the leaves on the windscreen. You open the glove compartment. How do you do this? With your thumb, maybe? Your elbow? Your teeth? Simple tasks are now ineffably difficult, and you curse my name yet again.

You root through the maps and the manuals and the diesel receipts. The amount of bits of paper that had built up in your car! Did you never throw anything away? No, of course you didn't. The conservator is keenly aware of the value of artefacts. Every document is evidence to you. The white envelope is not there. You go through it all once more. The note has definitely been removed. Now you know that I have found your message. Does this knowledge please or upset you? I don't know. Your head will inevitably start its throbbing again, so you'll fumble in your pockets for the front-door keys. You struggle to get the door open. I don't know how long this will take. I don't know how difficult it is to insert a key in a lock with splinted hands. It is a shame that the house doesn't unlock like the jeep, with the press of the central-locking button. I know that by the time you get inside, you will be in a black rage.

You stand in the hall, surprised at how little your surroundings have changed, when you have changed so much. Yes, I've already been down this road with myself – more than once. There is the phone seat. There is the unconnected phone. There is the rug on which we— You slam the front door and keep walking.

You make your way along the corridor through the different densities of light that spill into it from the adjoining rooms. You smell all the old smells. You push all the doors open with your foot. Just checking that the rooms are definitely empty. Just in case. You can never be too careful.

Relieved or disappointed to find them all uninhabited? Again, I don't know. But I would like to know.

Last of all you approach the bathroom, the room at the end of the corridor, the room in which I once hid. You try the handle of the door. It is unlocked, and swings open broadly onto nothing.

What's left of me in your house? A few long hairs on my pillow? The stiletto shoes? How I wish that I had held onto them! There is also that blue dress that you brought home to me one evening, and that I wore just once, and even then only for a few minutes. So you would have me wear silk and jewelled shoes, would you? You would have me be your girl? I wonder, have you destroyed these things or not? Have you had yourself a ceremonial bonfire? Have you passed them on to another woman? I'll bet the Nordic assistant looks awesome in blue. Have you even held onto the house? A terrible thing it would be to find you gone, to return one day and to have the door answered by a stranger, shaking his head at me as he stood in the porch. No, I will not let myself think of that, not today.

You'll finally be able to take down my case from wherever it was that you hid it. You'll be able to examine it at your leisure. You'll spread out its contents, and arrange and rearrange them on the kitchen table. What was inside? I can barely say. My memory is as unreliable as ever. There is a little money there, not as much as you thought would be left. How in God's name, you will wonder, did she manage to spend so much? Isolde's passport. And, of course, those photographs that I had done when I first arrived in the city. They are still slipped inside the document folder, I believe. Four of them, or did I give one to Kel? Yes, to say goodbye. Perhaps you have that one already. No doubt you removed it from the scene of the crime, stripped him of each and every trace of me. Will you even recognise me in those photos? That is the thing: I think that you will recognise me everywhere, just as I recognise you everywhere. In every calm face, in every quiet voice, in every lone figure that walks too fast.

Those postcards that I wrote in the village square are still secreted away somewhere. They'll probably flutter out of a book in years to come, smelling of summer, smelling of parched light. They'll flutter down gently and you'll pick them up off the floor and study my handwriting. You had never seen my handwriting before. That doesn't matter. I barely recognise it myself.

The note. There remains the question of the note. I couldn't face opening it until recently. Until last week, in fact. The eve of Christmas Eve. A Monday. When I got to the cottage, I stashed the envelope in the middle drawer of the dresser, and decided not to think about it again. But I opened the drawer the other night, and found it there, in amongst the tea box tokens and the Mass cards and the reams of garbled letters that I wrote and never sent to you. I sat with the envelope on my lap, looking at my name on the front. My name in someone else's hand was surprising. My name in your hand. You had printed it out in block capitals. It looked kind of witchy, with its stark symmetry and sharp angles. ANNA. It was even more sinister when viewed upside down. ∀NN∀. I can't imagine when you must have written it. It looked like it had been in the glove compartment for some time. There was an oil fingerprint and pale water stain on it, and the lip of the envelope was beginning to come unstuck, as if it had been left in the sun. When, if ever, had you planned on giving it to me?

I was terrified, of course, to open it. What sort of accusations would I find inside? Some threat of blackmail? Another newspaper clipping? Some essential piece of evidence that would have me locked up for ever? You can see why I delayed opening it until the other night.

The words themselves had an air of gravity about them, with their fountain pen ink on thick cream paper. Written in the same language as the message on the back of the painting.

I half guessed at one of the words. *Zomer. De hele zomer heb ik aan je gedacht*. I turned the page over, and read the translation.

All summer, I thought of you.

And then, of course, at the end of this long day of reckoning, there's Kel and me. Two small children playing together in a garden. A little boy and a little girl. Remarkably alike, the two of them. Everybody says so. Two peas in a pod. All the attendant childhood sounds are there – the birds, the humming summer insects, the barking of the neighbour's dog. And the two small children play with each other in increasingly hushed tones as the game turns nasty yet thrilling. I look up and Kel is no longer huddled over our assortment of toys. He is standing in front of me, blocking the sun.

'Get up,' he says, and immediately I get up, wiping my hands on my dress. He is a full head taller than me. He examines me for a moment and then leans forward, thrusting two of his fingers between my lips. His nails nick the roof of my mouth.

'Suck,' he says, and I begin to suck. His fingers taste horrible, like dirt.

'Bite,' he commands, and I tentatively bite. There is nothing I would not have done to be included in his games. My big brother. He is staring at me. There is a funny expression on his face, an embryonic version of what was to become his sneer. Even his milk teeth are pointy.

I will never have had enough of his memory. This I know, and I possess that knowledge in an absolute way.

The cat, by the way – my cat, that is, my dirty-white, inherited, leftover cat, Bert (allegedly) – my cat has had kittens, and her so old that she barely has teeth. There's hope for us all. Five or six nights ago now since it happened. She had them on the sofa where I sleep. A nest of tiny mewing little balls, all slimy and shut-eyed and terrifyingly vulnerable. Funny that – I'd had her pegged as a boy. The priest monitored her gestation with care. I didn't even know that it was a gestation. Just thought she'd been piling on the pounds. 'You've let yourself go,' I informed her one evening, and she'd turned fastidiously on her heel. It was the priest who'd been taking care of her before I'd arrived. That's why he'd shown up at the cottage that stormy morning back in October. Not to interrogate me. Just to make sure that the cat was being properly looked after. The poss-poss. The pretty poss-poss. He'd only stayed chatting at the kitchen table to make me feel welcome. He felt sorry for me, I think. Knew a lost soul when he saw one.

He dropped in a Christmas card the other night, the only one I received. He still calls in regularly to look in on the cat. 'Funny how she grew on me,' he commented as he was leaving one afternoon, almost apologetic that a grown man should have a soft spot for such a bedraggled creature. She was up on her hind legs kneading his leg as he said this. We both looked down at her, but must have seen different things. She truly is an unholy mess. But the priest doesn't care that her fur doesn't shine, or that there is a small tear in her left ear, or that some of her front teeth are missing. He doesn't even mind her stinky breath. And she doesn't mind that he's old and getting smaller, and that the jokes he tells aren't in the least bit funny. The two of them adore each other. I don't know why it makes me sad to see them together, but it does. It makes me happy, but it makes me sad too. It makes me sad for all of us. It makes me sad for the world. He is going to keep two of her kittens (the poss-poss's posseens) and has already found homes for the other three.

He went home to his family for New Year's. An invalid father with the same name as him, and a spinster sister several years his senior. The two of them still live in the priest's childhood home. A white, bare place with stone floors, I would imagine. One of the kittens is destined for there. He apologised before he left because he wouldn't be able to visit for a week or two. I told him that we'd miss him, me and the cat, and he considered this information for a long moment. 'Looks like snow,' he observed, and ambled off into the weather. I watched his hunched figure make its way down the road. Painfully slow. His walk has deteriorated to a shuffle. He was diagnosed a month ago with Parkinson's disease. I only know this because Mrs Mackey told me, but now that I know, I watch for the signs. I saw the teacup shake in his hand the week before Christmas, and what was worse was that he saw it too. He stared with frightened eyes as if the cup was possessed and had shaken itself. We were sitting across from each other at the kitchen table. He set the cup down, and glanced at me to see whether I had noticed. I just kept talking as if nothing had happened. As the condition worsens, he will need proper care. Around-the-clock professional care. His days on the island are numbered. We will miss him a lot, the cat and me.

I have another little surprise for you, you'll be delighted to hear. I had forgotten all about it. It only came back to me a few nights ago, while I was thinking of something else.

Remember the all-night café that I told you about? Not the one that we were in together, but the one that I ended up in the first time I ran away from Kel (which was not the first time, no). I'm sorry, I've no idea what the place is called, but you'll remember it once you see it. It's a few streets away from the Grand Plaza. Kel told me that you'd followed me the night I ran away from him. I wasn't sure whether to believe him or not. I thought that he was making it up. But he wasn't making it up. He'd have come along himself, had he the energy. I ended up in that café, remember? Crying my silly eyes out. It's a dingy old place. They never clean it, which is why I reckoned it'd be secure. Yes, dirt and neglect seem to offer safe harbour – what is wrong with my thinking? Go into the toilets and look over the door. You'll see a picture of the stars. It's just a big postcard, really, stuck onto a cardboard frame. It's not properly centred on the wall. It caught my eye because of its stunning incongruity. Yes, in my mind-boggling solipsism, I read it as a metaphor for my life. Get a chair, just as I did then, and place it under the postcard. See? I have you walking in my footsteps all over again, ghosting me despite your best efforts. I am clever that way, or should I say devious? Be quick about it. If anyone comes in, the chair will be knocked out from under you. Take the picture down. It's only pinned up with thumbtacks, though I pressed them right in when I was finished there. You'll need to bring something to prise them out. You'll need hands that aren't broken, for a start. Underneath the picture, you'll find a hole. Not a huge one. You could maybe fit a shoebox into it. But here's the thing that I remembered a couple of nights ago. In the hole, wrapped up in Isolde's paper face, is the missing money. Thousands of pounds of it. Hundreds of thousands. Countable in inches.

Be careful when you are unwrapping it. Don't rip the paper. I want you to look at Isolde's face. The photocopy of her face. I want to know if you see any of mine in it. For I confess: I could not.

Do me one last favour when you get the money. Find out where Kel is and bury him properly. I miss him, and all his beloved perfection.

And now? What am I to do with myself now? The word alone makes me laugh out loud. Now! It is another empty shell that I can place on the windowsill, or bang against the wall like a destructive child. I am full of stupid ideas, ones that will never work. I want to be a courier and speed along the city streets. I want to bring things that are in the wrong place to the right place. I want addresses and grid co-ordinates. I want to join the city council and spend my days tending the roads that I used to love. I want to go back to the café and get to that money before you do. Then I'll buy the café. I'll hang out with the customers, and hang out when the customers are gone. I want to be the only one with the keys to it. I want to have it to myself sometimes. Just stick up a closed sign when I feel like it. Watch the regular customers trying to push open the locked door and shake my head sadly at them as I sit in the chip-fat gloom. *Sorry, love – closed.* I want to have that café as my little oasis in the city. I want to belong to something. I want something to belong to me. I want to say that word again that I must once have loved so much, that troublesome word that must have caused the whole mess in the first place: mine. Mine mine mine. Say it enough times to finally rid myself of it for once and for all.

And then one day, just when you think it's all over, my card will arrive on your doorstep. It will be in amongst the other cards, as innocent as the rest of them. A snowy starry scene on the front, and emblazoned in silver across the immense midnight sky, *Silent Night*. Dear Sir, you'll read in my too-erratic hand, Dear Mr Conservator, Happy, oh Happy, New Year!

It is January, and everybody has resumed their lives after the holiday season. I have felt weightless all day. The place was all of a sudden busy with cars bumping around the tiny roads at all hours. Singing leaked out of every pub and house. The sound of it came to me as though I stood on top of a cliff, and civilisation was a thousand unnavigable feet below me. It was the loneliest sound that I had ever heard. I was jealous of them while it lasted, but it stopped quite abruptly, the merriment, a day or two after New Year's, and the island itself seemed to reel with the hangover. They have gone back to work now, and all that remains is a bruised silence. And then, maybe two or three days ago, it suddenly crept over me: this sensation of exhilaration that is still with me now. I am coming to see the empty space in front of me as freedom. It is a word that I never appreciated before, but I feel it surrounding me now like a mist, and I want to drown in it.

It is January. The wind is at the door. The snow that covered the east coast never made it here. The scrap of canvas waits on the top shelf of the dresser. Your note, all summer, is folded in the drawer. The priest's Christmas card is on the mantelpiece, and soon I will take it down. The cat is asleep in front of the fire, her kittens curled into her belly. The newspapers are spread out. 'O most beautiful flower, I beseech you from the bottom of my heart to succour me in my necessity. Grateful thanks for favours received, and about to receive.' It is January, and I am exhilarated because I am anticipating summer. I can taste it. I can smell it in my hair. I can count the days to it, and watch their number decreasing. The clock will go forward again and I will barely be able to contain myself. It is January, and I am full of May and June and July.

Think of me sometimes. Think of me when the phone rings and no one speaks on the other end. Think of me waiting for you in this empty room, listening for a knock on the door at dusk. Think of me when I am aching for you to come to my door unexpectedly in the night, all wet because you've been walking through the rain that never stops. Your limbs heavy, but pushing onward all the same. Full of the old determination, full of the old drive. Think of me in my startled state when I realise that the knock has at last come. It has at last come! I will not know what to do with myself. I will not know where to look. Think of me staring stupidly at the door in trepidation, as though I thought it might open itself. I want there to be just that inch of wood between us. Think of me opening that door and standing there speechless when I see your face.

I will take your hand and lead you in, and sit you in front of the fire. I will dry you off, and wrap my arms and legs around you. I will rock you to and fro. It will get late, and then later. The fire will die down. The embers will fall through the grate and turn to ash, but the Sacred Heart will burn all night. We won't fall asleep. We will sit in the red glow. Then I will say it. I will whisper it into your ear: I am sorry. I forgive you. And I forgive myself.

ACKNOWLEDGEMENTS

Deepest gratitude to Andrew O'Connor, Keeper of Conservation at the National Gallery of Ireland, for being so generous to me with his time, his expertise and his years of experience during the writing of this book. *All Summer* would be very different without him.

Thanks also to Roy Hewson, Photographer at the National Gallery of Ireland; the staff at the Gallery Library; to Brian Snow and Pieter Six for the translations, and to Marianne Gunn O'Connor, for being steadfast.

The author gratefully acknowledges the receipt of a bursary from the Arts Council of Ireland, An Chomhairle Ealaíon, to help in the completion of this book.